Other Books By Tim Callahan

KENTUCKY SUMMERS SERIES:

THE CAVE, THE CABIN, &
THE TATTOO MAN

COTY AND THE WOLF PACK

What a poignant story! I wish we could all live in a town like *Sleepy Valley* with a man like Nick. Thank you for an inspiring read!

—Nancy Ann Wall

It moved me many times to tears with the book's humor, sincerity, and faith in God. Outstanding job letting the reader get inside the heads of the fantastic cast of characters. Everyone who reads it will not be left the same. In order to be fully human we are to be persons in relation to others. The hallmark of *Sleepy Valley* is Callahan's ability to illustrate the importance of life-giving relationships and the need to recognize mutual respect, human worth and dignity and how God uses our relationships to show His love for us and others.

—Sebert A Guckian

TIM CALLAHAN

To Charlotte,
May your path be paved by God.
Blessings,
9.29.12

TATE PUBLISHING & Enterprises

Published by Tate Publishing & Enterprises, LLC
127 E. Trade Center Terrace | Mustang, Oklahoma 73064 USA
1.888.361.9473 | www.tatepublishing.com

Tate Publishing is committed to excellence in the publishing industry. The company reflects the philosophy established by the founders, based on Psalm 68:11,
"The Lord gave the word and great was the company of those who published it."

Book design copyright © 2008 by Tate Publishing, LLC. All rights reserved.
Cover design by Janae Glass
Cover Illustration by Nicole Seitz
Interior design by Kandi Evans

Published in the United States of America

ISBN: 978-1-60604-970-9
1. Southern Fiction/ Romance Comedy
2. Spiritual Journey
11.14.08

This book is dedicated to my wife, Charlene.

I love you.

ACKNOWLEDGMENTS

I would like to thank anyone and everyone associated with the Great Smoky Mountains National Park and Cades Cove. My love for the park was the great influence in my writing of this novel. While the village of Sleepy Valley is a fictional town, the park is not. My many trips over the past forty years have brought so much enjoyment and excitement to my life. I marvel each time I drive or hike through the wonders of the park as though it's my first time.

I thank my God for places such as the Great Smoky Mountains National Park that show His love for us and the beauty of His creative powers. I thank God for the bears, deer, foxes, elk, otters, birds, salamanders, butterflies, fish, and fireflies and the many trees and flowers.

Very special thanks to the lovely and talented author and artist, Nicole Seitz. The painting you created for the Sleepy Valley cover is perfect. Words can't express my gratitude. I love your writing and paintings. www.nicoleseitz.com

I pray God will continue to create in me a thankful heart for everyone who has helped me, for all He has made and for all the folks who read my writings. I pray that a person who reads a book of mine will come to the end happier and a sensing of God all around them.

Blessings,
Tim Callahan

I know, O Lord, that a man's life is
not his own;
it is not for man to direct his steps.

Jeremiah 10:23 (NIV)

1

Nick Stewart stood on the front steps of his new home on a beautiful Saturday morning. Looking out past his front yard, he saw only trees and the long gravel drive. The gravel lane led to Mountain Road, which led to the Tennessee state route and on to the village of Sleepy Valley. The village sat in a quiet valley fifty miles northwest of the Smoky Mountains, had a population of one hundred and thirty-six... now one hundred and thirty-seven.

Nick had moved into his new home the day before. This morning he spent unpacking boxes and hanging his favorite paintings and pictures, none of which were of his ex-wife, Melissa. He had given Melissa most of the furniture, and they had split the money. Nick had needed to leave Chicago, the town where he had lived his thirty-five years, and find a new beginning. Nick needed a new home and his heart needed a different place to heal. Nick also wanted to get away from people, he wanted time to think and mend alone. His faith in the human race was nearly exhausted. He knew what to expect from nature, surprises were to be expected. Nick didn't want the same from loved ones, but it happened.

It was April, and the woods around his small cabin-style home were in full bloom. The woods had white and red Trilliums, May apples, and plenty of small pink and purple flowers shooting up from the forest floor. Moss covered the fallen logs as they decayed forming new life. Birds flew by and landed in the trees within the yard. Nick had put out a bird feeder when he first arrived, and the birds had already found their new source of food. He wanted to sit and watch the birds for hours.

Nick had no immediate plans. He had no job, no money coming in, and he didn't care at the moment. In Chicago, he'd been a teacher at the local high school and coached different sports, basketball being his favorite. He didn't like quitting near the end of the school year, but after the divorce it had become unbearable, and he'd had to get away from it all. He had his savings, not much, and his half of the money from the sale of their house.

Melissa moved in with the man that she had been having an affair with for the past year. Nick had loved his wife, but couldn't provide her with the life she wanted. He could only provide his heart and love, which were apparently not enough.

As Nick stood on the front porch looking out into the woods he again thought of Melissa's words—*I want a divorce.* He'd thought of those words every day since. Anger was pretty easy for him to control, but not the emotion of her unfaithfulness. He never thought he would be single again… a divorced man. So he stood and looked toward Sleepy Valley and the feelings swept over him again. He shook them off. He was getting used to the thoughts of Melissa flooding upon him suddenly.

Nick had always loved the mountains, especially the Smokies, with the rock-filled creeks that flowed down from the mountaintops. He loved the different trees and vegetation at the various levels and the views of the blue gray cast that enveloped the valleys and mountains. Animals were plentiful and flowers shot up from every nook and cranny. He loved the quietness of the woods and the history of the past when men came there in search of a better life for themselves and their families. He too hoped for a better life and future.

Nick stepped off the porch and headed into his woods to do some exploring around the property. He had bought the fifteen acres that surrounded the small cabin and had not yet seen it all.

The real estate company said they would have ribbons tied to the trees that followed his property lines and stakes placed along the line so he would know what was his. He turned left off the porch and walked through the woods taking in the beauty. He quickly realized that he would never need to buy firewood for his fireplace. Trees and limbs were everywhere for the taking. He heard squirrels arguing in the trees and saw birds following him as he walked. Something yellow caught his eye near his right foot. He looked down to see a Yellow Lady's Slipper growing next to a stump. Nick knew how rare they were. He took the sighting of the Slipper as a sign that he had made the right choice in moving here.

He walked on into the woods until he saw pink ribbons hanging from trees and knew that the real estate office had done what they promised. It was a good start. He turned left and followed the ribbons along his boundary and found wooden stakes driven into the leaves left from last fall. Later he heard the bubbling and recognized the sound of the stream that ran through his property. The stream was rocky and beautiful but not very big. In places it widened to ten feet, but it flowed with plenty of water from the mountains that surrounded the property. Walking farther away from the cabin he came to a clearing. It wasn't far from the stream and he wondered if a home had been in the spot at one time. He looked around for clues, but found none. A doe and fawn stepped out of the woods and into the clearing. Nick lowered himself near the ground and watched them eat the soft grasses of the meadow. Nick found himself lost in the moment and the scene. At that moment his troubles were gone, the healing began. He loved the deer and the birds and squirrels and this place. Maybe people wouldn't get in the way.

Nick made his way back to the house leaving acres of woods yet to be explored for a later time. He had no food in the house, except for the powdered donuts he had picked up at the gas station on his way here. He decided to head to Sleepy Valley, look the place over again, and buy some supplies. Nick jumped into his '99 SUV and drove into the village. He saw a sign on Mountain Road that read "Puppies for Sale." He didn't pay much attention to it and drove along slowly looking at neighboring houses and farms. A small sign advertising an art gallery caught his eye just as he rounded the last curve before State Route 74. The artist's name was Morelli... Morelli Gallery. Sounded like modern art, and Nick didn't like modern art. When Mountain Road dead-ended into State Route 74, he turned right toward Sleepy Valley. Turning left would have pointed him toward the bigger town of Pineville.

Sleepy Valley had a small grocery, a post office, and the Tennessee State Bank on one side of the street. Trudy's Eating Place diner stood between a general store and an antique store named Sally's on the other side of the street. White, two-story homes began where the storefronts ended, completing Main Street. Large oaks, maples, and elms lined the street, their limbs overhanging the slanted parking spots. Lampposts lit the sidewalks for the few folks who liked to stroll the empty sidewalks after dark. There was a small gas station on the outskirts as you left the village.

Nick decided to treat himself to lunch at Trudy's. He pulled the SUV into a slanted parking slot between the restaurant and Sally's. This was his first journey into town except for his trip down to sign the papers for his new home at the bank and to open savings and checking accounts. He had also driven through town when he visited to look at the cabin and he liked what he saw, a clean, rustic village with few people.

He knew he would have to meet folks at some time, and he might as well start with Trudy. The truth about Nick was that he had always been very outgoing, loved being around people, and made friends easily. The divorce had hurt him, and his church had damaged him also. Members looked at him differently. He knew they whispered as he walked away from them. He expected support and help from the body of Christ, but it hadn't come. The pastor had been good to him and offered counseling and meaningful words, none of which really helped a lot. He had felt broken and betrayed, thus the move.

He walked into the diner and was surprised to see a room full of people. It was almost packed to capacity. He wondered where all the people came from. The whole village must eat lunch on Saturdays at Trudy's. Actually the place only had twelve tables and a lunch counter that seated five.

An attractive, busty, red-to-auburn-haired lady behind the counter yelled, "You can pull up a chair anywhere you would like, honey. I don't have time to seat you." Nick found a table with two chairs close to the jukebox and seated himself. "I'm busier than a hornet chasing a sugar crazed leprechaun. Why don't you people eat at home? It's a shame that the only person that cooks any longer is Trudy. What is this town coming to?"

An older gentleman at the counter answered, "You know you love us. What would you complain about if it wasn't for us?"

"Believe me; I'd have plenty to complain about. My back hurts and these breasts are getting bigger every minute."

"That's the only reason I sit up here, to get a better look at them."

The restaurant erupted in laughter. Nick found himself smiling for the first time in a long time around people. Nick could tell that Trudy was Irish as soon as he looked around the place and heard Trudy speak. The tables were covered with green and white checked, vinyl tablecloths and shamrocks hung from the ceiling, probably left over from St. Patrick's Day.

"Looking is the only thing you'll ever do. Tom, you old fool, you would drop over dead if you ever actually saw them," she said as she walked over to Nick's table. The restaurant was moving with laughter as Tom swiveled in his seat, watching her walk by.

When she got to Nick's table she plopped down a drink and said, "Here's your Pepsi. Have you decided yet?"

"Why the Pepsi?"

"You looked like a Pepsi guy."

"I was actually going to order a diet," Nick said.

"My name is Trudy. What's yours?"

"Nick."

"Be a man, Nick… drink the Pepsi," Trudy suggested.

A couple was sitting at the table next to Nick, and the husband turned around and put his finger to his lips, signaling for Nick not to say any more.

Nick took his advice and said, "Thank you. I'll have a burger, well done, and fries."

Trudy looked down at him and said, "And what would you like on it?"

Nick quickly answered, "Whatever you think I would like would do fine."

"Good boy. You learn fast." Trudy turned and walked away. As she got behind Tom she swung and knocked his cap off his head to the floor.

"Hey," Tom gasped.

"How many times have I said it's impolite to wear your hat indoors? This society is going to hell in a gold pickup."

The gentleman that signaled to Nick turned back around and offered his hand. "Hi, I'm George Sanders, and this is my wife Sally. Trudy doesn't mean any harm. She would do anything for anyone, a heart of gold."

Nick chuckled, "It's good to meet you. I'm Nick Stewart."

"We've been looking forward to meeting you. You bought the Gibbons' homestead. Great place," George offered.

"Thank you. How did you know?"

"Small town," Sally said.

"Would you be Sally of Sally's Antiques?" Nick asked.

"Yes. That would be me. My husband sells insurance in Pineville." Pineville was the closest town with any size to it. It was twenty minutes to the north and had a population of 4,500. Folks went there to shop for things they couldn't find in Sleepy Valley such as cars, clothes, electronics, and insurance. Pineville also had a new four-theater cinema and a few of the chain restaurants.

"It's nice to meet you George, Sally. I'll definitely be visiting your store. I'm a little low on furniture, perhaps you can help me."

"I'd love to. We're going to leave you alone now, have a pleasant lunch."

Nick instantly liked them. "Thank you, you've been very kind."

Trudy walked back to the table and placed the burger and fries in front of Nick. It looked great.

"You bought the Gibbons' home didn't you?"

"Yes, I did."

"Good for you. Listen up, everyone!" Trudy raised her arms above her head to get everybody's attention and then stuck two fingers in her mouth and whistled loud and long. The place came to a complete hush.

Nick quickly realized that Trudy had the complete respect of everyone in her place. They looked at her with admiration, and the men maybe with a little lust, which probably caused some of the admiration. She was thirty-seven years old and single. Her looks reminded Nick of Maureen O'Hara. The men always joked about Trudy's boobs. She would tease them back with, "Dream on." As Teri Hatcher said on the Seinfeld episode, "They're real and they're spectacular."

"You'll just have to dream on guys." Today, she had on a sleeveless Carolina blue blouse with the three top buttons undone, enough to give the men a peek of cleavage.

After getting everyone's attention she announced, "I would like for everyone to meet Mr. Nick Stewart. He's your new neighbor. He purchased the Gibbons' place on Mountain Road. Come by and say hello as you leave."

Everyone applauded. Nick had not expected such a greeting. He just wanted lunch. He had to admit it felt good. The best he had felt in the past year. He wondered why his old church couldn't have applauded him. They could have stood and clapped as he walked awkwardly into church. Someone could have said, "Let's hear it for Nick. He really needs us now."

Nick finally was able to take a bite of his sandwich. It had mayo on it. He hated burgers with mayo so he took the top bun off and scraped off all that he could. He replaced it with some mustard that was on the table. It then met his standards for a great hamburger. The fries, he knew, were the best he had ever tasted. Trudy brought him a refill of his Pepsi, but this time it was diet.

As he ate, customers kept stopping by on their way out to introduce themselves and welcome him to the village.

As Nick took his last bite of fries Trudy stopped by to ask if he was ready for dessert. "Best cobblers and pies in the state."

"Not today, maybe next time. You can give me the damages."

"No damage today. It's on the house. New neighbors always get the first meal on me. You sure you don't want the dessert now?"

"Thank you. That's very kind of you. Maybe I will have a slice of coconut cream pie to go, if that's okay."

"I'll get it for you. Good choice. Don't you dare leave a tip either. You can leave large tips from now on."

Trudy came back with a bag and said, "Glad to have you in the village. I believe you'll like it here in our quiet little village. Now get out so I can seat someone else."

As he left he looked at the hours posted on a sign in the window. It read:

Monday-Saturday 5:30 a.m. to 3 p.m.
Sunday—Closed Go to church!

Nick chuckled and walked next door to the general store. He opened the screen door and walked in. He was met with the most beautiful violin music he had ever heard. He was going to have to find out what stereo system they had. His cabin could use a stereo system with such an amazing sound.

He walked around looking at the old-fashioned wooden shelves filled with odds and ends and all the different tools hanging on the walls. Nothing seemed to be in any order. A hammer was hanging next to a hoe. A saw was hanging close to the garden spade. A shelf was filled with tools, hunting clothes, nails, a few fishing lures, and mixing bowls. Nick had never seen a store in such disarray in his life, but the stereo system was fantastic.

The music stopped and a man's voice called from the back, "Is someone there?"

"Yes, I'm just looking."

"I don't recognize the voice," Mr. Vincent Marconi said as he made his way from the back office to meet Nick.

"I love the sound system." Nick was looking at a shelf with Barbie dolls and mousetraps on it.

Vincent walked around the corner to face Nick and said, "I'm sorry, but I don't have a sound system."

Nick looked up to see eighty-two-year-old Vincent Marconi holding a violin under his left arm and a bow in his right hand. Vincent had gray hair combed neatly from front to back. He wore a bushy mustache that looked too big for his pleasant face. He didn't look nearly his age. Nick walked over and stuck out his hand and Vincent transferred the bow to his left hand and shook Nick's hand. "Nick Stewart, I'm new in the village. I bought the Gibbons' home. The music was beautiful. I thought... well, never mind what I thought. You play magnificently."

"Thank you. You're so kind. I'm Vincent Marconi. I like to take a break and play every now and then. As you can tell, it's hard to find time with the rush of customers I have to deal with." He laughed a hearty laugh. Nick knew right away that he liked Vincent.

Of course Nick was the only customer and had been for the past hour. Mr. Marconi only kept the store open for something to do. He had retired from playing in the New York Philharmonic Orchestra five years earlier and moved to Sleepy Valley away from the hustle and bustle of New York City a month later. He had said that no one should die in New York City. He had loved the Big Apple when he was younger, but he wasn't going to die there. The tragedy of 9–11 convinced him further.

"I'm sorry I bothered you. I was just looking around the village, checking out the places to get supplies."

"You can get most anything in here, if we can find it. If you can't find something, just ask. I know where most everything is kept."

"I can't quite figure out your system." Nick looked back at the shelf to his left.

"When I first bought the place I put everything in alphabetical order and now as something sells I just replace it on the wall or shelf with something new to sell, whatever it is that comes in, simple and easy. That's the way I like my life now. The reason I moved to Sleepy Valley. I'll give you a tip. You need to go eat at Trudy's."

"I just left there. Nice place," Nick told him.

"I enjoy them also. My wife, God rest her soul, would slap me for such thoughts. But our good Lord has blessed me with good eyes, even at this age, and I'm certainly going to keep using them."

"We'll have to enjoy the view together over lunch some day, Mr. Marconi."

"I would like that." Nick walked toward the door and Vincent said, "Have a wonderful day."

As Nick walked out and started across the street to the grocery, he could hear the sweet strings playing again inside the general store. He realized he still had the bag with the coconut pie in his hand and returned to his vehicle and placed it on the front seat.

Nick crossed the street again and entered the Sleepy Valley grocery and was surprised at how well-stocked and clean the store was. He was glad that the groceries were stacked in a normal manner. The vegetables were in the same section. The baking goods were all together and the breads had their own spot. It wasn't a very big market, but bigger than it looked from outside. The inside of the building was deep.

Nick gathered up all the supplies he could think of, including food, cleaning supplies, toiletries, and soaps. Melissa had let Nick keep the washer and dryer. She said they were old, and she wanted the new front-loading style. All Nick wanted was something that would wash his clothes.

After loading everything in the back of his SUV he drove slowly back toward his home. He only lived two miles outside of the village... still inside the city limits, but at his cabin it seemed he was miles from anywhere, and that's want he wanted. As he unloaded the supplies he thought about his visit to town. He had enjoyed it. He knew he would like his new life, maybe even better than his life with Melissa. He had grown tired of the bickering about money, how small their house was and her always wanting to take exotic trips they couldn't afford.

Nick and Melissa had met their junior year at DePaul University in Chicago and dated from then on until they married the fall after their graduation. Nick began teaching at the local high school and Melissa went to work for a large manufacturing company as an assistant to the production manager. Their marriage was happy and supportive until her salary grew to much more than his. She then constantly brought the fact up during arguments about the money she spent. Nick took the criticism but never backed down on his desire to teach and coach, she knew his aspirations when she married him. A year before the divorce Nick had known the marriage was in trouble. He just didn't know how much trouble. She had lied about needing to work late and having to go on company trips.

He had made it even easier for her to cheat, as he was always late at practice, gone scouting, or at games. He wondered why she had stopped coming to his games. He liked having her on the sidelines, being able to look up and see her smile. He figured she had just grown tired of watching the games after a few years. Nick accepted some of the blame for their divorce, but he never accepted the blame for her adultery, nor would he ever. He felt he didn't deserve being mistreated like that.

Melissa demanded the divorce in September. Seven months later Nick made the move to Sleepy Valley. He had received the final divorce papers in the mail on Christmas Eve.

2

Trudy locked the front door and said good-bye to Alice and Fred, the cooks, and left for home. She enjoyed Saturday evenings. She planned on taking a warm bath and then curling up on the couch and reading her new Adriana Trigiani book. She too had escaped from a bad marriage and found Sleepy Valley. Her good-looking, jock boyfriend had turned into an abusive, drunk, good-for-nothing husband. Ten years of marriage were nine years too many. She had finally had enough and left him lying in his vomit. She walked out the door with her clothing, valuables, and everything she could stuff in her car. She cleaned out the savings and checking accounts and drove. She ended up at Sleepy Valley and filed for divorce.

Trudy Ann Flynn had owned the small restaurant for eight years and made it her own. Folks came from neighboring communities to eat there. Her desserts were famous, and customers drove as much as an hour to get a piece of pie or a dish of cobbler. One tour bus made her place a regular stop so the retired sightseers could enjoy their best meal of the trip.

Trudy had settled into a comfortable life with her tomcat Scone. The cat was named after the Irish scones she made for breakfast each morning at the restaurant. Scone was the same color as her tan and black speckled treats. She worked most of the hours the restaurant was open - six days a week. She liked to spend her evenings with a good book or a good movie on television. Sundays she spent at church and visiting friends and walking through the hills and mountains. She had dated a few times since coming to Sleepy Valley, but nothing serious.

Trudy's home was a small, two-story farmhouse. The house was surrounded by the foothills of the mountains that enveloped Sleepy Valley. She owned the house and an acre of trees with a nice sized yard for flowers and a small garden.

~

Vincent closed the General store shortly after Trudy closed the restaurant. He knew no one would come into town just to shop his store. He walked a half block and turned right to his white Victorian home. The house was much too big for just him, so he rented the top floor to young newlyweds, Tom and Susan Brown. He had an outside staircase built to the top floor entrance.

He walked into the empty house, laid his violin on his piano, turned to the fireplace and said, "Good evening, my love." He went to his old record player and placed an album on it. He turned it on and watched as the arm moved over and dropped down onto the classical ridges and it began to play. Music filled the silence of his house, and Vincent walked to his favorite chair, sat down, and began going through his mail.

Vincent loved the quietness of Sleepy Valley, but missed the companionship of others. He was lonely, but he knew that not many of the residents had time to spend with an old man. Couples were either rearing their children or busy with everyday life. He had attended a few social functions in Pineville for retired citizens, but found them silly and funny smelling. He had told Trudy afterwards, "I'm not a big fan of old people. Not much fun. The men speak of past accomplishments and the women wear funny hats."

Vincent still had a zest for life and wanted to use it to make something good happen. He just wasn't sure what. A piece of his mail was the new Blue Ridge magazine. He read about future things to do in the states around him and listened to the beautiful harmonies that lifted off the record. He decided to take a nap and then maybe drive to Pineville for a nice dinner.

~

Nick was sitting on his porch watching the dark-eyed juncos and chickadees at the bird feeder. The evening was turning cool and he began wondering what he should fix for dinner. Maybe do without. He wasn't much of a cook yet. He heard a car driving up his gravel drive. A red Buick convertible came into view. The top was up. The car stopped and Vincent Marconi opened the door and waved. Nick waved back and walked to meet Vincent.

"Hello, Nick."

"Mr. Marconi, it's nice to see you again. Come have a seat." Nick pointed to one of his plastic lawn chairs on the porch.

"Thank you, Nick. I was on my way to Pineville and wondered if you would like to join me for dinner at the Oak Club restaurant, two bachelors out on the town."

Nick started to say no but quickly changed his mind. "I'd love to. What's appropriate attire for the Oak Club?" Nick had on a pair of Columbia pants and a T-shirt, his normal attire.

"A collared shirt and you should be fine," Vincent suggested. Vincent had on a white Nehru collared shirt and gray slacks with a black cardigan sweater over his well-trimmed body.

"I'll be just a couple of minutes. Please have a seat, Vincent." Nick quickly changed, freshened up, and brushed his teeth. He walked back out onto the porch and asked, "Would you like for me to drive?"

"No, no. I enjoy driving the roads."

Nick settled into the passenger seat and said, "Nice ride."

"Thank you. I never had a car in New York. Had to pass a driver's test when I moved here in 2002."

"Really? I can't imagine that. I mean not having a car."

"No need for one in New York. Cabs and the subway got us where we needed to go. Traveled the country by train or plane." Vincent turned left at the end of Mountain Road and headed toward

Pineville. Nick noticed how slowly Vincent drove, but he figured Vincent was in no hurry.

Nick looked out the window and studied some of the houses and farms for the first time. He was always driving. Seldom had he ever been a passenger in a car except maybe with his buddies on a golf outing.

"I enjoy driving very much. Most Sundays I take a long drive to a new town in the area. When it's warm enough, I like to drive with the top down and the breeze all around. I put a classical CD in and crank it up." Vincent laughed and Nick smiled and tried to imagine this stoic gentleman driving into a small town with the top down on his red convertible with his classical music cranked up as he cruised through town.

"I might have to join you on one of those trips."

"I'd love for you to."

Vincent pointed out different farms and crossroads and explained where each road went. Nick found out quickly that Vincent loved to fish as the old gentleman told him about the ponds at each of the farms. Nick enjoyed fishing also and asked, "Maybe you would take me with you on one of your excursions."

"You fish?"

"Yes. Not much lately. I used to go up to Ely, Minnesota, every year and fish the Boundary waters with some friends."

"Northern Pike and walleye?"

"Some. We mostly fished for smallmouth bass though."

"I'll call next time I go. The weather is good right now for the ponds. This week we'll go," Vincent promised.

"Count me in. I have nothing going on for a while."

The country road turned into a three-lane highway and soon they entered the city of Pineville. Vincent pointed out different businesses and pulled onto a street that led back out of town until they came to an old white mansion with an unlit sign that announced, "Oak Club." The restaurant was nestled under old oak trees with a mountain rising behind it. The sun was setting and lampposts lit up the walk to the entrance.

The young hostess smiled and said, "It's so nice to see you, Mr. Marconi," and they were shown to a table in front of a small stage. "Have a nice dinner."

"Thank you, Leslie."

"I see you have connections here at the Oak Club."

"She's a student of mine. I give violin lessons to a few of the more gifted musicians."

They ordered dinner and began talking. Vincent ordered a glass of wine. Nick asked for a diet Pepsi. Vincent shared his life as a musician and all the different towns and venues he had played. Nick shared his teaching experiences, which seemed minor in comparison. Vincent took great interest in Nick's stories. When dinner was nearly over a curtain opened on the stage and a string quartet was announced and played classical tunes and a few pop selections. One was a very good rendition of "Penny Lane."

Vincent gave all his attention to the music and would nod to Nick his approval during parts of the performance. Nick enjoyed the show and especially enjoyed watching Vincent. The dinner was delicious and the service wonderful. Nick wondered if it was because he was with Vincent. He wondered what Vincent must have been like on stage. He didn't have to wonder for long. The quartet invited Vincent to join them on stage and handed him a violin. The music they played was the same that Nick had heard Vincent playing in the store. When Vincent ended his performance he was given a standing ovation by the patrons, waiters, and waitresses. Vincent graciously bowed and returned to their table.

"You are truly a special musician, Vincent."

"Thank you, Nick. I love the music, and an entertainer never grows tired of the applause."

"I would guess not."

"The Oak Club has a different type of music almost every night.

On Fridays they have country. It's a totally different atmosphere. I rather enjoy it. A line dance might even break out. Bluegrass some nights and light rock once in a while. Monday is karaoke night."

"Well, it's a great place. Thank you for inviting me."

"It's my pleasure."

They talked for another hour and listened to the music until the quartet quit for the night. Vincent refused to let Nick pay for the meal or leave the tip. Nick decided not to push it. He figured he could offend Vincent and that was the last thing he wanted to do.

~

Trudy watched *Saturday Night Live* until it got too silly and she decided to turn in. Sunday school began at 9 a.m. and she taught the junior high class at her Southern Baptist church, Victory Road Community Church, named for the road it sat on halfway between Sleepy Valley and Pineville. The kids loved the fun-loving, red-haired Trudy, especially the boys. The class had more men volunteers than it needed.

The pastor used this to the church's advantage. If he needed a bunch of men for a project he would ask Trudy Flynn to head it up. The ladies of the church couldn't figure out why Trudy had been asked to organize the *parking lot black-coat sealing project.* It took no time to get the parking lot sealed with the large crew of men that showed up. Trudy poured some lemonade and went back to her restaurant.

The pastor smiled and winked at Trudy before she left and said, "Thank you, Trudy, couldn't have done this without you."

"No problem, pastor. We should use what the good Lord gives us the best we can," she said as she winked back.

Pastor Hill was only thirty-six, happily married to his wife Teresa with a twelve-year-old son, Jacob, and a ten-year-old daughter, Sara. The congregation loved the family. Pastor Payne Hill was not your usual fire-and-brimstone preacher. He had taken over the church as pastor six years earlier. The church held three hundred and fifty but had only a hundred attending when he arrived. With humor, love, caring about folks, and teaching Christ, the church was now bursting at the seams. He was unsure what to do about the crowds each Sunday. He didn't want to relocate or have a big fund-raising campaign to expand the building. He was prayerfully considering different options while lost souls were coming to repentance every week. He praised the Lord and kept serving.

~

Vincent dropped Nick off at his home shortly before midnight. They promised to go fishing the coming week. Nick sat on the porch in the night chill and felt happy for the first time in a long time. He knew this was the right choice; to get far from Melissa. But by doing so, he had left his parents behind. They still lived near Chicago, and it would be hard not seeing them as often. They wished him well and understood that he needed a change and a new life. They could see how the divorce had taken his spirit and twisted it to where Nick was no longer himself.

Nick's dad had retired six months earlier, and he told Nick to make sure and have a spare bedroom. They would be visiting often. Nick's sister, Laura, still lived near their parents with her family. He knew she would be there if needed. Truth was, during his marriage to Melissa they didn't spend that much time with his parents anyway. It seemed they spent a lot more time doing what she wanted.

Nick listened to the night sounds in the woods that surrounded his home. It felt welcoming. Nick had seen a sign advertising the Victory Road Community Church on the way to the Oak Club. It had read: "Worship begins at 10:15. Turn left." Nick wanted to find a church to attend, but not just any church. His plan was to attend several churches in the area and then join his favorite. He decided to go to bed and let Victory Road be his first.

~

Trudy rose at seven and curled her shoulder length hair under.

Applied her face, not much was needed, and put on her designer black slacks and blue blouse. She left the house at 8:15 and pulled into the church lot at 8:35. She had her blue leather Bible in one hand with her purse and her lesson in her other hand. Mr. "Red" Whitt, an older black gentleman, was at the door to greet her as he was every Sunday since she had been going to church there.

"Good morning, Miss Trudy."

"It is a good morning, isn't it Red? The Lord must be in a good mood today."

"I would say so, Miss Trudy."

Trudy walked down the hall toward her class, greeting people that she saw. Two kids were already in the room when she walked in. One was Jacob, the pastor's son, and April Grooms, who lived within walking distance of the church. They both were always waiting on Trudy to walk in. They loved to help with anything that Trudy needed done before the rest of the class arrived.

"Good morning April, Jacob."

~

Nick rose, readied himself, and put on a tie and sports jacket. He arrived at the church at ten. He liked the outside appearance of the church, an older looking, whitewashed, wooden, two-story building with a tall steeple and a cross on top, a plain but stylish look. There was a church cemetery located to the left of the building.

He wanted to get a feel of the church as others entered. He also wanted to look around and read any bulletins or material he could find in the lobby. He knew that most community churches had an affiliation with a certain denomination. What was this one? He wondered if he would agree with this church's teachings and beliefs.

He entered the sanctuary and sat midway and to the right at the end of the wooden pew. Folks began filling up the pews at a rapid pace. Nick had not expected so many people. He noticed that only a few elderly men had on ties or bowties. Suddenly he felt out of place. The congregation seemed to wear whatever they wanted, women included. The majority of attendees had on blue jeans and T-shirts. Everyone seemed happy and glad to be there.

Nick began going through the pamphlets trying to figure out what kind of place he had stumbled into. At Nick's old church, women never wore pants, and if they did, only once. They would be quickly informed that it wasn't correct behavior or stared at until they got the clue. Most men wore suits and ties. A few rebels would wear Dockers pants and golf shirts, but never T-shirts.

Nick looked up at the stage and noticed guitars, drums, and a keyboard. His old church had a piano. Most other instruments were frowned upon. Nick looked for a hymnal. Where did they keep the hymnals? Five minutes before the start of the service the place was packed. Men began setting up folding chairs around the sides and back. Nick thought that maybe something special was going on today. Nick had always disagreed with the legalism that his old church held onto so tightly. Women could only wear dresses at church, no clapping in church, members shouldn't go to movies, although everyone did, and the Kings James Version was the only Bible acceptable… and on and on.

A couple had settled next to Nick in the pew. The young man turned and introduced himself.

"Good morning. I'm Sam Wagner, and this is my wife Alice."

"Hello. I'm Nick Stewart. Nice to meet you."

"Good to meet you, Nick." Alice smiled and nodded, and they shook hands.

Nick asked, "Is it always this crowded?"

"Yes sir, for the past year or so," Sam answered. "I take it you're visiting us today."

"Yes. I am."

"We're glad you're here. I hope you'll enjoy it."

The musicians had made their way to the stage and the leader greeted everyone, "Good morning."

"Good morning," the crowd answered back.

"Let's worship the Lord." Before the drummer could count down, the congregation rose to their feet as the worship band began. It was like nothing Nick had ever seen in church. The music was loud with the people clapping and singing along with the verses shown on a screen atop the left side of the stage. The first song was "Open Skies" by the David Crowder Band followed by a Chris Tomlin song and "My Savior My God" by Aaron Shust. The building was rocking. The musicians were great. Nick felt as though he had been placed inside an Eagles concert.

Nick knew most of the songs. He listened to the nation-wide Christian *K-love* station on the radio at times. Nick didn't realize churches played this type of music in services. Some folks raised their arms in praise during the songs.

A gentleman took the stage as the band departed. He had on blue jeans, an old blue work shirt and tennis shoes. Nick wondered if they were having a drama act before the sermon. The man opened his Bible and prayed. He then had everyone stand out of respect for God's word as he read from Galatians. Everyone sat again and he began preaching. Nick wondered, *Is this really the pastor of this church?*

The pastor was funny, pointed, sincere, and his message was heartfelt. Nick enjoyed the message as much as any sermon he had ever heard preached. The worship band played again during the invitation. No one begged, but two ladies accepted Christ as their Lord and Savior when invited. Many went forward to pray.

After the service ended, Sam turned to Nick and asked, "Did you like the service, Nick?"

"Very much. Is it always this casual?"

"Yeah. Nothing fancy here. Come as you want. The important thing is to come and worship. We hope to see you next week."

Nick knew that Sam was right. God didn't care if he had on a tie. It was the worship that mattered. Nick took his time leaving the building. He was hoping to tell the pastor how much he enjoyed the sermon, but the pastor was in deep conversation with a young man that had come forward to pray. Nick didn't want to bother the pastor at that time. As he walked to his car he saw familiar red hair and realized that it was Trudy. He thought about the hours sign on her restaurant—*Sunday—closed—go to church!*

Nick drove home in a better mood. He felt he had made a great choice moving to Tennessee. He went home and spent the rest of the day walking his land and making plans for the woods and what was needed to fix up the house a little. Some fresh paint would be a good start.

3

Vincent spent Sunday afternoon driving with the top down. He decided to drive east. He took mainly country roads to the small town of Oak Ridge.

He wanted to call Nick and invite him to go along. He also thought that Nick might not be that interested in hanging out with an old man. He decided not to push it. He would invite him to fish with him on Wednesday.

Vincent was lonely for companionship. He loved Sleepy Valley, but missed his friends in New York, the get-togethers, small cafes, and afternoon lunches with other musicians. He missed their great debates about almost anything, but especially politics and the Yankees. He mostly missed the love of his life, his wife Maria. Here in Sleepy Valley the great passion was Tennessee Volunteer football. It meant nothing to Vincent, except he knew he could close the store on Saturday afternoons in the fall.

~

Trudy spent Sunday afternoon on her porch swing finishing *Home to Big Stone Gap*. Next she was going to read Fannie Flagg's *Can't Wait to Get to Heaven*. She spent the evening taking a walk with her good friend Gabry Morelli. Trudy and Gabry spent a lot of Sunday evenings together since neither had steady guys in their lives. They walked and talked of their dreams and how few men were available in Sleepy Valley.

There were plenty of single men in the area that would love to date Trudy or Gabry. But most of them had already been dumped by their first (or multiple) wives for good reasons.

As Gabry told Trudy, "The remaining bachelors are too young, too undate-able, too ugly, or just looking for a good time."

"Or *too* gay," Trudy added.

Trudy and Gabry were not those types of ladies. Although a good time was definitely wanted and probably needed, they wanted to hear *I do* first from the right man.

They both buried their lives into their work and waited for the right man to come along, hoping it would be before they became too old. While on their walk, Trudy told Gabry about a possibility that walked into her restaurant the day before.

"His name is Nick Stewart. He bought the Gibbons' place."

"His looks are?" Gabry asked with renewed interest in their conversation.

"Very nice, dark brown wavy hair. Nice body, I heard he coached sports in high school. He looked athletic."

"Did he have all his body parts?"

"The ones I could see." Trudy impishly grinned.

"Trudy. You devil."

"Sally told me he just got out of a messy divorce. He left Chicago and moved to Tennessee."

"So he's been married before?"

"So were we, Gabry."

"You're right. I shouldn't be so judgmental. Where is he working?"

"He's not right now. I guess he's taking his time."

"Well, judgmental or not. The whole thing sounds kind of strange. To move somewhere without a job or plans."

"You're probably right, unless he's very well-to-do."

Trudy nudged Gabry, "In that case, a little bit strange doesn't matter." They both laughed although they both knew it did matter.

~

Nick spent Monday and Tuesday painting the inside of his house. He was able to put a fresh coat of paint on every room. He had his Bose CD player blasting with Casting Crowns, Carrie Underwood, Keith Urban, and some Elton John among others as he painted. The two bedrooms he painted an off-white color. For the kitchen and table area he chose a soft greenish blue. The family room he painted a tan color. All the woodwork in the house had a hickory stain. The weather was perfect for leaving all the windows open to rid the house of the smell and help the paint dry. The third bedroom was upstairs and resembled a loft that overlooked the family room. Nick made it into a den for his computer. He painted it a dark tan, trying to make it feel like a man's hide-away. It worked. He liked it.

After he got everything, including himself, cleaned up, he poured himself a soda and went to the front porch and sat. His next project was to buy a porch swing and hang it from the ceiling rafters. The outside of the cabin was covered with wooden boards, stained dark, with gray wood shutters on the windows. Wooden fish scales, stained a little lighter, covered the gables of the home—a nice look.

Nick also needed to see Sally at the antique store about a bed for the guest room. He was sure his parents would visit soon to check on him. His mom called at least every other day to see if he was okay. He also needed some chairs. He actually needed a lot.

The phone rang around six-thirty and he answered, "Hello, Mom."

"No one has ever called me 'mom' before," Vincent replied. "I'm not sure where our relationship went wrong, Nick."

Nick laughed and apologized. Nick explained that the only person that had called the house since he moved in was his mom.

"No problem. Are you up for some fishing tomorrow?"

"I'm looking forward to it, Vincent. What time?"

"Around seven in the morning. You think you can drag yourself out of bed by then?"

"To give you a lesson, I'd rise at any hour," Nick teased.

"Is that so?"

"I'll pick you up at your place."

"Okay. See you then," Vincent said as he began to hang up the phone.

"Wait, Vincent, where is your place?" Vincent gave him the address and how many houses it was from the store. "How about meeting at Trudy's for breakfast? We can check out that great view you were talking about," Nick suggested.

"See you there around six-thirty."

Nick had bought Carl Hiaasen's new book *Nature Girl*. He went inside, relaxed on the couch, and read until *American Idol* came on the television. He was hooked, as was the whole nation. He watched Jennifer Lopez give advice to the contestants. Each of them had to sing a Latino song; of course it was awful because none of the contestants were Latino. Simon agreed they were awful. Nick wondered what the judges expected. His favorite winner so far had been Carrie Underwood. There was something about an unknown country girl blossoming before your eyes on the show that Nick thought should give everyone hope. Imagine all the people around the world that had greatness within them but needed that one break to showcase it; painters, singers, writers, humanitarians, and coaches with great abilities hidden in little villages and towns.

~

Vincent was at his favorite table in front of the window waiting for Nick when he walked in at exactly six-thirty. The small restaurant again was crowded. Nick expected to see Trudy when the waitress came to the table. But instead, a thin black lady with a pleasant smile settled up next to Nick and asked, "Coffee, honey?"

"No. Thanks. But I would like a glass of orange juice."

Vincent cut in before sixty-eight-year-old Miss Stella Baker could walk away, "Stella, this young man is Nick Stewart, our newest citizen. Nick bought the Gibbons' place."

"Sweetheart, it's nice to meet you. If you need someone to show you around the area, I'm available. I'm a lot of fun." She laughed a hearty laugh.

"Thank you, I'll keep you in mind," Nick teased back.

Stella turned to go get the juice. Nick said, "What happened to our great view, Vincent?"

"She'll be here soon. Trudy and Stella alternate days opening up the restaurant. They're both here by the rush at seven. Stella is a great lady. You'll like her."

"I already do. She called me 'sweetheart' and 'honey.'" They laughed.

"You two darlings ready?" Stella was back to take their order.

Nick ordered eggs, sausage links, and toast. Vincent asked for French toast and bacon. Suddenly a voice was heard behind the counter. "Don't you folks know how to fix toast at home? Paying me seventy-five cents to toast two pieces of bread isn't real bright. But I'll keep taking your money." Everyone laughed as Trudy made her way through the restaurant, welcoming each person.

Nick noticed that Tom was at the counter again. Tom loudly countered with, "It's the waitressing that we pay the extra for... to catch a glimpse of your smiling face, Trudy."

"Tom, that's not what you're trying to catch a glimpse of, you old fool." The place erupted in laughter. Trudy had arrived!

Tom's counter buddy Andy said, "She's got you pegged pretty good, Tom. She knows you're trying to catch a peek, and she knows you're an old fool."

Tom replied, "Yeah, and you're here for the great coffee, huh?"

Trudy came back around to them and stood in front of them.

"Don't fight boys. I've got one for each of you to stare at."

She turned and made her way over to Vincent and Nick. "Hello, gentlemen. I see you two have met."

Nick answered, "Yes. We've even been out on the town together."

"You two out prowlin' around together? Not a woman safe in the area."

Vincent smiled and told Trudy, "I've only got eyes for you." He reached for her hand and gently kissed it.

Trudy swooned and looked at Tom and Andy, "You two old goats could learn something from Vincent. He might actually get a peek." Laughter filled the place.

Trudy looked back at Vincent and Nick said, "I noticed you at church Sunday."

"You attended Victory Road and didn't even say hello?" Trudy asked.

"I'm sorry. But it was after the service in the parking lot, and you were headed away from me walking to your car."

"So what did you think of Victory Road?"

"I enjoyed it very much. It was refreshing. Have you gone there long?"

"Nearly three years," she said as she slid into the booth beside Nick. "I like it a lot. The pastor and his family are good people."

They small talked about the church and Trudy told him about the junior high class she taught. Trudy then asked, "What are you two up to this morning?"

Vincent answered, "I'm taking Nick out to Virgil Bowling's pond and giving him a fishing lesson."

"Is that so? I thought I was giving the lesson," Nick grinned.

"Sounds like we're going to have a few tall fish tales coming up," Trudy said.

Vincent asked, "Why don't you come along with us and referee? I'll even take along an extra pole."

"It would be a shame to have a lady out fish the both of you. You two have fun." Trudy rose and walked behind Tom and knocked his hat off his head again.

"Another love tap?" Tom asked.

"That's the only reason you keep wearing that hat indoors. I'm probably the only woman to ever put a hand that close to you," Trudy told Tom.

"The only woman I'd ever want to."

Nick and Vincent ate their wonderful breakfasts while talking about the local news and weather. Nick noticed how good Vincent's French toast looked and commented that he would have to order it next time.

Trudy and Stella yelled good-bye as they walked through the door. Virgil's farm was a couple of miles outside of town. Vincent had called Virgil the night before to make sure it was okay even though he had a standing invitation to fish the pond any time he wanted. Vincent wanted to be sure it was okay to bring Nick. "You can bring anyone you'd like at anytime," Virgil assured him.

The pond was large and triangular with tall reeds growing around the narrow end of the pond. Vincent used an open-face spinning reel with a minnow-looking lure that dove to a three-foot depth while being cranked in. Nick used a closed face Zebco reel with a light rod and decided to try a top-water jitterbug for a while. The jitterbug traveled from side to side as it gurgled through the water.

Soon Vincent had the first bass and, soon after, the second. Nick decided to switch lures and save the top-water for some late evening excursion. He tied on a lure much like what Vincent had on. On his fourth cast he caught his first bass of the day. By the end of the morning Nick had to thank Vincent for the lesson since Vincent had caught twice as many bass as he had. They released all of the fish to catch again at a later date.

They promised to make fishing a weekly event. Vincent said he knew plenty of ponds and streams to try. It was great for both of them to have a buddy to hang out with. Despite Vincent's age, Nick knew they would become good friends.

As Nick drove back into town Vincent said, "I think Trudy might have her eye on you."

"What do you mean?"

"There aren't many eligible good-looking men in Sleepy Valley. You'd be a nice catch."

"I thought we were doing the fishing," Nick suggested.

"I saw the way she looked at you. She gave you an extra sausage link this morning."

"What?"

"When a customer orders eggs and sausage, they always get three sausages—you got four. I'm telling you, she's got her eyes on you."

Nick grinned and shook his head, "Vincent, I'm a long ways from wanting to start another relationship. Trudy is a fine lady, but I want some space from women for a while." He pulled into the parking spot in front of Vincent's home. "Thanks for the morning. I had a great time. Come out and visit anytime. We'll sit on the porch and watch the birds."

"I'll do that."

"Oh, Vincent. Where can I buy a nice porch swing?"

"You could go to Pineville, but you really ought to drive by Andy's house out on Yellow Possum Road. He builds them, and they're sturdy and comfortable. Almost everyone goes to Andy when they need something built."

"Andy who?"

"Counter Tom's friend, Andy Spencer. He's quite handy with wood."

Nick went home and got cleaned up. He watched the birds for a while, and then checked the phone book for Andy's address. He studied the county map for Yellow Possum Road and headed out to buy a porch swing. Nick had to drive past Virgil's farm to get to Andy's road. He was pleased that he was learning his way around and recognizing a few of the landmarks.

The land was wooded with a few cleared pastures for cows and horses. He saw deer standing at the edge of a field. He slowed to a stop to watch them for a minute. It reminded him of Cades Cove in the Great Smoky Mountains National Park, his most favorite spot he had ever been. The road climbed a small hill, and at the very top was Andy's place. A sign hung from the homemade mailbox announcing Andy's Woodshop. It had a great view of the valley and the mountains beyond. He wondered if he should have called before stopping by.

Nick turned into the gravel driveway that led to the small barn with a sign on the door that read, "OPEN." Nick parked, looked around at the neatly trimmed yard and well-maintained, white farmhouse. Not what Nick expected. Nick walked to the door, opened it, and went inside. The shop was filled with Andy's wooden creations. Small tables and chairs, stools and benches, mirrors, a few beds and dressers, and jelly cabinets. Nick was amazed at the variety and quality of Andy's work. He walked toward the sound of what he recognized as a lathe turning in the back room. Nick had taught woodshop in school one year when the school was shorthanded. He learned more from the students than they learned from him.

He looked into the room and saw Andy standing at the lathe turning the leg of a table. A sign at the door read "Hit Buzzer for Service." He pressed the buzzer and Andy turned off the lathe and smiled as he turned around. The workroom was filled with stacks of wood and every imaginable tool.

"Is it Nick?" Andy said as he stretched his hand out to Nick.

"Yes, it is."

"Tom told me who you were this morning at Trudy's. It's nice to meet you."

"Thank you. You too."

"What brings you out here? Let me guess… you would like to fish my pond."

"No, although that isn't a bad idea. I'm looking for a porch swing and Vincent told me that you were the man to see. From what I can see, he was right."

"I have a lot to choose from, Nick. Follow me." Andy took Nick through another door and to Nick's surprise there were swings hanging from every rafter in the room. He had different styles and shapes. They were made from different types of wood. Some had designs cut into the backs. Some were painted. They all showed great craftsmanship.

"This is amazing, Andy."

"Everyone that walks in here for the first time has pretty much the same reaction. Keeps me busy and out of trouble. My wife appreciates that."

"I guess so."

"Try them out. That's why they're hanging like that. You need to see how it fits you. Everyone is different. Some you won't like. I can even custom make you one."

Nick tried out different ones. He saw a large natural stained swing that seemed longer than the others. "That one will seat three adults comfortably and a person can even stretch out in it and take a nap or read. I don't sell many, but it's my favorite."

Nick tried it out and found it very much to his liking. "This is the one. I'll take it. I also would like one of those coat racks with the antlers and a porch rocker I saw in the other room."

"Good choice. You want me to follow you home?" Andy asked.

"Excuse me, what?"

"The price includes delivery and installation. We can set up a time that would be more suitable."

"That's real service. I'm not used to that. Actually I was going to stop at Sally's for a while." Nick looked at his watch and saw that it was two. "How about four? Or you name a time if today isn't good."

"Four is fine. I'll see you then." Nick pulled out his checkbook and wrote a check.

"It was nice meeting you, Andy. I'll see you this afternoon. Oh, can I help you load the swing?"

"Thank you, but I can get it, no problem. See you later."

Nick liked Andy. He'd imagined Andy and Tom as men out of work and not up to much. Nick knew that he needed to get rid of the notion he had of Southern folks. In Illinois he had heard all his life that Southerners lacked education and most of their teeth, and that they were inferior in intelligence. He knew it wasn't true. He liked the people, the down-home atmosphere and Southern hospitality. But when you hear something so many times it creeps up on you at times. The way racism is passed from generation to generation.

Nick drove slowly back into the village and pulled into a spot in front of Sally's Antiques. Nick knew that almost all bedroom furniture was now being imported from China, Vietnam, or some other foreign country. It saddened him. He liked the idea that his furniture would be made from American trees by American workers. So an antique bedroom set would solve the problem or he could go back to a local woodworker such as Andy.

He walked into the antique store and was greeted warmly by Sally.

"Good afternoon, Nick. How can I help you today?"

"I'm looking for a nice bed for my guest bedroom, a nightstand and a dresser. They don't really have to be a set. I kind of like mixing pieces that I like."

"That's a good idea, especially with antiques. Let me show you what I have."

Nick found everything that he wanted and even bought a small rocker. Sally said she could have them delivered the next day. Nick told her he would be at home all day. As he left the store he noticed that Trudy's was still open with the last customer paying at the cash register. He decided to take some dessert home. He opened the door in time to let the customer leave.

"I'm sorry, we're closed," Trudy announced without looking up.

"Is there time to get a dessert to go? If not, I'll get it another time."

Trudy recognized the voice and looked up smiling. For Nick, she would open the store at midnight to get him a piece of pie.

"Come in, Nick. Of course I can get you that dessert. I have blackberry cobbler and a couple pieces of pecan pie."

"I'll take the cobbler. Thank you."

"You didn't come to town just to get dessert did you?"

"No, but I would. I was next door at Sally's buying some furniture and noticed that your door was still unlocked."

"How was your fishing with Vincent?"

"Very enjoyable. Vincent's a very good fisherman and schooled me pretty much the entire morning."

"He's a great person. He's gone fishing almost every week since he moved here. So he's got a bit of an advantage on you."

"No wonder he knew the best lures and spots. But he's a great guy. I also made my way out to Andy Spencer's woodshop. I bought a fantastic porch swing from him."

"He builds the best swings around here. Of course, he's probably the only one that builds them around here." Trudy said as she placed Nick's cobbler in a bag. "How do you like Sleepy Valley so far?"

"A lot. It's beautiful country with friendly people. What more could a person ask for?"

"Is Andy hanging your swing?"

"At four, so I had better be going."

"I'd like to see it some time, Nick."

"You're welcome anytime. We can sit, swing, and watch the birds."

"Sounds nice."

Nick paid and left. Trudy had almost three helpings of cobbler left and had given them all to Nick. There was no use letting it go to waste. She wondered if maybe she was trying to feed her way into Nick's thoughts.

4

Nick spent the next two days working on the house and yard. He spread some wildflower seed at the edge of the woods and raked it in hoping it would take. He spent a lot of time in the porch swing. One thing he really liked was the drink holders built into the arms of the swing. Two men had delivered the furniture from Sally's Antiques. He decided he liked the furniture better than what he had so he moved the antiques into his bedroom. The antique bed, dresser, and nightstand had much more character than the plain head-board and dull dresser Melissa had left him. He filled the guest bedroom with his old drab furniture for his parents when they visited.

He enjoyed the solitude of the days, the quietness of his place, and the chance to take pleasure from the nature around him. He felt unburdened and at peace at last. Arguing and shouting had become too much of his life over the past year. He hated it and was glad it was over. But he missed the good times. It hadn't always been fighting.

When he and Melissa first married they were so happy. They planned a life of caring for each other and a life of fun. They wanted three or four children and even had the names picked out. They laughed all the time and had plenty of friends. Nick loved his teaching position and had a good rapport with kids. Melissa moved up the ladder at the company she worked for. The first five years were good, but then things changed. The next four years weren't good.

Nick was sitting on the swing thinking about his past marriage. The evening sun was glowing on the trees that surrounded his front yard when a small blue Ford SUV emerged down the lane. He knew instantly who it was when he saw the red hair flying from the open window.

He walked off the porch and opened the door for her. Nick couldn't help but think what a good-looking woman Trudy was. She was wearing a simple yellow sundress scoped low at the neckline. She flashed a big smile at Nick and said, "You invited me to come sit on your new porch swing and watch the birds, so here I am."

"I'm glad you did. It's a perfect evening for it. The birds have been swarming the feeder. Hummingbirds have been flying to their feeder also."

"I love to watch the hummingbirds. I don't have a feeder, but they like my trumpet vines and honeysuckle."

"Please, come have a seat," Nick invited.

Trudy walked up the steps to the porch and carefully sat on the swing. Nick sit on the opposite end of the swing.

"Nick, this is really a great place. It's so peaceful."

"That's what drew me to it. I needed the quietness and privacy it offered."

"Until something barges up to your door."

"Your company is welcome. Sometimes being alone too long can bring back a lot of unwelcome memories. A person can begin to dwell on them."

"Then we begin to feel sorry for ourselves—a sad place to be," Trudy agreed.

Nick nodded his head in agreement. "You're right. It sounds like you've got experience at this pathetic existence. You went through it also, huh?"

"Not really. I never wanted to be alone. I like people too much. For me it was more doubting myself and my abilities."

"Explain."

"After I got rid of the no-good husband, I had no idea what I would do. I married Glen right out of high school and had no train-ing at all. All I knew how to do was be a wife, some secretarial skills, and being taking advantage of. I was so young and naive. It was easy for Glen to take advantage of me. When I finally left Glen, there I was on my own, doubting myself."

"I'd say you've turned out great." Nick pointed to a pair of cardinals that had flown to the feeders. The low rays of the sun was lighting up the bright red of the male and the true beauty of the female.

"They are beautiful, Nick. What kind of bird is that small one on the ground?" Trudy pointed to a spot under the feeder.

"That's a wren. She's built a nest in that little birdhouse hanging in the dogwood tree." Nick pointed to the small house he had hung from the lowest limb. "The pair sing all the time. I can hear them through my open window when I wake up."

"At least the birds got us off that terrible subject," Trudy said.

"I'm happier than I was. I think I'll enjoy living here. Would you like something to drink?" Nick offered.

"Okay. A Coke or Pepsi would be good if you have it."

Nick left for the kitchen. Trudy studied the front yard and porch as Nick prepared her tall glass of soda. He hadn't expected Trudy to visit so soon. Knowing that a beautiful woman waited for him on the porch made his hands tremble as he placed ice in the glass. He felt strange being alone with a different woman than Melissa. He took a deep breath and headed back to the porch. Nick handed the glass to Trudy and sat on the opposite end of the swing.

"I do have Pepsi for the *real women* that visit."

"You had to bring that up. Sometimes I don't know what I'm thinking or saying. It just pops out of my mouth. I'm sorry."

"That's okay. Made me feel like I was still in my marriage—*be a real man.*"

Trudy laughed. Did she really say that?

"In several ways. *Can't you do better than that? My father never would have done that.*"

"That must have been hurtful."

"Yeah." Nick handed Trudy the glass of Pepsi.

"I'd love to see the inside. Do you mind?"

"Not at all."

They walked through the front screen door into the family room. Trudy looked around at the paintings and pictures in the room. The room had a manly but comfortable feel. It was inviting.

"This is pretty much it," motioning around the inside of the house.

He showed her where the bedrooms were and pointed his head toward the loft. "My den is up there. That's it. All I need."

"It's a great place, Nick."

"Would you like to take a walk and see some of the land?"

"I'd love to." Trudy was already feeling very comfortable around Nick, like she had known him a while. He seemed like a man who could be trusted. It also helped that she liked his looks, a handsome, gentle, rugged look. She sensed he was a kind man. The type of man she could see herself falling for. Who was she kidding? Certainly not herself; she was already falling for him.

Nick held the door for Trudy and then led her along the back yard. Nick explained how much land he owned and that he hadn't had time to see all of it yet.

"Next time wear hiking shoes and we'll walk around the property. There's a small creek running through the woods. Saw a Yellow Lady Slipper earlier this week."

"Rare."

"Yes they are from what I understand."

They walked around the yard and back to the porch swing. The sun was setting. The last rays were lighting the tops of the trees as the air turned cooler. Nick and Trudy sipped their drinks and chatted as the darkness closed in.

They were talking about the church when car headlights appeared on the gravel lane. "I wonder who that could be," Nick questioned out loud.

"You've become quite popular."

The car parked behind Trudy's and Nick recognized the red convertible. Nick rose from the swing and stood at the edge of the porch as Vincent walked around the SUV. "Good evening, Vincent."

"Nick, my boy. Am I barging in?"

"No. The more the merrier. You are always welcome."

"Hello, Miss Trudy. Aren't you lovely this evening?" They held hands for a moment.

"Vincent, come sit next to me on Nick's new swing. It's very comfortable, and the evening is perfect. This swing is big enough for the three of us. I would love sitting between two handsome men."

"I can't speak for Nick. But I know one would be me," Vincent laughed. "I would ask what you two were up to, except that wouldn't be very gentlemanly."

Trudy answered, "I dropped by to see his new swing and watch the birds. Then we were going to run around naked in the moonlight."

"Sounds like I got here just in time. That's my kind of fun. Old Tom is going to miss out again." Everyone laughed.

"What brings you by, Vincent—besides the nudity?" Nick asked.

"Isn't that enough?" Trudy suggested.

Vincent answered, "Came to invite you to go to the Oak Club for dinner and some country music. Now I can invite both of you. Let's go show the locals how to line dance."

Trudy answered first, "I haven't had dinner yet, and I haven't danced in a while. I'm ready. Sounds like fun."

Nick then realized why Vincent had on cowboy boots and a slide tie around his neck. "Okay. I don't want to be the party pooper. But I left my cowboy boots in Illinois."

"Just bring your *yee-haw* and you'll be fine," Vincent said.

Vincent wanted to drive and Trudy rode shotgun. Nick sat in the back and marveled at how Trudy and Vincent teased and laughed all the way to Pineville. He tried to figure out what Trudy's intent was. She was such a nice person, he thought maybe she was just being neighborly, dropping by to make him feel welcomed. Maybe she needed someone her age to be friends with, someone to talk to, share secrets or confide in. Maybe, hopefully not, she was looking for a husband, and he was the newest candidate in the area.

This thought concerned him. He wanted to get away from involvements and being responsible for someone else's feelings. He felt he needed to concentrate on himself. He felt depleted of his needs and happiness. He didn't mind female company once in a while, but only once in a while. The other side of his brain thought, *every single man in Tennessee would give their right arm to have Trudy fuss over him, a chance to date her, even to marry her. She was gorgeous and built like a... well... she did have a nice body.*

Trudy laughed a little louder. "Nick. I think Vincent just made a pass at me."

"I'm sorry. I didn't hear," Nick apologized.

Vincent answered, "I told her we had the most beautiful date in the county."

"I can't argue that."

"Now you're both making a pass. How will I choose between you?" They all laughed.

~

Trudy was very flattered to have Vincent and Nick say how nice she looked. Men were always flirting in the café or at church. None of them interested her, though. Nick did. She began thinking Wednesday about dropping by Nick's place when he told her about the swing and she had pretty much invited herself. She had hoped he would ask her to come by on a certain date or time. Instead of a *drop by sometime and we'll watch the birds* invitation. Men!

She had thought about it almost non-stop the last two days. She was wishing he would be back in to eat or to invite her properly.

By Friday at quitting time she had had enough. She was going to make a move. She had hurried home leaving Stella to close the restaurant. She showered, shaved her legs, in case his hand happened to accidentally touch them, fixed her hair and make-up, and put on her sexiest casual dress with her best push-up Victoria Secret bra. If she was going to show a little cleavage she didn't want anything sagging.

During her drive to Nick's her stomach was all in knots, she knew it was nerves, she couldn't help it. She had even been dieting since Wednesday, trying to lose a couple of pounds. She didn't need to, but try telling that to a woman trying to impress her quarry.

She almost turned around when she got to the lane at Nick's house. *Ladies don't just show up. How desperate do you want him to think you are? I can't believe I'm turning in. Maybe he won't be home. I hope he's home. I shaved my legs.*

All her doubts disappeared when she saw him on the porch and then walking to her car to greet her. When he opened the door for her, she thought her heart would explode. *What a gentleman,* she thought. What a handsome gentleman. It was all worth taking a chance.

She was having a wonderful evening with Nick. Casual, laughing, and they seemed to be hitting it off. She found herself looking at him, almost staring at his strong jaw, kind eyes and lips. She even thought of what it would be like to kiss him.

Then Vincent showed up at Nick's. Trudy told herself to make the best of the situation. Vincent's idea of going to the Oak Club sounded like fun. She quickly thought about the chance to dance with Nick, maybe a slow dance. A very, wrap my arms around him slow, very slow dance. Plus, she was feeling hunger pains. She needed some food before she passed out in his arms while slow dancing.

Vincent wanted to have a fun evening and thought Nick might enjoy a night out. He enjoyed Nick's company. Having Trudy come along was a pleasant surprise. He thought he might get a slow dance from her. Never too old to hold a beautiful lady in your arms and dance the night away, at least for a few minutes.

Vincent pulled into the parking lot of the Oak Club. Nick quickly got out and opened Trudy's door.

"Thank you, Nick," Trudy said as she slipped her hand inside Nick's arm. It surprised Nick, but truthfully he didn't mind walking into the Oak Club with Trudy on his arm. They were quickly shown to their table even though there were customers waiting in the lobby for dinner tables.

The DJ had the country tunes cranking and the dance floor was half full with couples twirling and dipping and circling side by side around the floor.

"Have you two eaten?" Vincent asked.

They both answered that they hadn't. Vincent motioned to the waitress who promptly brought menus and took their orders.

"Great service," Trudy commented.

"I've learned that Vincent has a lot of clout here."

"Really," Trudy said. "Must be the charm?"

A Rascal Flatts slow song began to play as soon as they had ordered. Vincent rose from his seat and asked Trudy if she would like to dance. She stood and they walked to the dance floor. As the singer crooned about a *winding road,* Vincent gracefully led Trudy around the floor as gently as a person would walk with a butterfly perched on their finger not wanting it to fly away. His hand was carefully placed on the small of her back and his other hand held hers high, and he kept a proper distance between their bodies as they flowed along.

Vincent knew there was nothing worse than an old man acting as though he was chasing a younger woman on the dance floor, trying to get a cheap thrill at youth. He had seen it and thought "how pathetic" it was.

They returned laughing and Nick praised their abilities. The salads had arrived and they talked and laughed during dinner. The music was loud and fun and the wooden floor got more crowded with each song. A line dance finally broke out and they enjoyed watching the rhythmic steps back and forth, over and over. Everyone seemed to be having a great time.

Vincent laid his fork down and announced, "Excuse me, I hear the music calling my name." Vincent quickly found a spot in the front row between two older ladies and he knew all the steps as though he had been doing the dance all his life.

"I never realized Vincent was so outgoing. He's so much fun."

Nick agreed and added, "He surprises me every time I'm with him. I think I might learn a lot from him."

After three or four songs the line dancing broke up for a while and Martina McBride slowed things up. Trudy put her hand in Nick's and motioned with a nod for him to join her on the dance floor. Nick positioned his hands as Vincent had. They slowly moved around the floor. The lights darkened overhead for mood and Trudy took the opportunity to loosen Nick's grip on her right hand and place both arms around Nick's neck. Another minute into the song and her body moved closer, her head fell onto his shoulder.

Their feet moved to the music as their bodies blended into slow motion. Thoughts raced through their minds as they held one another on the dance floor:

"I might be acting too fast, but I can't help feeling this way."

"She's acting way too fast."

"It feels so comfortable with my arms around Nick's neck and my body pressed against his. I hope he's enjoying it as much as I am."

"I feel very uncomfortable. It's too soon after the divorce to be dancing this close to another woman."

"I hope I didn't use too much of my favorite perfume."

"Trudy smells wonderful, a soft and sweet aroma. Does she always smell like this, or does she have on perfume?"

"I love the feel of our bodies moving as one. It feels as though I'm floating on a cloud."

"Trudy must think I have two left feet. I know I've never been a good dancer. It feels like my feet are stuck in cement."

"Are we the only two dancing? With my eyes closed it feels as though we're alone."

Nick senses that everyone at the club is staring and whispering.

Trudy wonders if she had placed her body too close to Nick's. What must he be thinking?

Nick was thinking what a sensual pleasure it was having Trudy's breasts pressed against his chest.

As Martina sung the last note they untangled and walked slowly back to the table without talking. They smiled at each other.

Vincent was missing. The DJ announced that everyone should grab a partner and get ready for a square dance. "Your caller will be Jake Scooter and your music will be provided by Vincent Marconi. Let's have a warm welcome for both of them." Vincent was in front of the microphone with a fiddle and began playing. The caller called out the steps, and the dance floor took on a whole different look and feel. Trudy and Nick sat and watched the groups circle and laugh. Vincent was a big hit as always.

Vincent returned to the table after the square dance was done. He soon left for the dance floor and danced away most of the evening. Nick and Trudy relaxed, watched the different dances, and small talked over the music. The evening was tremendous fun, and they left the club a little before midnight.

Vincent dropped them off and Nick walked Trudy to her car. He opened the door for her. Then she smiled, leaned in and gave Nick a kiss at the corner of his lips.

"Thank you for a wonderful evening, Nick."

"I enjoyed it also. See you soon."

5

Nick woke to the wren's singing and quickly thought about the evening before. For the most part he had enjoyed the evening. He liked the attention that Trudy had given him. But he was worried. He hoped Trudy wasn't getting the wrong impression. He was concerned she was. Any man would enjoy Trudy's company and probably be stupid for thinking anything except for how lucky he was. Nick knew he just wasn't interested in any type of relationship except friendship. He wanted Trudy to be his friend and nothing more—at least for now.

~

Trudy woke feeling ashamed. *What A floozy I was,* she told herself. She worried about what Nick thought of her. She hadn't planned on going dancing or kissing Nick. Who was she kidding? She'd thought of kissing Nick since the first time she'd seen him at the restaurant. But she also thought that maybe Nick enjoyed the dancing and the kiss. He was a man, wasn't he? Perhaps he was shyer than she thought. Her mind went back and forth as she waited on her customers. She needed to talk to Gabry. Gabry was her support and rock, but she was out of town for the weekend at an art show.

Trudy paced the restaurant taking orders and bringing plates of food as if she were just another waitress. Tom asked, "What's wrong with you this morning? Aren't you going to knock my hat off? I haven't heard you yell at anyone since I walked in. Twenty minutes of quiet—I think that's a record."

Trudy walked around to the opposite side of the counter and faced Tom and stared at him. Tom stared back and demanded, "My hat. Aren't you going to do something about my hat?"

Trudy looked at him and reached over the counter and carefully removed his orange Volunteer cap. She picked up the water glass that hadn't been touched by Tom and poured it into the cap. She then placed it back on his head and the patrons erupted in laughter. "Can't you see I'm not in the mood today—you old fool?" Water ran down his head and face, and he grinned.

"That's my girl," Tom gurgled through his grin.

Trudy was really worried about coming on too strong with Nick. *Why did I do it?* She thought to herself. I always come on too fast. She knew she was impulsive and it had cost her plenty in her life. Ten wasted years with her marriage to Glen. She had married Glen two months after meeting him. Her parents warned her that he was "no good" and that she was "too young" to get married. She didn't listen and jumped into the marriage to escape the criticism.

She had lost her virginity when she was a sixteen-year-old sophomore in high school to the senior star quarterback. She had thought it was true love after one date. At the end of the date he'd gotten what he was after. There was no second date.

She now realized she had these impulsive tendencies and had tried her best to unburden herself of them. Becoming a Christian had helped her with her decision-making. She was much better. She regretted coming on so strong with Nick the night before and worried that she may have driven him away before anything even started. She couldn't blame him. *What kind of woman just shows up at a man's house uninvited, puts her body against him during their first dance together, and then kisses him goodnight?*

She had to apologize. She knew she had to apologize. She thought about going to his house after work to apologize. She quickly thought, *Not again, you dummy.*

Trudy continued her work with all the troubling feelings going through her head. Her customers knew something was wrong.

~

Nick spent all day Saturday working in his yard. It was a beautiful spring day. He went to a nursery and bought red impatiens and a couple of red azalea bushes that were in full bloom and planted them on the northeast corner of the house.

He gathered some fallen limbs, cut them into firewood size and started a woodpile. He would stockpile until the next winter, a little at a time. He thought about church while he was working. He really liked Victory Road Community Church but decided to stick with his plan and visit a different church Sunday.

Toward evening, he walked his property and followed it all the way around the edge. He saw plenty of small wildlife such as squirrels and chipmunks. He scared two deer near the creek. Their slender white tails rose and they vaulted away. Birds were everywhere and seemed to follow him again. He thought about how beautiful his land was; a great place to live and die. It was exactly what he was looking for.

A thought went through his mind of Melissa. He questioned whether she would like the place and the seclusion. What did it matter now? He reasoned that she would never see the place anyway, but maybe if she did... He knew he had to stop thinking about her coming back to him. It was over, long over. The hurt of the divorce leapt onto him again. He went to the front porch and sat on his swing and watched the sun shining on the eastern trees in front of his house until it set.

~

Monday morning Nick decided to head into Sleepy Valley and buy groceries. He wanted to see Vincent and check on him. He planned on spending the afternoon driving around the surrounding towns and counties to see what was around. He had only lived in Sleepy

Valley for nine days. Going to a different church turned into a disappointment. It was a dull service with a humanistic sermon. The gatherers looked bored sitting in their pews.

Nick was proud of himself for all he had accomplished in such a short time. The house and land looked better. He had made friends. He knew he needed to make attempts to continue the friendships. He couldn't expect them to always make the first moves.

Mid-morning Nick jumped in his vehicle and drove toward the village. He passed the sign that had read "Puppies for Sale" the first time he saw it. This time it read "One Puppy Left—Free to a Good Home." Nick drove to the next drive, pulled in and turned around. He turned into the lane with the sign. He stopped and read it again. He decided to see what kind of pup it was. He knew it had to be a mongrel to be free.

He loved the house, a nice small timber frame log home, a house he might have built. A lady came out of the house with a toddler next to her. Nick got out and walked toward her.

"Good morning. How can I help you?" she asked pleasantly.

"I saw the sign about the free puppy to a good home. Thought I might take a look at it if you still have it."

"We do. Follow me. He's in the barn."

"I'm Nick Stewart. I bought the Gibbons' place. We're almost neighbors."

"Where are my manners? I'm Betty Carter, and this is Noah. Say hello, Noah." The little boy hid behind his mom and waved his little hand from around her leg.

"My husband is Jerry. He's at work."

"What does he do?" Nick asked, trying to small talk till they reached the barn.

"He works for the local phone company. He's a lineman."

"Hard work."

"You'll have to stop by and meet him. He just said we should come over and introduce ourselves. We were waiting a proper period of time to let you settle in." Nick didn't realize there was a proper period of time.

"I'd very much like to meet him. You have a lovely place."

"Thank you. This place has always been our dream." Betty said as she opened the barn door. They walked down the center path through the barn. Nick could hear the whimpering as they neared. A beagle walked from the far end to meet them. Nick bent down to pet her.

"That's Lill. She's the mother of the pup." Nick had nothing against beagles. The fact was he had always liked them, but it wasn't what he had in mind for his dog. They made it to one of the cribs and there was the pup.

"He's a cripple. No one wants him. We may have to put him down."

Nick noticed that the pup limped badly on his back left leg. It looked a little shorter than the others. The pup didn't look like a beagle. It was a yellowish-tan color and had a white stripe from his nose to the top of his head. "This pup isn't a beagle."

"He's a mix. Lill apparently had a fling with the yellow lab down the road. Some of the pups were marked like beagles and others were like this. The kids say we should call the puppies beagledors."

"How many were in the litter?"

"Six," she answered as Nick stepped inside to play with the little guy. The pup licked Nick's hand and jumped up on him. The pup seemed normal to Nick except for the limp. He was a friendly, outgoing pup.

"How old is he?" Nick asked.

"Ten weeks today."

"If you don't mind, I'll take him." Nick couldn't believe he said it.

"Not at all. We've been hoping someone would have the heart to take him. He's a sweet dog. I didn't want to say anything unless you took him, but you're the first person he's made over. He has pretty much ignored everyone else."

Betty gave Nick a cardboard box and they placed it on his passenger seat. Nick placed the pup inside. Nick thanked Betty and Noah and drove away and again headed to the village. Nick pulled into an empty spot in front of the general store. It was a nice cool April morning so Nick cracked the windows a little and left the pup in the SUV and went inside. Vincent was waiting on a customer.

"Thank you, come again," Vincent said as the customer turned to leave. "Nick, my boy, what brings you into town?"

"Just wanted to drop by and say hello. I wanted to thank you for Friday night. Had a great time."

"The Oak Club is quite a place, isn't it?"

"Yes, it is."

"You and Trudy seemed to hit it off, huh?" Vincent smiled and nudged Nick on the arm.

"Maybe too much."

"A beautiful woman is a good thing, Nick." They both laughed. The obvious seemed so funny.

"I don't want Trudy thinking that I'm looking for a serious relationship, and she was moving in awfully fast."

"It's simple, my son."

"Explain."

"Tell her. Better to tell her how you feel. Women like honesty. It might hurt when she first hears it, but after Trudy thinks about it, she'll understand. She's a smart lady."

"You really think that will work—honesty?"

"I don't know. It sounded good though, didn't it?" Vincent smiled. "Who knows what women think. They're a wonderful but strange group of people. God created them from man, and I'd bet he himself doesn't always understand them." They laughed in agreement.

"I've got something to show you." Nick motioned for Vincent to follow him outside. Nick opened the door and pulled the pup from the cardboard box. "What do you think?" Nick handed the pup to Vincent.

Vincent made over the pup and got licks to his face in return. Nick placed the pup on the sidewalk. He ran to the grassy area and peed.

Nick explained how he got the pup and what Betty had told him about the limp and maybe putting the pup down.

"Nick, I think the pup is great. We all have flaws. No one has put us down yet. What are you going to name him?"

"Haven't thought about it yet. Any ideas?"

"No."

"Where can I get a dog cage?" Nick asked.

Vincent looked at Nick with a shocked look on his face and said, "You are at the general store. Come on, bring the pup with you."

Vincent led Nick to the aisle that also had the dustpans, Dirt Devil vacuums, and other things starting with a "d." There it was; a dog cage. Nick bought it along with a dog collar which was in the "c" aisle and two dog bowls in the "f" aisle.

Vincent told Nick he could get dog food at the market across the street. Before Nick left he invited Vincent to dinner at his house around six-thirty. "Nothing fancy, we'll grill some hamburgers and I'll make some potato salad."

"Can't pass that up. I'll bring the wine."

Nick placed everything into the car and walked across the street to the market. Trudy was waiting on a customer while facing the window when she saw Nick walk across the street. Her heart sank. Was Nick going to come into town and not stop by to say hello? She figured she was right in her thinking. She had driven him away already.

Trudy kept an eye on the street as she worked. When she saw Nick coming out of the market she told Stella, "I'm taking a break. Will you watch my customers?"

She didn't wait for the reply. She placed her apron on an empty chair and walked out the door. Nick was placing the bags in the back of the SUV when she said, "Hello, Nick."

Nick pulled the door down into place and turned to Trudy. He smiled and said, "Good morning, Trudy."

His smile made her forget for a moment what she had come out to say. She hesitated and then began, "I'm sorry. I feel like a fool."

Nick was caught by surprise. He knew what she was saying but didn't know how to respond. He stood there looking at her. Finally she continued, "I know I came on a little too strong Friday night. I embarrassed myself. We barely know each other. I'm so sorry."

Nick was struck by how sincere Trudy was and how worried she looked. Where was the Trudy smile and personality? At last he spoke, "Vincent is coming over for a cookout at six-thirty. I would like for you to join us. If you could come between five-thirty and six we can talk. I feel we need to talk."

"I'll bring the dessert."

"Okay."

Trudy felt like kissing him again, but refrained. Her smile returned and she thought maybe she hadn't ruined things between them. She turned and headed back to the restaurant. She said over her shoulder, "See you then, Nick."

"Bye."

Nick jumped into his seat and told his pup, "We're going to have a cookout. Burgers for everyone. The pup excitedly tried to climb up the box to Nick. Nick reached over and scratched behind the dog's ears.

Nick's plans were now changed. No driving around the area in the afternoon. Nick wanted to go home and make a place for the dog and give him a bath to get the barn smell off him. Nick wanted the pup to look his best for their visitors. On the way home the sign "Morelli Gallery" came into view. He decided it was time to check the place out. The pup was fine in his box.

Nick pulled down the lane. It seemed as though everyone had a long lane to their residence. Privacy, he guessed. It seemed strange for a gallery though. He followed the lane almost a quarter mile before he came to a small two-story home with a small barn-style shop beside it. He parked in the shade under a large oak tree. The barn had been either fixed up or was new, Nick couldn't tell for sure. A sign over the door read "Morelli Gallery" in bright red lettering. Two large windows let the morning sun shine into the shop.

Nick opened the door to a marvelous showroom with paintings hanging on the walls and on the floor leaning against the walls. Tables were placed around the room filled with an unusual style of pottery. It was fantastic. The paintings were mostly of landscapes and faces. It seemed the artist liked to paint unique faces of older men and women, faces that had weathered through years of suffering and toil. In each face the eyes seemed to tell the story. Nick had never seen paintings of such tales.

The pottery was molded mainly for accent pieces, not to be used for cooking. The coloring of each piece was distinctive from the next. Nick heard noise from the adjacent room. He noticed a bell on the counter and a sign that read "ring for service".

Nick was reaching for the bell when the door swung open. Gabriella Morelli smiled and walked through the door. "Good morning. You must be Frank Simeon."

Nick answered, "No, No. I saw the sign and just stopped in to look. I just moved to the area and was checking things out."

"I'm sorry. A collector had called and said he would be here soon from Atlanta." Gabriella now knew instantly who he was. Trudy had described him on their walk. "I'm Gabriella Morelli. The owner and artist," she said as she held out her hand.

She had on a painter's smock and her shoulder length black hair pulled back into a ponytail. Still, Nick thought she was beautiful. He shook her hand and said, "I'm Nick Stewart. I bought the Gibbons' place up on Mountain Road."

"It's nice to meet you, Nick. Can I help you with anything?"

"Are all of these your creations?" Nick asked motioning around the room.

Gabriella liked the way Nick asked the question. She liked thinking of her work as creations. To take paint or clay and make something that others wanted felt empowering in a self-satisfying way. "Yes," she answered. Gabriella was far from arrogant though. She was very talented and thankful for that talent. She was even surprised at her success.

"They're beautiful. Not what I expected."

"Why is that?" she inquired.

"My assuming nature I guess. The name Morelli suggested modern art to me for some reason."

"Do you like modern better?" Gabriella asked.

"Not at all, or I should say mostly not."

"I understand. I feel the same."

Gabriella showed him different paintings, and he asked questions about each one. The eyes of the faces amazed him. She told him most of the faces were real people she had met. She had asked if she could take their picture. She would paint from the image on the photograph. The landscapes she painted were mostly around the Sleepy Valley area and other places she had traveled. They talked nearly thirty minutes. Nick knew he would have to buy a painting one day and told her so.

"I hope I'm not being forward, but I'm having a couple of friends over this evening for a cookout. I would love it if you and your husband could join us. It's just a cookout, nothing fancy."

"I'm afraid I can't bring a husband. I'm not married. I would be happy to come myself though, if that's okay."

"Great. Around six-thirty."

"What can I bring?" Gabriella asked.

"Nothing." Just then the door opened and Nick assumed that Frank Simeon was walking in.

Nick said as he was leaving, "See you this evening, Gabriella."

"Bye, Nick."

6

Nick thought about having the guests over for dinner as he drove home with the pup. He actually looked forward to it. He was glad he would get a chance to talk to Trudy. He was happy Gabriella was coming so it wouldn't be as awkward with only one woman there. He thought maybe Trudy could relax and be more her fun-loving self. He figured they had to know each other. Small town, surely they had met. Then a thought hit him. What if they knew and hated each other? Still, that wasn't his problem. He was just inviting friends for a nice relaxing evening.

Nick took the pup out of the box and introduced him to his new home. The pup limped around the yard with his nose to the ground, checking things out. He watered different spots in the yard and tried to hike his leg against one of the azalea bushes and fell over. Nick laughed at him. The pup came running to Nick, not embarrassed at all at his mishap. The pup's limp was even worse than it looked in the crib. But it didn't seem to cause him pain and he seemed happy.

Nick was watching the limp when the name for the pup came to him. Chester. Chester was a good name for the pup. Nick was a fan of westerns shows and movies. Every now and then he watched reruns of *Gunsmoke* on *TV land*. His favorite character on the show was Chester, the deputy, Marshall Dillon's sidekick. Chester had a bad limp on the show. The name was perfect.

"Come here, Chester," Nick told the pup. The pup came running again. "Good Chester, good boy, your name is Chester the beagledor."

~

Gabriella thought Trudy's description of Nick was right-on. A nice and handsome, rugged-looking man. It caught her by surprise being invited to dinner on their first meeting. She almost declined the invitation, but the fact that others would be coming made it a party instead of a date. She wanted to call Trudy and let her know she had met him and that she had been invited to his house. She would wait till later when Trudy got home.

Gabriella's business was good. She sold paintings all over the world. Her work was collectable and her reputation grew in the art world every day. Frank Simeon spent six thousand dollars on four paintings and four pieces of pottery. Hardly anyone in Sleepy Valley knew how well-known Gabriella was. They wondered how she made a living. Few of them could afford her one-of-a-kind paintings. Some bought her pottery as gifts.

Gabriella had lived in Boston while she mastered her painting and pottery. She met Jimmy at a starving artist sale one Saturday. They married a year later, to the day, and lived in a small apartment near Fenway Park while struggling to make ends meet. She painted, and he was a fireman for the city. Three years after they married he died after getting trapped in a burning house when the roof collapsed.

She took their savings and insurance money and moved away from the city to Sleepy Valley. Gabriella was like others in Sleepy Valley, escaping bad memories and similar stories. It was a good place to grieve and heal, and she was still on the mend. She had met Trudy not long after her move. She had lived in Sleepy Valley seven years now and Trudy had become her best friend and hiking buddy. They shared most everything.

~

Nick made potato salad and placed it in the fridge. Nick didn't have a gas grill for cooking out. Melissa had wanted it. Nick pulled out a small black charcoal grill and stacked it with the coal. Chester roamed around the yard while Nick readied the place for guests.

~

At five-thirty Trudy got in her car and headed to Nick's. Her phone in the house rang as she pulled away. Gabriella wondered where Trudy could be.

Trudy drove up to Nick's house just as she had done Friday evening. She wasn't sure what to expect. She told herself to be ready for anything.

~

Nick left Chester in the bedroom in his cage. He would introduce him when everyone got there. He wanted to talk to Trudy with no interruption. Nick walked out to the drive and greeted Trudy. Trudy had her hands full with a basket filled with two pies.

"I'll take those inside. Have a seat on the swing and I'll be right back. The birds are feasting this evening."

"It's a great evening for a cookout," Trudy noted.

"It is."

Nick came back out and sat at the other end of the porch swing and turned to face Trudy. Trudy was spectacular this evening. She wore a cotton button-up sleeveless yellow blouse and blue shorts. Stylish sandals finished the outfit. Her full lips smiled at Nick as he turned to her. Nick was tempted to sweep her into his arms and kiss her. He knew he wasn't ready for that though, and he had to tell her so.

"I wanted to talk to you," Nick started.

"Me too."

"I felt you may have gotten the wrong idea from me. I'm sorry if I led you into thinking I was interested in a relationship."

Trudy was shocked. She was the one that needed to apologize, not Nick. Nick didn't do anything but be a gentleman. Here he was taking the blame for her behavior. *How sweet,* she thought. She couldn't speak.

Nick continued, "My divorce hasn't been that long ago. I really need time. It would be easy to say I need time to heal. I'm not sure if it's healing. I just know I need time before I get into another relationship."

Her eyes began to moist. Not from sadness, but because this man was so sweet. She wanted him more now than ever.

"What I need now are friends. I would like for you to be my friend because I really like you. Don't cry."

Trudy wiped the tears away and said, "Nick, you are the sweetest man. You did nothing wrong. I came on too strong. I've always had that problem. I knew it while I was doing it. I'm the one that's sorry."

"I didn't want you to think I was rejecting you. I'm just not ready for a relationship yet. You're a special lady. Can we just be friends and forget what happened?"

"I can't forget what I did. I can try not to let it happen again."

"Maybe not forever, I enjoyed the dance," Nick smiled.

"You did, huh?"

"I'm still a man, and you're still a very desirable lady."

"You think so," Trudy baited.

"Yes. Just ask Tom and Andy." They both laughed. "I think I need to put the burgers on."

Trudy teased, "So you liked my boobs pressed against your chest?"

"I'm cooking the food." Nick laughed and walked away.

"Isn't it fun being friends and talking about my boobs? Let's talk about shopping and my many moods."

"Trudy," Nick shouted from inside the house, "I don't want to be the kind of friend that shares everything."

"Can I tell you about the men that I think are hot?"

"Sure, I would love that," Nick answered as he walked through the door with a plate of raw hamburgers and a smile on his face.

Trudy felt a lot better. Nick made it so easy. She was hopeful that sometime in the future Nick might be ready, and she could be the one.

Nick was amazed at how well Trudy accepted his words and that they could joke about it. *Trudy was truly a special gal,* he thought.

Nick was at the side of the house grilling the burgers when two cars drove down the drive. Trudy wondered who all was coming. She thought only Vincent would be joining them. She recognized Vincent's red convertible in the front and what looked like Gabry's blue mustang behind him.

They parked, and Trudy greeted Vincent with a kiss on the cheek. Trudy then ran to Gabry as she got out of her car and hugged her. "What a surprise that you're here! How did this happen?"

Nick heard the cars and walked around the side of the house to welcome his guests. Nick shook Vincent's hand and welcomed Gabriella to his home.

Vincent spoke up, "What a nice surprise to have the two prettiest ladies in the county here in my company this evening. You two must have known I was coming."

Trudy winked at him and said, "I'm stalking you Vincent. I even put my restaurant right next to your store."

"I imagined that was it. It feels good to be wanted."

"Excuse me ladies, I need to get the burgers off the grill."

Gabriella commented to Nick how beautiful the red azaleas were. They were in full bloom.

"Thank you. I just planted them this week. Red has always been my favorite color." Gabry and Trudy both took note.

The ladies went to the swing and Vincent followed Nick to the grill.

Trudy asked, "I'm so happy you're here. I have so much to tell you. I missed our walk yesterday. How did you get invited here tonight?"

"Nick walked into my shop today to check it out. We talked for about thirty minutes, mainly about my paintings, and he said he was having friends over this evening and invited me and my husband." She laughed.

Meanwhile in the side yard Vincent was quizzing Nick about how he got Gabriella to come. Nick explained everything.

"She's hardly ever seen out of her studio. Works hard, pours all her energy into her art. She's a real go-getter," Vincent informed Nick.

"She's a real looker also," Nick said. Gabriella had on a light blue pull-over sleeveless cotton top with white shorts and sandals. She had the Italian dark skin. Her legs glistened against the white shorts.

"Two great-looking women, you lucky dog. I can sense trouble brewing."

"Why?"

"They're best friends." Nick looked stunned as Vincent walked away. Nick had thought that they might know each other. But he had no idea they were best friends. It didn't matter; he considered them both his friends. They could all be friends. Couldn't they?

"I'll be right back. I've got something to show everyone." He walked inside, placed the plate on the table and went to the bedroom and took Chester out of the crate. Chester was excited to be out. "We have someone else joining us for dinner," Nick announced as he walked through the screen door.

Trudy and Gabry both were quickly up to see the pup.

"He's so cute."

"Look at the white stripe on his face."

Nick put him down on the porch and Chester ran limping straight to Vincent despite the ladies calling him.

Gabriella sighed, "Oh, he limps, poor thing."

Nick explained where and how he got him. Trudy asked, "Have you named him?"

"Chester."

Vincent knew instantly where the name came from. "You must be a fan of *Gunsmoke*."

The ladies said, "What?"

Vincent explained who the character Chester was and that he limped in the show. "It was the actor, Dennis Weaver."

Trudy answered, "I know who he is. He was Sam McCloud."

Vincent quoted one of his sayings. "'To get what you want, *stop* doing what isn't working.'"

Gabriella asked, "How would you know that?"

"It struck me as true when I heard it. Isn't that how we all got here in Sleepy Valley?"

"That's deep, Vincent," Nick teased.

Trudy defended Vincent, "He's got a point."

Nick announced that dinner was ready. They gathered around the table and Nick asked, "Do you mind if I ask grace?"

"Not at all," Trudy spoke.

"Father. Thank you for this food before us and your blessings to each of us. Thanks for blessing me with these friends and for this new home. We love you. In the name of Christ, Amen." Nick then said, "Dig in. We can eat inside or take it outside to the picnic table."

"Let's go out, it's so nice," Trudy said.

"Your place is great, Nick. You're making it very homey," Gabriella told him.

"I'm doing my best. Trying to make it work with what I have. I didn't get a lot in the settlement. Didn't really want a lot."

An old picnic table was left on the property. Nick had cleaned it up for the picnic.

"You need a job don't you, Nick?" Trudy asked.

"Someday."

"You can cook for me. This all is delicious, great potato salad," Gabry complimented.

"You'll make a great wife to someone, someday, Nick."

"That's funny, Vincent." Nick thought to himself, *Maybe better than I was as a husband.*

Nick had cooked a small hamburger for Chester and broke it up in little bits and fed it to him. Chester then took off to explore.

Nick asked Gabriella and Trudy, "When did you two become such good friends?"

"We met on a trail a few years ago while hiking. We began talking and now we hike every Sunday evening," Gabriella answered.

"We've been best friends ever since," Trudy added. "We've even vacationed together."

"Total disaster is what it was," Gabriella explained. "We went to New York City. I wanted to see all the sights and art galleries. Trudy wanted to see the plays and David Letterman."

"We fought like sisters the entire trip."

"We spent half the time separated."

Vincent asked, "You're still friends?"

"Sure, we just have different tastes in the finer things," Trudy said. They both looked at Nick.

"How about a game?"

They spent most of the evening playing bid Euchre, the boys' verses the girls, laughing, eating the desserts and telling stories. They moved inside when it got dark. Vincent told stories about life as a musician on the road. Chester lay at Nick's feet when he wasn't being held by Gabriella or Trudy.

Vincent looked at Chester nuzzled between Trudy's breasts and said, "To have the life of a dog."

Everyone looked at where Chester was lying and laughed. Trudy gave Vincent the invitation. "You can lay your head there any time you want. But you also have to lick my face."

"I would do that," Vincent said and laughed.

"You nasty old man. I say that in the nicest way, Vincent."

"I understand, dear."

Gabriella noticed the time. "It's eleven-thirty. Where has the time gone? I'd better go."

Vincent agreed, "I need my beauty sleep. Nick, my boy, a sign of a good party is that your guests lose track of the time. I truly enjoyed myself."

Everyone agreed. Nick walked everyone out. "It was nice that you could come. We will do this again. Vincent, we're fishing Wednesday morning?"

"Yes. See you at Trudy's Eating Place at six-thirty." Nick waved goodbye as they drove away.

Nick sat on his porch and listened to the night sounds. He thought about the party and the fun he'd had. The friends he had made this past week were already special to him. His idea was to move to Tennessee to get away from people, have solitude and heal from the hurt. It hadn't worked. Instead of getting away from people, he'd found people, true friends such as Vincent. Instead of solitude, he'd found happiness in friends and nature. He was in the healing process.

~

Trudy's whole outlook on things from this morning had changed. Nick forgave her and even took the blame himself. It made him more appealing than ever. She knew she was the one at fault, but it was nice not having to beat herself up over it. There was hope. She now could talk to Gabry about Nick. She would understand.

~

Gabriella had a wonderful evening. It was true, she didn't get out much. She knew that she needed to do more social activities. Her work had been so important and a refuge for her. She decided on her way home to try and balance her life more. How would she ever get to know a guy such as Nick if she didn't?

~

Vincent was thankful that Nick had moved to the village. He hadn't enjoyed himself so much in years. Before Nick arrived, most of his free time was spent driving the roads and at the Oak Club playing some music once in a while. It meant so much to him to have someone to share friendship. He wondered if he was a bother to Nick. An old man trying to relive his youth; was that the way Nick saw him? He hoped not.

If Nick pulled away, he would understand.

7

Nick woke up early and turned on the morning news and listened to the sports results from the night before and the weather report. He straightened the kitchen as he listened and then left for the restaurant to meet Vincent.

Nick pulled up in front of Trudy's Eating Place at exactly six-thirty Wednesday morning. Vincent already had the table and to Nick's surprise Gabriella was sitting with him. Trudy was serving their drinks.

Nick waved through the window and walked in. "Starting without me, huh? I'm thrown to the gutter and replaced with a beautiful painter." Nick had a choice of sitting in the booth next to Vincent or on the other side next to Gabriella. He chose Gabriella.

Gabriella blushed for a moment. She wasn't positive if he meant beautiful as a woman or that the paintings she did were beautiful. Either way, it was a compliment. "Are you going fishing with us this morning?" Nick inquired.

"No, just having breakfast with you two, if you don't mind."

"Not at all."

Trudy ventured over, greeted everyone and took their orders.

Gabry smiled and said, "I used to fish as a young girl. My dad would take me with him to the lake. I did enjoy it. I suppose mainly because I was spending time with my dad, watching him smile and laugh as he reeled fish in. It was nice seeing him relaxed, and I loved being outdoors breathing in the fresh country air."

Vincent urged, "You should join us one day. We have extra equipment."

"I'll do that," she promised.

Tom was at the counter complaining to Trudy about his fried eggs being too runny.

Andy told him, "You'd better just eat them. You remember what happened to your water the other day."

Trudy told him, "Those yellows would look good running down the side of your head. Hush up and eat them, they'll go down easier this way."

"I don't know what's happened to the service in this place."

Trudy suggested, "Why don't you stay at home and fix your own eggs? Instead of bothering me."

Nick's table was laughing at every word. It was great entertainment. Most of the customers came in early just to hear the banter between Trudy and Tom.

"Well *excuse* me for thinking this was a restaurant where you waited on customers."

"You're not a customer," Trudy waited.

"Then what do you call me?" There it was; her straight line.

"You're just an old fool." The place erupted with laughter with Tom leading the way.

Stella walked in and Trudy asked her to take over while she took a break. "Tom has worn me out."

"In your dreams," Tom came back quickly. Again the laughter filled the restaurant.

Trudy walked to the table and sat in the seat next to Vincent. "When are you two opening in Vegas?" Nick teased.

Trudy answered, "We are pretty funny, aren't we?" Everyone nodded and grinned.

Gabriella asked, "I was wondering if everyone would like to come to my house Saturday evening for dinner, same time. Vincent, I'll cook Italian."

"You couldn't keep me away, my dear."

"I'd love to," Nick said.

"Count me in for a party," Trudy followed. She was surprised by Gabry's invitation. She knew that Gabry had never asked anyone to her house except her. Trudy had meant to call Gabry Tuesday, but she got busy in her garden and forgot. She definitely would have to call her today after work and see what was up between her and Nick.

Gabriella had taken her promise to herself to heart, make time for more social activity. Thus the dinner plans and showing up at Trudy's this morning to invite everyone personally. She had planned a trip to Nashville this weekend for an art show. She decided this was more important.

Stella brought the breakfasts and began handing them out. "Here you are sweetheart. French toast for my darling," she said to Vincent.

"No. Not today."

"It looked so good last week I had to try it today," Nick reached for the plate.

"This plate must be yours then, maestro."

"Thank you, my sweet Stella," Vincent flirted.

"He's so *good*," Stella told everyone as she walked away.

Tom yelled out, "Come over here, Stella, and I'll tell you how good I am."

"That's all you can do…tell people. I don't see any action," Stella challenged.

~

The fishing was good all morning. Clouds rolled in around eight-thirty and a light drizzle fell against the surface of the pond that Vincent had chosen. Nick and Vincent fished on with great success. Nick decided to catch a mess of bluegills for dinner. He had brought two cane poles and handed one to Vincent and they sat and caught a large stringer full. They split them up, and they both had fish for dinner. Nick ate his in front of the TV as the beautiful Haley got voted off *Idol.*

~

SATURDAY, APRIL 21

Saturday came quickly. Nick looked forward to the dinner at Gabriella's. Good food and friends. *What could be better?* He thought.

Chester was growing and happy. Nick had taken him to the vet to get checked out. The vet said nothing could be done about the limp. A bone was formed incorrectly. He said Chester appeared not to be in any pain and should live a happy life. He wanted to check it every month as he grew. Nick agreed.

Nick's mother had called yesterday to check on him again; every other day like clockwork.

"How's the weather, Mom?"

"Windy," his mom answered. She always answered the same way, "Windy." She told Nick that she had seen Melissa at the mall. Melissa seemed happy to see her and asked how he was doing.

"That's nice, Mom." How dare Melissa act like she was still a part of the family. *How is Nick? Good to see you. I miss you.* How annoying it was. It frustrated Nick hearing his mom speak her name.

"Your dad and I would like to visit you the first part of May. I'm looking forward to seeing your new home. Do you like it down there?"

"Yes. I do, Mom. Let me know the exact date when you decide, and I'll make sure I vacuum before you come."

"Nick."

"Just kidding, Mom, I'll let you do it while you'll here." Nick's mom laughed. "I'm looking forward to seeing both of you. I love you. Tell Dad."

Talking to his mother stirred up emotions he hadn't felt for a while. The familiar feeling crept upon him again, but he shook the thoughts off. Nick decided physical activity was what he needed.

He took Chester into the woods behind his house and let him

roam. Nick wanted to create a hiking trail through the woods, a trail he could hike every day. He decided to try and lay out the path. He took bright ribbon and tied it to trees marking the path. He would come back through and clear small trees, bushes, and limbs. He was going to buy a chipper, cut up the limbs, and put the chips on the trail so he could walk when it was raining or wet.

Chester loved roaming around the woods and climbing over the smaller limbs and trying to climb over the bigger fallen logs. His bad leg didn't seem to bother his endurance. He kept going as long as Nick did. He would rest when Nick rested. He would walk when Nick walked.

Nick and Chester worked in the woods during the afternoon marking the trail. Nick would change his mind and remark parts of it. Around three Nick decided to head to the house and start getting ready for dinner. He left time to watch the Bulls defeat the Miami Heat in the playoffs.

~

Trudy had finally called Gabry Wednesday evening and they talked for over an hour. Trudy told Gabry what she had done in throwing herself all over Nick.

"You didn't!"

"I did. I was so ashamed of myself the next day. But Nick was so sweet about it. He even tried to take the blame," Trudy explained.

"Trudy, we have to give him space and let him decide when the time is right. It's different for everyone. Neither you nor I want to be the rebound girl. That never works out."

"I know. But you know my impulsive nature."

"Yes, and you've done so much better," Gabry praised her.

"Are you interested in Nick also?" Trudy was afraid to ask the question, although she already knew the answer.

"How could I not be? Is that a problem between us?"

"No, of course not. Nick may not be interested in either of us."

"How could he not? Two of the hottest chicks in Tennessee," Gabry teased and they both laughed.

Trudy added, "I'm looking forward to Saturday evening."

"I am also."

"I'll host a dinner party the next Saturday."

"That's it. We'll keep him booked up on Saturday nights until he is ready." They laughed.

~

Vincent closed his store early and headed for Pineville. He made it to the flower shop just before they closed. He purchased a dozen red roses and a single white rose and drove back to Sleepy Valley in time to get showered and dressed for the dinner party. The single white rose he carefully placed in a bud vase and positioned it on the mantle next to the urn that held the ashes—her favorite. "Good evening, my love."

~

Trudy arrived a little early to help Gabry with last-minute preparations. The table looked fantastic. White cloth napkins inside red napkin rings. Italian plates of bright colors decorated the table. Smart wine glasses stood beside each plate. Gabriella had on a stylish short red sundress with a yellow belt.

They both laughed when they saw each other's outfit. Trudy wore a red button up blouse with the top four unbuttoned. With it she wore white pants that went just below her knee. Both women would stop traffic in their outfits.

Nick arrived at exactly six-thirty. He wore a nice red golf shirt with tan pants. Trudy was at the door to greet him. Nick brought a box of mixed chocolates for later.

Vincent arrived wearing a white pressed shirt with a red dinner jacket over it. He presented Gabriella with the red roses and a bottle of wine. She swooned over them, kissed him on the cheek, and placed them in her family room on the mantle.

"Dinner will be ready soon. Make yourselves at home."

Nick had already started studying the paintings and artwork about the house. She had nothing of her own art in her house. They were all from different artists around the world. A painting of schoolgirls in what looked like Italy caught his fancy.

Soon Gabriella walked in to tell them dinner was served. "Gabriella, I love your art collection."

"Thank you."

"I especially like this one," pointing to the schoolgirls.

"It's my favorite. I'll tell you about it later. It will take awhile."

Gabriella asked Nick to say grace and they dug into the lasagna, salads, and homemade Italian bread. Vincent poured wine for everyone. The red outfits went well with the table.

Vincent finally noticed, "We all have red on this evening."

Gabriella explained the best she could come up with, "Nick said his favorite color was red. So we wore red to welcome our newest neighbor."

"Thank you very much. You ladies look much too lovely, and Vincent, as always, you look *magnifico*," Nick lauded. "The dinner looks wonderful."

Vincent noticed that Nick hadn't touched his glass of wine. "Do you not like the wine, Nick?"

"It's not that at all, Vincent. I don't drink alcohol at all."

"But it's good for your heart," Vincent said.

"I don't doubt it, but I would rather drink cola or water, no disrespect."

Gabriella asked, "Would you rather we didn't?"

"Not at all. I really don't mind. Enjoy, it looks delicious."

"Can I get you a cola?"

"Later. Let's enjoy this terrific meal."

After dinner Nick helped Gabriella clean the table while Trudy entertained Vincent on the porch.

"Thank you for the delicious dinner, Gabriella."

"It was my pleasure. I should be thanking you."

"For what?" Nick asked.

"I've hid in my shop and this house far too long. My artwork has taken over my life. Your party last week made me realize I was missing out on so many important things."

"What brought you to Sleepy Valley? Seems like a strange place for such an amazing artist."

"Same as you; a new start in a new place. I was looking for seclusion and quiet surroundings, a spot in which I could be creative and not be bothered." Nick nodded as though knowing what she meant. Gabriella continued, "When my husband died I thought my life was over."

"I'm sorry. I didn't know. I figured you were like Trudy and me, broken marriage, bad break up."

"Jimmy, my husband, was a fireman. He died when a roof collapsed on top of him. He was trying to get a young girl out. She was trapped, and he ignored the warnings and went back in to save her."

"What a shame. It sounds like he was a great guy. "

"That was Jimmy. He had a big heart, and when he died it broke mine. It's taken a long time to recover. I'm getting there though… slowly."

"Good for you. That type of grief has to be more heartbreaking than losing an unfaithful wife. I guess I should be happy I know and that it's over."

"You still lost someone you cared about. Someone you promised to love forever, a person who promised to love you forever. It has to hurt. It takes time when you're healing a broken heart."

"You're right."

"You're doing the right thing, though. I needed friends, but hid. You've discovered how much friends can help you move on with your life."

"It was purely an accident. I came here with the same mindset as you. I wanted to be left alone. Then Vincent entered my life. I couldn't say no."

Gabry agreed, "Who could? Vincent is a great fellow to have on your side."

"He is. But I think all three of you are."

"Thank you. We're done in here. Let's join the others."

The sun had already set, so the four went into the family room and spread out. Vincent took the easy chair left of the couch which faced the fireplace. Trudy nestled into the big brown leather recliner to the right and Nick and Gabriella sat on the leather couch on opposite ends. It was a cool evening for the middle of April in Tennessee, so Gabry had placed a fire log in the fireplace and lit it.

Gabry informed the men, "Trudy says she has come up with a game to play this evening. I'm going to let her explain."

Trudy began, "We go around the room and a person gets to ask a question about anything. Each person has to answer it truthfully. If a person refuses to answer the question or the majority thinks they lied, they get a point. The person with the fewest points wins."

Vincent asked, "And what do they win?"

"The nothing-to-hide award. The main purpose of the game is so we can learn about each other. It will be fun learning about each other's lives. We'll keep going until we tire of it."

"Sounds like fun," Nick said and actually did think it would be interesting.

"I'll start to give you an idea what it's like. I would like for you to tell us the favorite place you've ever been and explain why it was so special. We'll go around the room clockwise. Gabry, you get to go first. If you think a person has lied, yell out when they're done."

Gabry quickly answered, "That's easy. My father took me to Tuscany, Italy, when I was sixteen. I met our relatives and saw the beautiful countryside. The colors were so amazing. I remember the colors so vividly. It was there in Tuscany I realized painting was what I wanted to do."

"Did your mother go?" Nick asked.

"She had died a year earlier. It was just Dad and me. It was probably why he took me. Something he could give—with Mom gone. That's my answer." No one objected to Gabriella's answer.

Trudy then said, "Your turn, Nick."

"I haven't been overseas. I would like to go to Europe and New Zealand some day. But that's a different question. So, I would say it would be Cades Cove in the Great Smoky Mountain National Park. It's a lot like here. It's a valley full of wildlife and beauty. Every day it looks different. Every changing season gives it a different look. It's so peaceful, if you can get away from the crowds. Perhaps, one day, we can have a field trip and we can all go. It's not that far from here."

"That would be fun. As close as we live, I've never been there."

"Count me in," Gabriella agreed.

"You could paint there forever. You're next, Vincent," Nick pointed to Vincent.

"Carnegie Hall in New York, the first time I played there. I have never had a feeling like it. It is so magnificent, the curvature of the stage, the bright lights, and the boxes above us. The thrill to sit on the same stage where the greatest musicians in the world had performed was beyond belief." He looked at Nick, grinned, and said, "Maybe I could take us on a field trip there." Everyone laughed.

It was Trudy's turn. "I'm not sure why I asked this question. I've been nowhere. I guess I wanted to hear about places. My family never went anywhere. We were too poor. When I married I wanted to travel, but it wasn't what my husband wanted to do and we didn't really have the money to go away. Since the divorce I've run the restaurant."

Vincent began acting as though he was playing the violin to her sad tale of woe. Nick and Gabry began laughing.

"Okay. Okay. My favorite place is the mountain that Gabry and I hike all the time. I love it. I've had so much fun on those trails."

Nick raised his hand and objected, "I vote she gets a point. If she's not lying then she deserves one for asking the question without an answer. Besides, she just told us she went to New York with Gabriella." Gabry and Vincent raised their hands in agreement. Everyone laughed.

"Okay. I deserve it. I forgot about New York." She marked it down. "Gabry, it's your turn to ask a question."

Gabry poured herself another glass of wine and grinned. "Okay. Let's cut to the chase here. If you could have sex with anyone in the world—"

Everyone began laughing. Diet Pepsi came out of Nick's nose. He grabbed a napkin to clean up.

"—who would you chose? No strings attached. No sin to be accounted. Present company excluded. They have to be living at this moment. Your fantasy partner. And Nick, you're first."

Nick finished cleaning himself up and laughing before answering, "Talk about cutting to the chase. Hold on, I'm thinking. Okay. It would be Scarlett Johansson, the actress in the *King Kong* remake. It seems she's in every movie lately. The reason is she seems like fun, and she's beautiful. I would also do Jennifer Garner, Angelina Jolie, Diane Lane, Lucy Liu, the tall blonde on *Grey's Anatomy*..."

"Enough all ready," Gabry cried out. "Men!"

"Wasn't the actress in *King Kong* Naomi Watts?" Trudy asked.

"You're right. Add her to the list," Nick grinned and waited for hands to shoot up. None did.

"I guess no one thought I was lying." After the laughter died down it was Vincent's turn.

"I would have sex with Bea Arthur." Everyone raised their arms quickly as the laughter continued.

Trudy offered, "We definitely do not want you to explain that one."

Nick said to Trudy, "I'm anxious to hear yours."

"I'd have to say Brad Paisley, the country singer. I like him and I think he's sweet. Have you heard his song that says, "I want to check your body for ticks?"

"No way! Is that true?" Gabry asked. "That's a song?"

"Yes. I've heard it also," Nick confirmed.

"And this is who you would pick?" Gabry asked.

"Apparently, you haven't seen him," Trudy affirmed. "So, who are you picking?"

Gabry was next. "I would pick Carson Palmer."

Trudy yelled out, "Who is that?"

"He's the quarterback for the Cincinnati Bengals. He's handsome, young, and a nice guy."

Nick raised his hand, "I don't buy it. Of all the hunks in the universe I don't believe you would pick a football player."

Trudy blurted out, "I don't know, I did in high school." Everyone began laughing again.

Gabry asked if they could take a break and have some dessert. She had made a cheesecake and everyone took a piece and sat back down to continue. All were enjoying the game. Nick was amazed at how quickly everyone was at ease with each other, like longtime friends.

"I guess it's my turn to ask a question. I want to know your most embarrassing moment," Nick said. Everyone moaned at the thought of having to answer.

Vincent was first. "I was asked to play at a wedding of a friend's daughter; a very proper, formal wedding. I got up to play as the bridesmaids began entering the center aisle followed by the flower girl and a small boy who was the ring bearer. The young boy took his place on the floor right in front of where I was playing on the edge of the stage. The boy looked up at me and with a startled look he turned to find his mother in the crowd and he yelled, 'Mom, I can see his red underwear.'"

Everyone laughed as Vincent explained. "I had forgotten to zip up my trousers and there I was wearing my red boxer shorts which were working their way out as I moved with the playing of the violin. The boy was correct. I quickly turned and zipped up and turned back in time to play for the bride as she walked down the aisle."

"How awful, Vincent," Trudy comforted him.

"I survived it, my dear. I always double check now. You are next. Surely you have done nothing so embarrassing."

"You have nothing on me, Vincent. I'm just trying to decide which to pick from. Okay, I know. I can't believe I'm telling this. I went to the doctor when I was around twenty. I was having some health problems. The doctor was asking me questions, and his nurse was taking notes while he was poking around. He then asked me what color my stool was."

Gabry snickered.

"I thought, what a strange question to ask, must be a medical reason for the question. So I answered *white.*"

"What do you mean white?" Nick asked as Gabry laughed.

"That's what the doctor asked. I told him that by toilet was white."

By then Nick and Vincent were howling with laughter. Nick was holding his sides in pain from the laughter.

Trudy continued, "The nurse was laughing and the doctor seemed aggravated with me and he said, 'No, I'm talking about your excrement, feces, your bowel movements.' I had never heard it called stool before. I was embarrassed and upset and I told him, 'You should just call it *shit or poop* so a person knows what you're talking about.'"

That did it. It got to that point where a person just can't laugh anymore. Tears were running down everyone's cheeks… even Trudy's. They took a few moments to settle themselves. Gabry opened up the chocolates and placed them on the coffee table.

"Gabry, are you hesitating because it's your turn?" Nick asked.

"Yes I am, for good reason too. Okay. I was seventeen and it was my dad's birthday. When I asked what he would like for a present he told me he needed some new golf balls. He even wrote down the name of the golf balls for me, *Titleist*. But he spells it wrong and forgets the 'e' in Titleist. I went to the sporting goods store to find them. A senior guy that I sort of knew from school was working there.

"He asked if he could help me. I asked, *'Can I see your balls?'* Of course he looks at me in shock. I then realized what I had said and began blushing and apologizing. I quickly said that I meant golf balls. I said to him 'Wait, I've got what you need.' I reached in my purse and pulled out my father's note and said 'Tit List.' He looked at me and said 'Yeah, I could use that.'"

Again everyone was rolling in laughter.

Gabriella finished by saying that the guy explained that the note was written wrong and how to pronounce Titleist. Nick realized that Gabry was still embarrassed while telling the story.

It was Nick's turn and he started by explaining, "When I first began teaching and coaching I was signed to coach a junior high boy's team. I compiled a list of what the boys needed for the first day of practice, and I used that list for the two years I coached them. The third year I was promoted to the varsity high school girl's coach.

"We had our sign-up meeting and I took out my list and began telling them what to bring for the first practice. I read shorts, T-shirts, good socks, basketball shoes, and a good jock strap. I didn't even realize what I was reading. I was already thinking about the next announcements. Soon one of the girls raised her hand and said 'Coach Stewart, why do we need to bring a jock strap?' I was reminded of that from then on. It spread from year to year, team to team. Every year at the first meeting some girl would ask if they should bring their jock straps. At the awards ceremony that year the team signed a gigantic jock strap and presented it to me. I couldn't believe it."

All four were having such a great time. The laughter rolled out unforced and continually. What a great idea the game was. It was Vincent's turn to ask a question.

"What do you want to be doing ten years from now? Trudy, I guess you would be first," Vincent directed.

She thought about the question for a moment and began, "I would like to be married and still living here in Sleepy Valley. I can't imagine living anywhere else. I love my restaurant, but I would like to stop being the waitress and just own it. I want to still have my friends near." She opened her arms to show that she meant those that were in the room.

Gabry was next, "I would like to meet the right man, have a family, and still work on my art. I would like to be recognized in the art world as a talented artist."

Vincent asked, "Aren't you already?"

"In a way I am. I can always be better."

"Can't we all," Vincent nodded. "Nick."

"This is hard. I don't really know. I'm just now starting over. I'm wondering what I'll be doing next week. I know someday I'll want to marry again. I would like to have kids. And I want to be fishing every week with Vincent."

Vincent raised his hand and said, "As much as I liked the last part, I don't buy it. I think he should get a point."

Trudy's hand shot up, "I agree, point for Nick."

"Hey," Nick objected. "Why?"

"We all know you want to teach and coach," Vincent explained.

"Okay, you're right. Give me a point. It's up to you, Vincent."

"At my age, I would love to be fishing with Nick in ten years also. I want to be able to stay on my own. No retirement homes. Maybe I'll marry and start a family—me and Bea." He laughed with the others. Everyone looked at Vincent with envy; such a full life, and still going strong at eighty-two. There was no doubt for anyone he would be fishing with Nick in ten years.

Vincent raised his glass and said, "A toast." The other three raised their glasses near Vincent. "May all our dreams come true!"

They clanked their glasses and the other three repeated, "May all our dreams come true."

At the end of the evening, when everyone was saying their goodbyes Trudy announced that she would like to host a party the next Saturday evening at the same time. Each person said they could make it. As they were leaving Vincent kissed Trudy and Gabry on their hands and said goodnight. Nick went to Trudy and kissed her on the cheek. He then thanked Gabriella for a wonderful evening and kissed her on the cheek also. Nick had truly enjoyed the evening and had almost forgotten about Melissa.

8

After church the next morning Nick was able to meet Pastor Hill. They talked for a while and the pastor invited Nick to lunch with him and his family. Since Nick had no plans for the afternoon and really wanted to get to know Pastor Payne Hill, he accepted.

The pastor had Nick follow them to a Mexican restaurant, The Big Burrito, in downtown Pineville. The pastor told Nick how he got into the ministry and came to Victory Road. Nick explained how he ended up in Sleepy Valley and at Victory Road. The two men were almost the same age and had a lot of the same interests.

"My search for a church is over, Pastor. I would like to become a member."

"Nick, we are a little different in that regard. Our church actually doesn't have membership. Our worshippers just come. We want it to feel as though folks can come as they are and feel as much a part of the church as the person who has been coming for the past twenty years. Of course we know who the regulars are. We're not naïve, though. We have to have regulars that teach, serve on committees, and play in the worship band and so on."

"That's different from what I'm used to. Most churches talk about how many members they have and post the attendance on the wall."

"All you need to do is call the office and give them your name, address, phone number, and email, and we will make sure you get announcements and are asked to volunteer when we need help. We have home cells, which are smaller groups that meet usually once a week to form a closer knit of people. We have some small informal study groups. I would like it if you could join mine. We could use another man. We meet at seven a.m. on Thursday mornings."

"Let me think about it."

"Call me anytime if you decide you'd like to."

Mrs. Hill said, "They usually end up talking about sports and fishing."

Nick laughed and said, "A man needs other men to do that."

The pastor said, "Amen."

"Do you know anyone at the church, Nick?" Mrs. Hill asked.

"I've introduced myself to a few folks before service, and I have one friend that attends, Trudy Flynn."

"We love Trudy," Mrs. Hill said. Teresa Hill was a petite attractive blonde. She was very polite, and at the same time friendly and outgoing.

Jacob's ears perked up and his sister Sara said, "Jacob loves her too."

Jacob threw his napkin at her. "I don't love her."

Pastor Hill said, "I think most of the kids like Trudy. She's a favorite in our church with everyone."

Mrs. Hill asked, "How do you know Miss Flynn?"

"We met at her restaurant and have become friends. We also have mutual friends Gabriella Morelli, the artist, and Vincent Marconi. He owns the General store in Sleepy Valley."

"We've met both of them. They seemed very nice. You've made some good friends," Pastor Hill told Nick.

"Yes, I have."

Nick enjoyed his time with the family and was happy to have the chance to relax and talk with the pastor. He was a great guy, Nick thought.

As they left the restaurant and walked to their cars Nick asked, "I know how crowded the church has become. Excuse me for asking, but have you considered having a second service on Sunday or one on Saturday evening to relieve the crowds?"

"I had thought about an early service on Sunday, but that's the first suggestion I've heard to have one on Saturday evening. Thank you, Nick." The Hill family waved good-bye as Nick walked to his vehicle.

~

When Nick arrived home there was a message from Trudy asking him to call her. He did. Trudy explained that she had a sixth-grade boy, Josh Wagner, in her class that always seemed depressed. She said she had tried everything to reach him. Trudy had talked to his mother and been told that the father had not been in their life since the boy was four. The mother said there were no men in his life, and Trudy wondered if Nick would act as a big brother to the kid for a while. Nick told Trudy he would like to think about it.

~

That evening Vincent didn't feel well and decided to lie down for a nap. He had spent the day traveling the roads in his red convertible and thought his lunch may not have agreed with him.

~

Nick spent the late afternoon and evening with Chester in the woods. Nick began clearing the small trees and shrubs for his trail. Nick knew he would enjoy the work in the woods and looked forward to the many days he would spend there.

~

Gabry and Trudy met for their walk on the mountain. Not long into the hike, the conversation turned to Nick.

Gabry asked, "How long has it been since his divorce was final?"

"Nick told me he received the final papers on Christmas Eve."

"Santa wasn't very good to him," Gabry suggested.

"You never know. It could have been the best gift he's ever received."

"He's seems like such a genuinely nice guy. Don't most women dream of a man like that?"

Trudy added, "Yes. His looks don't hurt anything either."

"He is a good-looking specimen of a man."

"I think he might be the one I've been waiting for," Trudy said, shocking Gabry. Gabry wasn't sure what to say, so she just nodded.

Gabriella thought she and Trudy had an unspoken understanding about Nick. She thought they would give Nick space and not make it a competition for his attention. Be happy for the other if something worked out with Nick. To say that Nick was the one she'd been waiting for was the same as saying that her knight in shining armor had arrived to save her. What could she say to that? Gabry wasn't sure if Nick would be interested in either of them, as far as something long term. She also knew Trudy had no claim on Nick, and neither did she.

Gabry thought Trudy realized that she also was interested in seeing if anything developed between herself and Nick. Gabry figured Trudy had the inside edge for a number of reasons. Trudy had met Nick first and they now went to the same church. Trudy had such a pleasing personality; everyone fell in love with her. Plus Trudy's beauty and body could probably win over almost any man, some because of pure lust.

As for herself, she wasn't sure about God. When she and Jimmy were first married they went to a church in Boston. Jimmy told Gabriella that he became a Christian when he was a teen. But Jimmy didn't like the views that had crept into the churches they attended. So they quit attending, and then he was killed in the accident. She was angry with God for taking Jimmy. She didn't understand why God would take him away from her. She was still searching for that answer.

Gabry knew she was more protective of herself than Trudy. But there was something about Nick that made her want to open up to him. He had the type of personality that a person wanted to be near. It was easy to be friends with him. People wanted to be liked by Nick. Few people possessed that trait.

They hiked in silence for a time, both of them thinking of Nick. The evening was still and cool on the Tennessee mountain path. The trail wound uphill for a couple of miles to a clearing where the village could be seen in the distance. Trudy's Eating Place looked like an insignificant spot from the overlook.

Trudy asked, "Do you think he likes me?"

"How could he not?" Gabry answered. Her words were sincere.

As Gabry looked up through the tree limbs she noticed that blue filled the sky.

9

Nick rose early on Thursday morning, fixed a couple pieces of toast and drank some orange juice. He played fetch with Chester for awhile in the yard until Chester decided to change the game to keep-away and mainly just ran around the yard with the stick.

Vincent and Nick had fished Andy's pond with good results the day before. Vincent had called and asked Nick if they could skip the breakfast. Nick picked him up at seven after deciding to skip breakfast also. Vincent never mentioned that he hadn't been feeling well. He had felt listless during the days even after getting a few good night's sleep. He decided to see a doctor if it kept up.

Nick decided to head to Trudy's for a good breakfast, toast and coffee wasn't enough. Nick had been working on his trail since Sunday and needed a break.

~

Gabriella was up and had decided to paint. She was depressed and felt like painting the saddest face with the most mournful eyes yet. She wondered why she hadn't said something to Trudy on the mountain trail. Why didn't she share her feelings with Trudy? She did like Nick's company. He made her feel good about herself. This, she thought, was silly. Why did she need a man, or anyone to make her feel good about herself?

Gabry was a successful artist and had been doing exceptionally well on her own since Jimmy died. She had need of nothing financially; her art sold extremely well around the world. But something was missing in her life since Jimmy died. She knew what it was, even if she thought it silly. She wanted to feel like a woman. She needed to be wanted by a man. She wanted someone to share herself with other than talking to a friend. She wanted a man in her life and a lover. She wanted to feel like a desirable woman. She sensed those feelings when she first saw Nick in her studio. The way Nick had smiled and said hello while looking down her body, not in a lustful way, but in a way that reminded her that men still found her attractive. All women realize when a man is checking them out. It's flattering when it's done in the right way. Trudy got it a hundred times a day. She even flaunted it... more than a little. Maybe that was why Trudy was so sure of herself; the reason she thought she could get any man she wanted.

The phone rang as she headed to her painting. "Hello."

"It's Nick."

"Hello, Nick. What a pleasant surprise."

"I was heading to Trudy's for breakfast and wondered if you would like to join me. I could pick you up in ten minutes. I'm sorry I sprung this on you."

Many things went through her mind. *I can't. I'm busy. I've already had breakfast. My hair isn't done. I'm not dressed correctly for a date. I was going to paint my depressing masterpiece and now this will ruin it.* But she said, "Sure, I'd love to. See you in ten minutes."

She hung up without saying good-bye and ran to the closet to put on something more appropriate, nicer, no holes, and well, sexier. She then hurried to the bathroom mirror to do something with her hair and makeup. Nothing was right. She knew Nick would be sitting across from her at the table and would question why he had invited the toad. *Should I even sit across from him?* Trudy would then come and sit next to him. Sitting next to him would be a bit forward, wouldn't it? But Trudy would certainly do it.

She heard Nick's car in the lane. She was almost ready. A little lipstick was still needed. The doorbell rang too soon. *Hurry, he's here, no more time.* Done! She opened the door and there he stood, as handsome as ever. She suddenly felt envy for men. They could show up in a flannel shirt and sloppy jeans, with their hair tousled, their faces unshaven, and still look great.

"You always look this beautiful in the mornings?" Nick asked as Gabry started out the door.

"Always," was all she could say.

"Are you going barefoot?" Nick asked as he looked down at her feet.

Gabriella wanted to melt into a puddle. No shoes, she knew he had to think she was a country bumpkin. She turned and ran into her closet and quickly stepped into her sandals. She did a quick check to see if she was missing anything else; bra, shorts, blouse, her teeth, yep… all there. She thought, *Okay, let's go so I can embarrass myself some more.*

They small talked on the way, which was only a minute or so to the café. When they walked inside they were greeted with hellos and stares as always. Nick led them to a small table for two by the window. Gabry hadn't thought of that. She wondered if Nick chose this table purposely. There were other tables open. The place was not that crowded.

Stella arrived at their table and looked at Nick and greeted him, "Hello, handsome."

"Good morning, Stella. How's it cookin' today?"

"Whoa, what a sweet talker you got here Miss Gabry. How are you?"

"I'm fine, Stella."

"I guess you are with a smooth talker such as this at your table. How's it cookin' today? Did you come straight out of the fifties, dear?" All three of them laughed. "Wait until I tell Trudy that line. We keep a list of the lamest lines we hear."

Gabriella asked, "Is there an actual list on paper?"

"Oh yeah, it's in the back and about three pages long. We can now add another to the list."

Nick promised, "I'll work on it. Next time I'll have a better one."

Stella shook her head sadly, "You'd better. I'd hate to ban you from the restaurant." Stella took their order.

After she left the table Andy came over. Nick greeted him with, "The porch swing is fantastic, Andy. It's been a big hit."

"It's a good one. I knew you'd like it."

"Andy, you know Gabriella, don't you?" Nick asked.

"Hi, Andy," Gabry smiled.

"Of course, hi, Gabry. We craftsmen stick together. Although I wouldn't put myself anywhere in her class."

"You're very modest, Andy. Your work is fantastic."

"Thank you, Gabry. Sorry to bother you." Andy turned to address Nick, "Trudy told me you needed a chipper. I've got one you can borrow."

"Thanks for the offer, Andy, but I really need one for more than a small job. With the property I have I'm going to need one all the time. I might as well buy one."

"If you change your mind, let me know."

"I will. Thanks." Andy walked back to the counter to sit with Tom.

"That was nice of Andy," Gabriella said. "He's a good man."

"He is."

Gabry said, "I wonder where Trudy is." She looked toward the kitchen.

"Stella will tell us."

Soon Stella was bringing Nick's French toast and Gabry's pancakes. Stella told them that Trudy had to go to Knoxville for the day on some business. She turned away to wait on another table.

"That's strange. Trudy always tells me when she's going somewhere. She usually calls to invite me to go along."

"Maybe it was personal."

"Never stopped her before, she shares everything with me."

As they completed their breakfast Nick asked, "Do you have to go back to the studio?"

"What do you have in mind?"

"It's such a beautiful day. We could take a drive or go hiking," Nick said excitedly.

"Take me to Cades Cove," Gabriella suggested. She couldn't believe she had just asked him to take her away for the day. What was she thinking?

"Really! You would go?"

"Yes. Let's go get Chester and take the trip. I've never been there. You made me want to see it when you talked about it at the party."

After finishing their meals, Nick left money on the table and they said their goodbyes and left. Everyone waved.

"Do you need to go by your house for anything?" Nick asked.

"No, unless I need different shoes."

"Yeah, if we do any hiking you may want to take some walking shoes." They stopped at her house and she ran in and came out carrying socks and soft hiking shoes. Nick drove to his house and got Chester. He put his cage in the back with the door facing them. Gabry wanted to be able to get him out and hold him on the way.

The thought of taking Gabriella to Cades Cove excited Nick and it showed. To see Nick so excited thrilled Gabriella. Nick grabbed binoculars and his digital camera, threw some drinks in a cooler, and they were off.

The day was perfect and Nick put Keith Urban's new CD into the player for some sound. They decided to roll some windows down and let the air in. Chester enjoyed sticking his head out the window while sitting in Gabry's lap. They talked very little except for pointing out sites and talking about Chester. They both were content in enjoying the ride together. An ease seemed present in their companionship. There was no need to force the conversation.

It wasn't long before Nick was driving through Marysville and then Townsend, advertised as "The Peaceful Side of the Smokies." On the other side of Townsend, Nick told Gabriella that they were entering the park, and then the sign came up on the right side of the road. A little later they came to a dead end and turned right toward Cades Cove. A sign said they were seven miles away.

"I already love it."

"You haven't seen it yet."

"If it's anything like this, I know I'll love it," Gabry explained. "The rock-filled creek is just beautiful." The road followed the small river almost all the way to the cove.

"Just wait till you see the cove," Nick promised. "Let's stop at the campgrounds for a quick break before we go through the cove. There's a small store and restrooms." "Good idea," Gabry agreed.

Nick bought soft-serve ice cream cones for the two of them and they went back to the vehicle. He had also picked out some Vienna Sausages for Chester and a bottle of water. As they entered the loop road through the cove, Nick stopped and bought a brochure at a self-serve box. The map showed trails and the name of the log cabins that were still maintained in the cove and told some of the history of the place.

Horses grazed in the first fenced-in field. Nick explained that the park offered horseback riding in the cove.

Gabry quickly exclaimed, "Nick, this is more beautiful than you described it. I love it." The day was perfect, temperature in the low seventies and not a cloud in the sky. Still, the smoky haze drifted through the mountains that gave them their name. They slowly made their way along the one-way lane taking in the sights. Nick would make way for cars to pass if they seemed in more of a hurry than Nick was. Four deer with two small fawns covered with white spots stood in a field to their left. Nick pulled the car to the side and handed Gabriella his binoculars.

"They're wonderful, Nick. The fawns are adorable."

"Late in the evening or early morning almost every field will have herds of deer. This time of day a person doesn't see nearly as many."

"What other animals are here?" Gabry asked.

"I've seen turkey, black bears, and red foxes. Wild boars are a problem in the park, but I've never seen a live one. I found a carcass of one while hiking in the cove one day. A few years ago they introduced red wolves into Cades Cove. But for some reason they didn't do well."

"Did you ever see one?"

"Once, he walked past me in a field while stalking a calf. The mother stayed between them protecting the calf. It was quite a scene. I was hidden behind a tree and was able to get a good picture of him."

Nick pulled into the parking area to the first landmark on the map, John Oliver's cabin. "Let's take a walk."

"Okay." Nick put Chester on a leash, and they followed the trail a few hundred yards toward the cabin.

Nick said, "This is the kind of day that confirms there's a God."

Gabry asked, "What about the bad days?"

"Those are the days that a person's faith kicks in. You know the day sucks, but you still know there's a God." Nick smiled at Gabry.

Gabry thought about it as they walked. When Jimmy died, she knew there was no God. How could a caring God take her love away? What little faith she'd had slipped away that day. She asked Nick, "Nick, you've had hard times, haven't you, times when you didn't know if you could go on?"

"Sure."

"Didn't you ever doubt there was a God? Didn't you lose faith?"

Nick stopped and looked into Gabry's eyes, "I've never lost someone like you lost Jimmy. I lost a wife that cheated on me. You lost a loving husband. There's a big difference. I can't ever imagine what you went through. I wouldn't pretend to think I could." He turned and they continued walking. "I know that God says that he is there for us, through the good and the bad. I don't believe God would take Jimmy from you. I believe accidents happen. Bad things are happening in the world every day. God created a perfect world for us, and man blew it."

"I guess my faith was never that strong to begin with," Gabry said.

"I think mankind likes to blame God when things go bad. But we never give him credit when things go well. I do the same at times. Martina McBride sings a song called 'Anyway.' The chorus says; "God is great, but sometimes life ain't good." Kind of sums it up."

"How can I know that God cared about me during all the pain and suffering I went through?"

Nick looked at Gabry and answered, "You said you didn't think you could go on."

"Yes."

"But you did go on. God gives us strength through the toughest of times. He lets us mourn. I believe he also mourns with us... in his way."

Nick reached for her hand and they continued to the cabin. Gabriella had never had it explained to her like that. It made sense. Over time she had regained her strength, and she even had happy days now. Today was one of them.

The old log cabin stood with no doors and old wooden shakes that covered the roof. Dogwoods and pines surrounded the old house. Oak trees and maples filled out the forest floor around the cabin's yard.

"Imagine what life was like when old John built this house for his family."

Gabry said, "Life would have been hard. But look at that view." Nick and Gabry looked from the cabin's yard across the field and valley to the mountains that jutted up into the clear blue sky.

Gabriella had been surprised when Nick took her hand into his and they walked hand-in-hand. She was pleasantly surprised. She wasn't sure if he did it to console her thinking about Jimmy or if he just wanted to hold her hand. Maybe it was both. It felt nice to have her hand melt into a man's touch. Not since Jimmy had she wanted a man to touch her in any way. Nick was different. She wanted his touch. Even though it was only his hand to hers, she wanted it.

They returned to the car and continued the drive through the cove. Gabry marveled at the landscape that surrounded her. Nick parked in a raised pull-off where others were parked. It overlooked almost the entire cove. Nick saw movement in one of the fields. He put the binoculars to his eyes and gently said, "There's a black bear."

"Where?"

"Crossing the field by that fence line." He pointed toward it and opened his door. Gabry followed. The other folks that were there had not seen it yet. Nick handed the binoculars to Gabry and told the others of his sighting. Soon everyone was motioning and looking through their binoculars at the same spot.

Gabry was nearly jumping up and down with excitement. "My first bear," she said elatedly to Nick. They watched the bear for a while until it disappeared into a thicket of woods.

Halfway around the loop was the visitors' center. They stopped and bought souvenirs. Nick bought Gabry a small stuffed black bear to remember their day together. They then walked around the grounds of the old farm that stood nearby. A water mill was turning in the same way it had for a hundred years. A stream flowed nearby supplying the power with its current.

The rest of the afternoon was spent roaming the old cabins and taking small hikes. Nick had a blanket tucked away in a storage compartment for emergencies. He spread it on the ground overlooking fields of grass softly swaying in the light breeze. Chester had to stay on a leash because of park regulations. He soon settled next to them on the blanket. The scene was beyond words, and both Gabry and Nick were silent in their comfort with each other. Nick lay back on the blanket. Gabry placed the back of her head on Nick's chest.

"Do you mind?" she asked.

"Not at all. You know we might fall asleep," Nick advised.

"Hush, I'm halfway there."

~

An hour later, Nick swatted at something crawling on his ear. Soon he swatted at it again. He opened his eyes to see Gabry holding a blade of grass near his head.

"Are you having fun?" Nick asked.

"Immensely."

"I'm glad." He grabbed her hands as she started toward his nose with the blade again. He pulled her toward him. They looked into each other's eyes for a long moment. They smiled at each other and Nick said, "I couldn't have asked for a better day or companion."

He slowly released her hands and she rose back up on her knees. "You were right. We fell asleep."

"How long?" he asked as he looked at his watch.

"About an hour."

It was close to six. Nick rose to a sitting position and looked out over the field to see a herd of fifteen deer filter out of the woods and into the pasture to eat. Nick reached for his camera and took pictures. He had Gabry stand so he could take her picture with the deer in the background. Gabry helped Nick fold the blanket and they walked back to the parked SUV.

Nick asked a couple from one of the cars parked next to his if one of them would take his picture with Gabry and Chester. The gentleman agreed if Nick would do the same for them.

Nick said, "I'd be glad to, except I don't know if I really want a picture of you two."

The elderly couple laughed and laughed like it was the funniest thing they had heard. The wife finally said, "You know I meant for you to take the picture with our camera."

"Of course," Nick smiled. Nick obliged them and then took a picture of them with his camera also. They laughed again and the husband said, "Okay then, I want a picture of you and your wife, and don't forget the cute pup."

Nick grinned at Gabry and they posed for their picture. The lady told them before they left the pose, "You two are such a lovely couple."

Gabry said, "Thank you."

Nick said, "Have a nice evening."

The husband said, "How could I not? Gorgeous day, wonderful scenery, and a beautiful wife."

"You're right." Nick and Gabry waved good-bye as they pulled away.

They agreed that they both were starving. Nick said he knew of a hole-in-the-wall restaurant in Townsend with the best pulled pork barbeque sandwiches. Gabry thought it sounded great. Within forty minutes they were eating sandwiches and coleslaw and having iced drinks.

As they ate Gabry said, "I've lived this close for all these years and I never came to the park. I feel like I've been stuck trying to gain success, and I've missed so much. Thank you for inviting me today. It's truly been the best day I've had since I left Boston."

"I can't take all the credit. You suggested coming here. I agree. It's really taken my mind off the past."

"What past? I don't know what you're talking about."

"You're right, a toast to the future," Nick said as he held his diet Pepsi out so Gabriella could clink her mason jar of iced tea against his.

10

Rain came the next two days. Nick lounged around the house and finished the Hiaasen book he was reading. He began reading *An Arrow Pointing to Heaven* by James Bryan Smith about the life story of singer Rich Mullins. Nick couldn't put it down. He thought to himself that it was the best book he had ever read.

He looked up at the clock on the mantle and saw that it was five thirty. He hadn't taken a shower or shaved. He knew he needed to get ready for the dinner at Trudy's. He actually wanted to stay on the couch and finish the book. But he also was anxious to see Gabry again. He had called her on Friday evening and they talked for almost a half hour. Mostly reminiscing about the day they spent together. He wanted to invite her over for the rainy evening but decided not to push it, knowing they would see each other the next evening.

~

Gabry painted all day Friday, inspired by her day with Nick. She thought of inviting him over Friday evening but decided not to push it, knowing they would see each other the next evening.

~

Vincent was feeling better and wanted to see everyone again. He looked forward to spending time with the other three. Being around them certainly had made him feel younger.

Vincent debated all week about selling the store. He knew the place was a shambles, and he really didn't want to put the energy or money into fixing it up. He thought he might have an idea.

~

Trudy left work early to get ready for the dinner party. She had talked to Gabry the day before. Gabry called to find out why she went to Knoxville without letting her know. Trudy couldn't tell her the truth and just said it was a spur-of-the-moment thing. When Gabry pressed the issue, Trudy lied and said it was business related. Gabry reluctantly told Trudy about her day with Nick. She didn't go into great details. She didn't tell Trudy how she felt when Nick held her hand, or how wonderful it was napping on the blanket with her head on Nick's chest, or how she thought Nick was going to kiss her, and how she wished he had.

She told Trudy that she and Nick had a nice day at the park and that she wished Trudy had been able to come along, which was actually not entirely true. Gabry didn't know how Trudy would feel about her feelings for Nick. She hoped Nick wasn't playing with them both. She didn't think Nick would do that. She wasn't even sure if Nick had feelings for her or Trudy beyond friendship.

Trudy had bought a new, very low-scooped, tight flowered pull-over top for the evening. It was the type of top that would have sent Tom into convulsions upon seeing it. Trudy wasn't a bit modest about flaunting her attributes even though she wasn't about to let a man get at them without a ring. She wore a light green skirt to complete the outfit.

The rain brought a cool chill to the evening. Gabriella was going to wear a checkered, colorful blouse and navy blue slacks. It never mattered what Gabry wore. She was always beautiful and classy, even without trying. She could have worn bib overalls and she would have looked elegant. Gabriella was a natural beauty but didn't realize how beautiful she was.

Nick called Gabry at the last minute. Gabry was walking out her front door when the phone rang. "Hello."

"Hello, Gabry. This is Nick. Would you like for me to pick you up on the way?"

"Sure. I was just leaving."

"Me too. See you in a minute." Nick hung up and said good-bye to Chester and left.

Gabriella was waiting on her porch when Nick drove up. Nick ran around the car in the rain to open the door for Gabriella.

When Nick got back into the car he said, "At the last minute I realized I didn't know where Trudy lived. I'm glad I caught you."

"So, I'm your map and directions this evening," Gabriella laughed

"Sad to say, I guess so."

"I had thought about calling you earlier today but got wrapped up in a book. When I looked up it was almost time to leave."

"It's been a good day to read," Gabry agreed.

"How was your day?" Nick asked.

Before answering, she told Nick to turn right and follow the road to the first house on the right. "I painted almost all day."

"A portrait?"

"In a way," Gabriella answered.

Nick wasn't sure what she meant, but he was pulling into Trudy's drive. Nick grabbed his large black Shaker umbrella and went around to the passenger door and helped Gabry to the porch. Vincent's car was already there. Nick looked at his watch and it was precisely six-thirty. He rang the doorbell.

Vincent opened the door and greeted them.

"I see you two came together."

"I didn't know how to get here. Or anyway, that's the excuse I used to get her to come with me."

"Good one," Vincent smiled, and Nick laughed.

"I'll remember that," Gabry said.

Vincent in a loud voice said, "Wait till you see our hostess. She will leave you speechless."

"You're such a charmer, Vincent," Trudy said as she entered the room from the kitchen.

Gabry couldn't believe her eyes. The top Trudy had on left nothing to the imagination. "I might as well leave now. No one will even notice I'm here this evening."

Nick grinned and said, "Did someone hear muttering?"

"Didn't hear a thing," Vincent went along.

"I can believe it," Gabry laughed as she gazed at Trudy's breasts.

Nick did enjoy the viewing but at the same time he felt uneasy. Vincent and he would have to watch where their eyes went all evening. A gentleman certainly wouldn't want to be caught staring by Trudy or Gabry. Nick figured Trudy wouldn't care as much as Gabry since she put it on for a reason, but he also wondered why Trudy would wear such a revealing top, as did Gabry.

"I can't believe everyone is making such a big deal out of these old things," Trudy said while looking down at her own chest. "Dinner will be served soon."

Gabry wondered if Trudy was making another pass at Nick. She decided to find out. Trudy turned toward the kitchen and Gabry followed closely behind.

"I've never seen you showing so much, Trudy."

"You really think it's a bit much?" Trudy asked Gabry.

"Are you trying to get Nick's attention or give Vincent a heart attack?"

"I guess that means you do."

"What gives?"

"I don't know. I just felt like wearing something sexy and different for the party. I didn't realize it was so revealing until I put it on. Then I thought, oh well."

"It's certainly sexy. You look great. I wish I had half of that."

"You don't need these. Perhaps I should put an open blouse on over it" Trudy suggested.

"It's up to you. It really doesn't bother me. I think it might make the guys a little uncomfortable though."

Trudy put on a short sleeve white blouse and left it open. When she returned Gabry gave her a hug and said, "You still look great and as sexy as all get out."

"Thank you. Let's eat, guys!" she called into the living room.

Trudy had made a pork roast, mashed potatoes, and green beans with homemade rolls. Homemade applesauce completed the meal. The meal was delicious and of course she had her famous cobbler for dessert later. Vincent had again brought wine and flowers.

The four sat at the table long after the meal was over. Trudy's table just seemed so inviting that they sat there for a couple of hours and just talked. The conversation moved from books to music to travel. Trudy brought up Nick and Gabry's trip to the park. Vincent was unaware of it and asked many questions, especially about the bear they had seen.

Vincent asked, "Will you take me sometime, Nick."

"Any time you would like to go. During the week would be best due to the crowd," Nick suggested.

"I want to go," Trudy said excitedly.

"You guys aren't going back without me," Gabry smiled. "I'm taking my camera next time."

"I'll take everyone anytime all three of you can go," Nick offered.

Trudy said, "I'll check the weather forecast and call everyone with a day." Everyone agreed.

Vincent suggested, "Let's play some cards." Everyone liked the idea since they were comfortable at the table anyway.

Vincent looked at Nick, "I want to put you on the spot, Nick. I would like for you to work for me at the store until you find a real job."

"You don't have to do that, Vincent."

"You would be doing me a favor. I've been thinking about selling the store. I need to fix it up and then decide what I want to do with it. You would be great at organizing the store."

Trudy offered, "You would be great at that, Nick."

Vincent studied Nick as he considered the offer. "You don't have to work every day. Make your own schedule. Two days a week if you want."

"Okay. I'll do it." Nick knew he would have to find work soon anyway. Money was not something he had a vast amount of.

They played cards and talked and laughed. The four were becoming easy around each other, a lasting friendship. They joked about Vincent's store and about Trudy's top. Trudy and Gabry were constantly looking at Nick and imaging a life with him. Nick would sometimes catch one of them watching him, and he would just smile. He thought maybe he had food stuck between his teeth or something out of place, not knowing they were just looking at him because they liked to.

Nick had grown fond of them all. Vincent like a father and Trudy as a sister. His feelings for Gabry were growing. He fought the feeling because he thought it was too soon after the divorce to have strong feelings for another woman. But Gabriella was hard for Nick to get out of his head. His physical attraction to her was there the moment he saw her. Each hour spent with her increased the attraction and brought with it an intellectual attraction. The day they spent together in the park felt so natural and good; he couldn't escape that fact.

"Vincent, what do you look for in a woman?" Trudy asked.

Without hesitating Vincent answered, "Women with skimpy tops and large breasts," he laughed.

After the laughter died down, "Other than that," she continued.

"What more is there? Okay, I'll be serious," he pondered for a moment and continued, "A woman such as my Maria. She was special. She was respectful of everyone despite their role in life. She never talked bad about anyone. She trusted me to make the right decisions, and I tried my best to do so. I never wanted to disappoint her. She was a beauty up to her last breath."

He hesitated, taking a handkerchief from his pocket. "She had dark hair when I met her and silver when she left me, always kept it long; pinned up in her later years. She was faithful to me and to her God. She had a great love for simple things and friends. The one thing that amazed me about her was that she always knew how to make me happy. Or maybe, just seeing her face made me happy."

The ladies had napkins wiping the tears from their faces.

"I didn't mean to make you cry."

"She sounds like an angel," Gabry said.

"Indeed, she was my guardian angel," Vincent agreed. The card game had paused as Vincent spoke.

Trudy turned to Nick and asked, "What would be your perfect woman?"

"I would like a Maria." When Nick said this his thoughts quickly went to Gabry. Nick thought she shared the same traits except for one; the faith in God. Nick knew in his heart that in time Gabry would share that trait also. The last piece in her healing that was missing.

As the evening closed, Vincent asked if he could host the next party. It was decided to meet at his house the next Saturday evening at six-thirty.

The rain had stopped during the evening leaving the air fresh with an earthy scent in the air. Stars were twinkling in the clearing sky. Nick drove Gabriella to her home and walked her to the door.

"I've really enjoyed the parties with everyone. I couldn't ask for more fun."

"I feel the same," Nick agreed. Gabriella fumbled for her keys to unlock the door. Nick held the strap of her purse as she looked for them.

She located them and looked up at Nick and asked, "I'll see you soon?"

He leaned toward her as he released the strap. Gabriella looked into his eyes and her breath caught as Nick bent his head down and she met his lips halfway. Nick softly and slowly kissed her. Gabriella dropped her purse to the porch and put her arms around his neck. He pulled her closer to him and deepened the kiss, pulled his lips slightly away and took her bottom lip inside his, and they kissed again. She laid her head on his shoulder and kissed Nick's neck. His hands moved up to caress her head and he held her beautiful face in front of his, and he kissed her again more passionately.

Again her head fell to his shoulder, and Nick said, "I had better go."

Gabry had trouble speaking. She wanted more but knew where it could lead. "Call me."

Nick turned to leave and their hands lingered and hesitated to let go. They finally slipped apart and Nick walked to his car. It took all he could muster not to turn around and go back and kiss her again and hold her in his arms. Not knowing what to say he finally managed, "Goodnight, sleep tight."

"Goodnight, Nick."

11

Nick had trouble going to sleep. He thought about what had happened between him and Gabriella. He hadn't planned to kiss her. It felt right at the time though. He was excited and nervous at the same time.

~

Gabriella had trouble going to sleep; she lay in her bed and hoped the phone would ring. She longed to talk to Nick after what had happened. She thought of calling him. Gabry reached for the phone several times only to stop herself. Once she dialed five of the seven numbers and then backed out. She didn't know what to say anyway. Gabriella kept thinking of the tender way Nick had kissed her. She didn't feel they had known each other long enough. Yet, she felt as if they had always known each other. She wanted him to come back over and kiss her again. She went back and forth.

~

Nick decided to turn on the nightstand light and read. He read for a couple of hours. He even thought of calling Gabry. Finally he turned off the light and slept.

~

Gabriella couldn't sleep, so she got up and painted. She had an energy she hadn't felt in years. Paint flowed from the brush. Images raced across her mind, visions that were easily fixed onto the canvas. Light entered through a window and she wondered who would be arriving. *Was Nick coming back for more?* The notion crossed her mind. She looked to the panes and saw that it was the sunrise. She suddenly felt the lack of sleep. She cleaned up and slid into bed.

~

Nick arrived at the church early, wanting to catch the end of Trudy's Sunday school class. He had decided to meet the sixth-grader, Josh Wagner, and talk to him. Nick was directed to her classroom and peeked inside. Trudy had everyone's attention as she finished her lesson. She asked one of the boys to close the class in prayer. Trudy saw Nick and motioned for him to come in. After prayer the kids gathered around her for good-bye hugs as they left the room.

Nick whispered to Trudy that he would like to meet Josh. Trudy looked around the room and saw him skipping the line for hugs and heading for the door. "Josh Wagner."

He turned and looked toward her and she motioned for him to come. The other kids quickly filed out leaving only Josh. "Josh, I would like for you to meet my friend Mr. Nick Stewart."

"Hello, Josh. I'm happy to meet you," Nick said as he offered his hand.

Josh looked at Nick and without shaking his hand said, "Hi."

Nick quickly dropped his hand and said, "I'm new to the area, and Miss Flynn thought you might be the guy to show me around a little."

Josh looked up at Nick with a puzzled look and asked, "Me?"

"What do you like to do? Bike, hike, or play baseball?" Josh continued looking at Nick like he was the strangest person on earth. "Fish?" Josh's facial expression changed. "What if I call your mother and set up a time that we could go fishing together?"

Josh looked at the floor and quietly said, "I guess that would be okay."

Nick pulled a pen from his Bible and wrote down Josh's number and promised to call that afternoon.

"I'm happy to meet you, Josh."

Josh turned and walked slowly from the room. Nick looked at Trudy and she held her hands up as if to say, *See what I mean?*

Trudy then said, "Nick, you're a good man. How about escorting me to the church service?"

"I'd be happy to, Miss Flynn. I've always had a thing for Sunday school teachers since I was a wee lad," Nick teased in an Irish accent.

"You sure are in a great mood," Trudy observed.

"I am, must be due to seeing the sun again."

They entered and Trudy saw spots open near the front. As they made their way down the aisle many people waved and said hello to Trudy. When they were seated Trudy said, "It's nice of you to help Vincent with the store."

"I would do anything for Vincent. But actually I can use the extra money. I'm just not sure where to start in the place."

"It's going to be a big project."

"Yeah, I'm afraid so. Think I'll take Chester and let him poke around during the day."

The service was beginning as everyone rose to sing with the praise band when Trudy added, "It will be nice knowing you'll be right next door. We'll get to see more of each other."

Nick started to answer when the electric guitar blared out the beginning of the first song. He nodded to her.

When the service was over Trudy asked Nick out to lunch. They decided to try the new Applebee's in Pineville.

Nick drove toward the restaurant. Trudy talked about how wonderful the day was. Nick thought about telling Trudy his feelings for Gabry.

Trudy talked about how long it had been since she went out with just her favorite guy. Nick thought about how he got in this mess and that he needed to tell Trudy about Gabry.

But Trudy was happy.

Nick was weak. He knew he wasn't the only man that would be

weak in this circumstance. He figured most men would. You just had to look at Trudy to know why. *My God, she was beautiful.* She was fun to be with. She was the salt of the earth and the most out-going woman Nick had ever met. There was no phoniness to her at all. You got what you saw, and every man liked what he saw.

Applebee's was crowded when they arrived. Nick saw a high table in the bar area that was empty. He knew they were usually first-come first-serve. They took the table and Nick had the hostess take their name off the waiting list. The restaurant was loud with talking and music. "Happy Birthday" was sung several times by the crew…badly. Nick and Trudy casually talked about Vincent, the church, and the evening before.

"The four of us will have to go to the Oak Club for karaoke night some week," Trudy suggested.

"That would be fun. Would you sing?"

"I do the best Patsy Cline in Sleepy Valley."

"I can't wait," he laughed.

"You just wait Mister Stewart, you'll be very impressed."

~

Nick worked on his trail the rest of the afternoon while thinking about Gabriella. He had made up his mind to give her some space and call her in the evening. Chester enjoyed running around the woods and barked when Nick fed the limbs into his new chipper. He enjoyed being out of the house and working after the two days of rain. Chester heard noise at the front of the house and took off to investigate. Nick didn't hear over the noise of the limbs being ground into chips.

A few minutes later Chester was leading a lady toward Nick. Nick was still busy with the chipper and didn't see her walking through the backyard. Chester ran to Nick and barked.

"Hi, Nick."

Nick looked up to see Melissa in front of him. It shocked him to see her standing there. He had never wanted to see her again, and there she was. She looked sad and lost. He knew right away that something was wrong, not that he should care. He wondered how she found him. His next thought was Mom.

"Hello, Melissa. You're a long way from home."

~

Melissa couldn't believe she was standing there in front of Nick either. Months earlier she knew what she wanted and needed to do; leave Nick and make a better life with Adam. Adam was more aggressive, had bigger plans and he wanted it all, including Melissa. It sounded like what Melissa wanted.

She thought she would grow tired of Nick's simple lifestyle. She was already tired of watching kids bounce basketballs and watching Nick grade papers and make out lesson plans. She wanted the bright lights, big parties, cruises, and jet-away weekends. Adam wanted that also. What Melissa hadn't counted on was that Adam also wanted it with Sara, Victoria, and others. He had hid it well that she wasn't his only weekend get-away guest, even after she moved in with him.

And now here she was, willing to beg Nick to take her back. The only true love she had ever had. While standing in front of Nick she thought of all the happy times they had while dating and the first eight years of their marriage. Surely Nick wanted those times back. She knew she could make Nick happy again. She had made him happy before and she knew Nick hadn't wanted the divorce; at least not until the very end. She had to find a way to get Nick to forgive her and take her back. Surely Nick didn't like living in this backward hick place. She figured he had to miss the excitement of Chicago.

Chester took off again toward the front of the house.

"It's good to see you, Nick," Melissa started.

"Sorry. I can't say the same thing," Nick replied as he continued cutting down branches. The comment stunned her. She had imagined in her mind that Nick would be forgiving and accepting when he saw her there. She hesitated and fumbled in her mind as to what words to say next. She wasn't actually thinking very well.

"Nick I wanted to—" Chester interrupted as he came barking back around the house leading Trudy toward Nick and Melissa.

Trudy looked fantastic in her open blouse and tight-fitting shorts. She saw Melissa standing near Nick and wondered who she was. Maybe Nick's sister. She had seen the Illinois license plates on the car parked in the gravel drive.

Melissa stared at Trudy as she smiled and bounced toward them. *Who is this bimbo? Is this what Nick has hooked up with?* She thought.

"Hi, Trudy," Nick said, without introducing Melissa.

Trudy offered her hand to Melissa and introduced herself, "Hello, I'm Trudy Ann Flynn."

"I'm Melissa." She ignored her outstretched hand.

"It's a beautiful day. Those big old white puffy clouds are just wonderful. How could someone not love a day such as this," she commented, not really wanting an answer. "Am I intruding?"

"Not at all," Nick answered. "Melissa was leaving."

"But Nick, we need to talk," Melissa insisted.

Chester took off again toward the drive, tongue hanging out. Trudy then realized who Melissa was. She hadn't heard Melissa's name that often, but she could see the tension between the two. "I was dropping off a pie for you, Nick. I'll place it in the kitchen and see you later."

At that moment Gabriella appeared in the back yard being led by Chester.

Nick wondered just how much weirder the afternoon could get. He wanted to spend the afternoon working on his path. All these women could leave now. He looked at Chester with a little contempt. *Why do you keep bringing women around the side of the house? I should have left you in the stinking barn.*

Melissa now was outnumbered. *Did Nick have a harem?* To her it looked like Nick wasn't very lonely here in Tennessee. So much for hoping he was lonely and wanted a woman's touch. She would have to use the "in God's eyes we're still married" card. She knew Nick thought divorce was wrong. She would do whatever it took to get him back, and these wretches had better stay out of the way.

Gabry said, "Hello, Nick, Trudy." She reached for Melissa's hand and said, "Hello, I'm Gabriella."

Melissa looked past the hand and said, "I'm Melissa Stewart, Nick's wife."

Gabry and Trudy looked at Melissa with shock on their faces. They turned and looked at Nick. Nick took off his gloves and threw his handsaw down and walked toward the women.

"I believe you left out an ex, Melissa. It's ex-wife, and don't you think it's time for you to mosey on up the road to wherever you were headed."

"We need to talk."

"No, we don't!" Nick raised his voice.

"I need to explain. I wanted t—" Melissa began.

Nick interrupted her with, "I have nothing to say, and I don't want to hear anything you have to say. I talked all I wanted last year. Please just go away."

"I have nowhere to go."

Trudy, being the nice person that she was, felt a little sorry for Melissa. She figured the woman realized what a great guy Nick was and was trying to correct her mistake. But at the same time she wanted Nick to get rid of her. She had seen the look Melissa gave her when she walked up, and she noticed the icy glare she gave Gabry.

Trudy and Gabry stood huddled together watching the battle, fascinated, but embarrassed to be eavesdropping. But they couldn't leave.

"There are hotels in Knoxville, and then you get up in the morning and head north on I-75."

"Nick, please, give me a half hour. I'm begging you, please. You owe me that much."

Nick looked at her with daggers. She would be dead if his eyes could have thrown them. "Excuse me, ladies." Nick turned and walked away, leaving the three of them standing there together. Chester watched Nick walk away and looked up at the women and then ran after Nick.

Melissa began to cry loud enough that Nick could hear. She was good at bringing tears whenever she thought they might help her. Trudy looked at Gabry with her brows raised. Gabry didn't know what to do either.

Trudy asked, "Can we do something for you?"

"He can be so stubborn, same Nick," Melissa said, and then she cried more. She looked up at Gabry and Trudy and asked, "One of you dating Nick?"

Trudy looked at her and answered, "We both are."

Melissa was shocked and turned her face and stared at them for a moment to see if they were teasing. "You both are?"

Gabry added, "It's complicated, but we've worked it out. I get him on even days, and Trudy gets him on odd days."

Melissa continued to stare at them. Trudy put her arm inside Gabry's and went on, "On Sundays, we share him." They couldn't keep it up and began laughing.

"Very funny. Is that backwoods Tennessee humor?"

"So what's your next move?" Trudy asked. Trudy suddenly stopped feeling sorry for Melissa and decided she didn't much like her. Feeling sorry for Melissa was now not part of what she thought of her.

"What do you mean?" Melissa questioned.

"Well, you tried begging and you've tried crying. You got any more tricks, missy?" Gabry looked at Trudy. She couldn't believe it. Gabry realized Trudy would probably say anything to anybody. She wasn't afraid to speak her mind. She admired that in Trudy; she could never say something that forward, even though she thought it.

Melissa stepped up close to Trudy and pointed her finger into Trudy's face and said, "He was my husband, he'll be my husband again."

"You want to keep that finger, missy?"

Melissa quickly dropped it to her side and continued, "I'll be back. A two-bit floozy doesn't stand a chance with Nick. There's only one thing I can think of you'd be any good for." Trudy took a step toward her and Gabry held on. Melissa continued, "I still have a card up my sleeve." She turned and walked away.

"You had better have more than a card with that boney butt of yours."

Nick thought the same thing when he saw Melissa. She looked like she had lost twenty pounds. Melissa had always been trim and fit. A lady that men would turn their heads to watch walk away. Nick wondered if she had taken up smoking or drugs. Or had life been hard on her with Adam? It wasn't in Nick's nature to be so rigid with someone, but he was fed up with her. He was just getting over her and had put her out of his mind. Nick was happier than he had been in years, and then she had shown up wanting to talk like long-lost friends. She had made her choice despite his pleas and warnings. She had changed so much in the past years. She would have to live with her choices.

Melissa went straight to her car and sped off, throwing gravel as she left.

"Well, that was fun, like I was back in high school. I definitely had a few catfights back then. You think she really wants him back?"

"Yes," Gabry feared. "But Nick's not that stupid."

"I think we should ask Nick to go hiking with us this evening," Trudy told Gabry.

"I've got to tell you something first, Trudy." Gabry knew she needed to tell Trudy about her feelings for Nick. She couldn't keep it from her best friend.

"What? It sounds serious."

"I've really fallen for Nick, and he kissed me last night."

Trudy smiled and said, "Tell me more, lucky girl."

Gabriella went on to tell Trudy about the kiss, and the embrace, and the second lingering kiss. "I think Nick has feelings for me also."

"Girlfriend, I sure hope so if he's giving out kisses like that."

"Are you upset? I mean, I don't know how serious we are, or he is, or if something will go on, or if I should."

Trudy laughed, "You sound like a schoolgirl passing *do you like me* notes. No. I'm not upset. You two are perfect for each other. I'll be here for you the whole way. I love both of you. I could see it coming. The way the two of you look at each other. I would have to have been blind not to see it."

"I thought you would be more upset. I knew you had feelings for Nick."

"Gabry, the Lord does know best. I'm sure He's leading Nick. Besides, you can't force these things and someone is out there for me. Maybe, Vincent or…Tom." They both laughed as only best friends could. "You had better hang on to him, because I'm still around."

Gabriella hugged Trudy, "Thank you Trudy. You're the best."

"Where's that pie?" Nick hollered from the back door.

"Let's go feed your man," Trudy suggested.

They sat at the kitchen table eating coconut cream pie. Nick talked about how sorry he was that they had to see what went on. Gabry explained to Nick that he missed the real fireworks. They laughed till it hurt as they went over the catfight.

"I think you could take her, Trudy."

"There's no thinking about it. I'd shove that boney finger…"

Gabry interrupted, "Trudy, Trudy, watch yourself."

"I'm sorry. She got me all worked up."

Gabry changed subjects, "Go hiking with us this evening, Nick, and bring Chester. He would love running the trails."

"He would like that. I'd love to. You sure I'm not imposing?"

Trudy then said it, "As long as you and Gabry can keep from making out in front of me." Gabry shot Trudy a look. Nick shot Gabry a look.

"I told her about the kiss last night."

"I figured I would make it more comfortable for you two to be around me. I didn't want it to be awkward."

"Thanks," both Nick and Gabry said at the same time.

~

The hike was great fun. Nick and Gabry held hands at times and Chester would run ahead and then run back to make sure Nick was coming. He did it over and over. Nick loved the view overlooking Sleepy Valley, a view with no Melissa in site.

12

Nick and Chester ended up spending the entire week with Vincent working on the general store. They came up with a plan and decided to close the store the next week for ten days to reorganize the store. Gabriella volunteered to help with some of the work that needed to be done. Nick told her they might need her help later. Vincent ran an ad in the newspaper and advertised a grand re-opening for Wednesday, May 16. They ordered a lot of new supplies, and they hired Andy to build a few new tables and shelves for the store. A painter was coming in to paint through the weekend so it would be done by Monday morning.

Vincent and Nick skipped the Wednesday morning fishing trip to work, but Nick took Josh fishing Friday evening. It went well. Nick bought Josh a new rod and reel and taught him how to use it. They went to Andy's pond and caught plenty of fish. Josh never said much, but the smile gave him away. Nick showed him how to clean the fish and Josh went home with a large package of fillets. Nick told Josh that he would call and they would do something the next weekend.

Nick had been so busy working in the store that he only took time to call Gabry twice during the week and talk on the phone. Gabry was busy with her painting and pottery. She had always become so involved in projects that she would throw herself into them, sometimes working until she became too tired to continue. They both looked forward to seeing each other at Vincent's that evening. Nick told her that he would pick her up. Around three, Nick left the store and headed for home to relax a little before going to Vincent's for dinner.

When he drove down the lane to his home a car was parked near the house. He recognized the 2001 blue Oldsmobile that his dad drove and loved. Nick couldn't believe his parents were there.

They were sitting on the porch patiently waiting for him to get home. His mom waved as he got out of his SUV and headed toward her. They hugged and then Nick embraced his dad in a manly hug.

"You're here."

"Yes. We said we were coming the first weekend in May."

"I guess I expected a call or a warning."

"A warning, you smart aleck?"

"How long have you been here?"

Nick's dad answered, "Around two hours. We've walked around the yard, watched the birds, and sat on your porch."

"What do you think of the place?"

"I love it," his dad said.

"I like it, but it's awfully secluded," was his mom's reply.

Nick opened the front door and took them inside to show them the place. Chester began whimpering in his cage and Nick let him out. Nick had left Chester home for the day, knowing he would be home earlier than usual. Chester pranced up to Nick's father and bounced at his feet until Nick's dad bent down to pet him. Nick made the introductions and then let Chester outside to pee. Nick's parents settled into their bedroom and began freshening up. He quickly called Vincent to see if he could make room for two more. "Of course, I would love to have them at my party. What's a little more spaghetti? Maybe I'll learn some secrets about you."

"I'm sure you will."

Nick went to the front porch and settled into the porch swing enjoying the moment of peace and quiet. Chester was still exploring the edge of the woods in front of the house.

Nick's mother came out onto the front porch, and Nick motioned for her to sit with him. Nick's mother was a lovely woman at fifty-eight. She kept her hair dyed a light brown and had kept her figure despite a little filling out over time. She was a good, loving mother to Nick and his sister. She was always at home when they were kids and involved in their comings and goings. Her only shortcoming to Nick was that she had a tendency to get too involved at times. She wanted to help everyone and fix everything when she felt they needed fixing. She figured that's what mothers were supposed to do; make everything all right.

"Mom, it's good to see you and Dad. How is Dad doing?"

"Retirement has been hard on him. He moped around the house and complained about everything. He needed something to do, so he's taken up playing poker."

"You're kidding."

"No. He was watching it so much on *ESPN* and the *Travel Channel* that he figured he could do it. He's actually pretty good at it. He's even won some money."

"Should I start watching for him on TV?"

"Maybe on *Divorce Court,* depends on whether he wins or loses." They both laughed.

Nick looked toward the door and asked, "What's Dad doing?"

"He was tired after the drive down and wanted to take a nap. Are you happy living here?"

"I'm very happy. I love my home and the church I'm attend-ing. I've made some great friends. You two will get to meet them tonight."

"What do you mean?"

"We're going to dinner at Vincent's house. I've told you about him."

"Yes, but we shouldn't impose."

"He's already told me that he would love to meet you. Besides, I want you to meet my friends and see what my life is like here. Isn't that why you came?"

"What should I wear?"

"Casual is fine, nothing too fancy."

Nick wanted to ask his mom about Melissa but decided to wait. The moment was perfect, so why ruin it? They talked about his sister Laura and her family. She told him the news about relatives and friends. His cousin Ray had a testicle removed. Nick squirmed on the swing. His sister's eight-year-old son, Samuel, broke his arm while trying to jump his bike over a ramp. His aunt Bernice caught her cat in the act of shredding a living room curtain with its claws and threw the cat out the window, forgetting that she had cleaned the window the day before.

"Bernice claimed, "Well, my window was so clean it looked like it was open when I threw Tabby." The clean window shattered and the cat is now bald on one side where they had to shave it to stitch up the cuts. It now limps on a broken leg and has only one ear. Bernice proclaimed, "I bet it won't shred another curtain."

~

Meanwhile, Gabriella finished the painting that she felt might be the best work she had ever done. She was very anxious to see Nick again. It was amazing how the heart grew when you missed someone. She also thought it strange how strong her feelings for Nick had become. She wanted to look her best for Nick at Vincent's dinner. She decided to wear a white sundress with natural sandals. She took great pains in getting ready. Applied just the right amount of makeup and fixed her hair just so, but she could have worn a pair of baggy jeans and a sweatshirt and Nick would have considered her beautiful.

~

Vincent hired a lady to clean his house. Normally she came in twice a month, but he asked her to make a special trip to get things ready.

Vincent was nervous even though he looked forward to having his friends to his home. They were the first guests he had invited to his home in Sleepy Valley. He felt so much more alive after spending time with Trudy, Gabry, and Nick. He liked to think of Nick as the son he'd never had. He became even more anxious after Nick's call asking if his parents could come. He welcomed them to come, but they were strangers coming into his house. He wanted everything to be perfect. The table was set in crystal stemware that his wife had bought. Wine glasses at each spot except Nick's. White china plates and polished silverware over a lace cloth completed the table. This was the first time any of it would be used since Maria's death.

He walked to the mantle and stood before the urn and said, "I hope you enjoy our guests, my love." He repositioned a fresh white rose next to the urn. He returned to the kitchen to check the sauce.

~

No one would ever know that Trudy sat at the edge of her bed and cried. She told herself to pull it together for the evening. She knew she had to tell them tonight.

~

Nick's father wanted to drive when it was time to leave. Nick's mom said she would sit in the back and let Nick ride shotgun.

"No, Mom. That's okay. We need to pick someone up on the way. I'll sit in the back with her."

"With her? Who is this mystery woman we're picking up?"

"Don't start, Mom. She's one of the friends that we're having dinner with. The same four of us have dinner every Saturday evening. Her place is on the way."

"Is she pretty?" Nick's father asked.

"Very."

"Good."

"Mike, you're going to get in big trouble," Nick's mom threatened.

"Nothing wrong in using my eyes, is there, son?"

"Not at all, Pops."

Nick's mom noticed the gallery sign. "Does she run a shop?"

"She's the artist, a great painter and potter."

"Artists are generally a bit on the strange side."

As Nick opened the door he said, "Be sure and tell her that."

Nick rung the bell, opened the door, and walked in calling, "Gabriella." She walked into the room and Nick's heart jumped. Gabry was the vision of an angel in white. She was beyond beautiful. They met in the middle of the room, and she slipped her arms around Nick. She kissed him with passion. "I've missed you this week."

"You look absolutely incredible, Gabriella." She had the classic Italian look; dark skin with a slight hump in her nose and spectacular, mysterious eyes hidden behind black hair.

"Thank you."

Nick kissed her again. They started toward the door. "I have a surprise."

"A good surprise?"

They walked through the door and Nick motioned toward his parents and answered, "Depends." Gabriella quickly dropped Nick's hand.

Nick's parents saw them walk out of the door holding hands. Nick's dad said to no one in particular, "Nick said she was pretty, but wow!"

Nick's mom said to Mike, "Did you see that? They were holding hands. I think something's going on."

"I hope so!" Mike exclaimed.

Nick opened the door for Gabriella and introduced her to his parents Mike and Sue. "It's nice to meet you Mr. and Mrs. Stewart."

"Please call me Mike." Nick's mom only nodded hello.

They arrived right at six-thirty. Vincent answered the door and greeted everyone. He kissed Nick's mom on the hand and welcomed Mike with a strong handshake. The house was filled with the aroma of Italian spices, marinara sauce, and garlic.

"Vincent, your house is lovely. The smell brings back so many memories of my home as a child. Is Trudy here?"

"She hasn't arrived yet." Vincent answered Gabry. Vincent's home was filled with a mixture of wooden antique furniture and flowered couches and chairs. A baby grand piano sat in the corner near the fireplace.

Soon the doorbell rang and Vincent hurried to the door to welcome Trudy to his residence. Trudy was lovely as always. She also wore a sundress. The bottom on the skirt was covered with colorful wildflowers and there was a large yellow sun covering her left breast with rays extending down the dress onto the flowers. It was a sight to see.

Gabry embraced her and said, "Your dress is adorable."

Nick kissed her on the cheek and said, "You two ladies have outdone yourselves."

Trudy said, "Vincent deserves the best."

Mike chipped in, "This is the best vacation I've ever been on. I can see why you moved to Sleepy Valley, Nick. Are all the women here as beautiful as these two?"

Trudy shook Mike's hand and said, "Aren't you a charmer? You must be Nick's father. I can see where he gets his good looks."

Mike stood a little taller and Nick's mom quickly reached her hand to Trudy and announced, "He's taken."

"You are a lucky woman, Mrs. Stewart. You had better keep an eye on him. You probably have to beat the women off him all the time."

"Yeah, they're beating down the door to get at him," Sue said dryly.

Vincent arrived back in the room and announced that dinner

was ready. The group followed him into the dining room. Everyone "oohed" and "aahed" at the spread before them. They all stood and gazed at the table. It was too wonderful to disturb and eat.

Two large platters of spaghetti were placed at each end of the table, and a large bowl of meat sauce and Italian meatballs sat in the middle with steam rising. Baskets of warm, sliced bread were positioned in different spots. A large salad was waiting for them to dig into. Vincent and Mike sat at the ends of the table. Nick and Gabriella on one side and Trudy and Sue on the other side. Vincent placed Nick to his right and Trudy to his left. Vincent asked Nick to say grace.

The dinner was delicious. The wine was magnificent. The girls asked lots of questions about Nick. They discussed his childhood and his high-school days. Sue told about Nick's first date. "Lily Chalmers, they were in the eighth grade. Mike drove them to a school dance and said he would pick them up at ten. Nick said they were sitting in the gym's bleachers when she turned to Nick, said she felt sick, threw up in his lap and then she passed out." Everyone laughed.

Gabry said, "Poor girl."

Nick sighed, "Poor girl, what about poor guy?"

Sue continued, "Nick called us at eight fifteen and said that he thought the date was over, and could his dad come get him. Lily's parents came to pick her up."

"I didn't even get a kiss on my first date."

Trudy commented while laughing, "Sounds like she was all over you." Everyone laughed.

"Trudy, that is so bad, but funny," Vincent said.

The dinner was fantastic and very filling. After dinner, Nick talked Vincent into performing for them despite his slight objections. Everyone settled into the living room to listen. Nick and Gabriella sat together in a love seat. Vincent stood at the corner of his piano. He played the violin so beautifully and confidently, as if he was playing in front of thousands. It didn't take much to get him to perform another. He began fiddling as though a square dance had broken out and then another classical piece. Vincent was at his best; hosting and entertaining his friends. The smile could not have been knocked off his face.

After Vincent put the violin down upon the piano, Gabriella asked about the beautiful covered vase on the mantle.

"That's where I keep my wife." Everyone looked at him in silence. "Maria's ashes are in that urn. It's as if she's still with me," the smile never left his face as he explained. "You may think it's a bit strange for me to still have them after five years. I just haven't found the right place to scatter her remains. One of the reasons I travel the roads every Sunday is to search for the perfect spot."

Nick offered, "Vincent, perhaps we'll be able to help you."

"I would like that."

The ladies in the room wiped tears from their eyes and Vincent asked, "May I sing you Maria's favorite song? She would like for me to."

"Please do," Mike answered.

Vincent took a seat at his piano and began playing. He played a long introduction and then began singing, in tune, with a raspy aged voice, "Moon River." Nick saw his dad put his arm around his mom and kiss her on the cheek as Vincent sang. Nick held Gabry's hand and they watched Vincent pour his soul into the singing of his Maria's favorite song. Trudy positioned herself behind Vincent and lightly held her hands on his shoulders. When he finished Trudy bent down and gave Vincent a light kiss on his cheek.

"Your Maria was a lucky woman, Vincent," she told him.

"I was the lucky one."

Vincent then began playing show tunes and everyone gathered around him and sang. He even played a couple of songs from *Grease*. He surprised them by saying he thought *Grease* was the best musical ever. Nick agreed. Others didn't.

Vincent went into the kitchen and brought out bowls of ice cream for everyone. "There's nothing like ice-cream after an Italian meal."

After the ice cream was gone Trudy asked if she could have the floor for an announcement. Everyone began to smile anticipating her usual cut-ups. She tried not to cry. She wanted to be strong for everyone. The smiles left the faces in the room. They quickly knew something was wrong. She couldn't hold it together when she spoke.

"I've been having some health problems. I went to Knoxville to see a specialist and to have tests done. He says that I've got cancer." Tears ran down her face.

Gabry jumped to her feet and ran to her best friend and cried out, "No!" They embraced each other for a long while.

Trudy then continued after the tears subsided, "I'm having a hysterectomy on Wednesday. The doctors are hopeful that I'll be fine after the surgery. I'm so sorry to have to tell this in front of your parents, Nick. I had to tell everyone tonight. I was running out of time."

A portion of the evening was spent comforting Trudy. They found out that her secret visit to Knoxville had confirmed her fears. The operation was scheduled during that visit. Gabry told her she would spend the entire time in Knoxville with her.

"I knew you would," Trudy said, "even if I had to force you to." Within an hour Trudy was back to flirting and telling jokes.

As they left, everyone thanked Vincent for a wonderful evening. Gabry said Trudy wanted to take her home and talk for a while. Nick asked Gabry, "Come to church with us tomorrow, and we'll pray for Trudy."

"Okay."

13

It was Wednesday, and Trudy's surgery began at seven thirty. Nick, Gabry, and Vincent were waiting for word on the outcome from the surgeon. Gabry paced back and forth down the hallway and back. Nick silently prayed off and on. Vincent talked to the other people in the waiting room, providing welcome relief to them while waiting for other outcomes.

Nick's father was staying with Chester, and his mom had volunteered to work at the diner and help Stella wait on tables. Tom and Andy had been waiting at the front door when Stella arrived to open. The restaurant had filled quickly with patrons waiting for word. No one left after eating breakfast. The place was bursting at the seams. Customers got up after eating and offered the tables to others and then stood around talking, waiting for the phone call. Stella had hung a prayer poster on the wall, asking customers to sign up promising to pray for Trudy since Monday morning. It was filled with names. Trudy had been touched by the love and concern every time she walked by it. Tuesday had been very emotional for Trudy as customers had stopped by just to wish her well and tell her they were praying for her. All day long she'd kept telling everyone, "Don't you people have jobs that you have to be at?"

Trudy and Nick had gone forward to pray during the invitation at the church the past Sunday. Pastor Hill had the church body take a few minutes to pray for Trudy. It had taken Trudy an hour before she could leave after the service due to all the well-wishers wanting to talk to her.

Gabry was so impressed with the love and sincerity she saw.

She had never seen anything like it in her life. Trudy had talked about her involvement in the church, but Gabry didn't realize how involved and adored she was at the church. She liked the church, but it left her feeling empty for some reason. She knew she didn't have the faith they had. They all acted as though they knew God would look over Trudy in her time of need. She wished she had that kind of faith. She worried about her best friend even though she knew worry wouldn't help anything.

~

At the café, Tom asked Stella, "Shouldn't we be hearing something by now?"

"We have to give the surgeons time to operate. They're not magicians." Stella knew that Tom and Andy were just concerned as were all the others crowded into the small restaurant. The phone rang and everyone became silent in anticipation.

Stella slowly walked to the phone. Sue was wringing a table rag in her hand. Tom removed his cap and placed it on the counter.

"Hello, Trudy's Place." She listened and then said, "I'm sorry, Betty. We haven't heard a word yet. We're trying to keep the phone line... Yeah, I know you are. We'll call you after we hear."

The diner let out a collective sigh.

"I can't take much more," Tom complained. He threw his cap to the floor.

"She's going to be fine. Trudy's a fighter. You of all people know that," Andy said as he stirred his cold coffee for the umpteenth time.

~

In Knoxville, Pastor Hill and Teresa walked into the waiting room at the hospital. Nick rose to meet them. "It's so nice that you came all this way."

"We had to, couldn't stand just waiting by the phone," Teresa said.

"Didn't I see you at church Sunday?" the pastor asked Gabry.

"Yes, I was there with Nick praying for Trudy."

"I'm sure Trudy appreciated your coming. She has told me so much about you."

"She has?"

"Told me you were her best friend and that she didn't know what she would do without you. You must be a special person."

Gabry's eyes began to tear up. Nick held her in his arms as she gently wept. She wasn't sure why she was crying except that she felt like a phony. Gabry knew she didn't have the faith in God that Nick, Trudy and the Pastor had, but she did feel the love of God through them. She felt she didn't deserve the love she received from Trudy or Nick. She wondered why they loved her so.

"Can we all gather and pray for Trudy?"

"Of course, Pastor Hill," Nick answered. They went to a corner in the room and either sat on the furniture or knelt on the floor. Pastor Hill prayed. He thanked God for Trudy and such great friends in her life. He prayed for the doctors and nurses that were taking care of Trudy. He prayed for forgiveness of his sins so that his prayers would carry to the throne of God with no hindrance. He prayed with the assurance of a man that knew God was hearing his prayers and would answer them. Gabry knew she wanted that kind of faith.

Lastly he prayed thanks for Trudy's testimony and that through it, her friends and customers would see Jesus and be brought to a relationship with Him.

~

Back at the diner, Tom had torn his paper napkin into a hundred little pieces. Andy finally realized his coffee needed a fresh filling. By then customers were standing outside the restaurant and folks were seen praying and talking, laughing, and crying. They were comforting each other with pleasant clichés. *Everything is going to be fine. She's a strong person. God is with her.*

~

At 9:40 the surgeon, Dr. Walker Green, walked into the waiting room and asked for them. They followed him into the hallway and he smiled and said, "Trudy is out of surgery; she's doing well." Gabry was hanging tight to Nick. He continued, "We're very confident we were able to remove all the cancer and she should be back to normal in a few weeks."

Gabry turned and hugged Nick and cried with relief into his shoulder. Vincent shook the doctor's hand and told him what great news it was. "She's a special person, doc."

"I know she is."

Nick asked, "When can we see her?"

"A nurse will come get you when she's awake and back in her room. It usually takes a couple of hours. Just relax now."

Gabry let go of Nick and hugged the doctor, "Thank you so much," she told him.

"I've got to make a call," Nick said.

Nick and Gabry headed down the hall and out the front door to a spot with better reception for his cell phone.

~

Everyone in the diner jumped when the phone rang again. It rang a second time as Stella looked at it. She looked scared to answer it.

"If you don't answer it, I'm going to jump over this counter."

"You couldn't jump over a dime," Stella said to Tom as she picked up the receiver. Faces from outside were pressed against the front windows. Heads were poked inside the open door. Everyone stared at Stella waiting for the news. "Hello. Yes. Yes… glory to God!" Stella gave the thumbs-up sign to the crowd with her empty hand and everyone erupted in shouting and laughter. People began hugging each other and patting each other on the back. Tom climbed over the counter and picked Stella up and swung her around. She was still trying to hear Nick as Tom and she were being wound up in the long black phone cord.

"Get off me you old cuss," Stella said when she realized they were tied together facing each other. Tom gave Stella a big kiss on the lips. Dancing broke out in the village street outside the diner when someone turned a radio up loud.

Nick and Gabry laughed as they heard all the excitement and shouting through the phone. Nick had to move it away from his ear. Their laughter increased when they heard Stella tell Tom to get off her. Nick turned and kissed Gabriella. They hugged each other, not wanting to let go.

Pastor Hill and Teresa left at eleven, and around noon the others were led into a private hospital room to see Trudy. Gabry quickly made her way to the bed and kissed her. Nick and Vincent stood beside the bed. They couldn't help but notice how good Trudy looked. Her hair looked like she had just come from a beauty shop. She didn't have on a normal green hospital gown. Instead she had on a beautiful pink low-neck gown. Even two hours after surgery she looked wonderful.

They told her about the scene at the diner and how happy they were for her. Trudy then said to Gabriella, "Isn't the surgeon cute? Not married either."

Gabry asked, "How do you know?"

"I asked him."

"Typical Trudy," Gabry exclaimed and Nick and Vincent agreed.

Nick and Vincent stayed until two thirty and then left. Gabry was spending the night with Trudy in the hospital. Gabry kissed him good-bye and said she would call him that evening.

14

Friday afternoon Gabry took Trudy home. Gabry had stayed in Knoxville and spent visiting hours with Trudy until she was released. Trudy was so thrilled to be back at her home, although, she liked seeing Dr. Walker Green twice a day. He even brought her and Gabry dinner Thursday evening, claiming the hospital food wasn't very good. Trudy asked him, "Do you do this for all your patients."

"Shh... Don't tell them," he answered.

Gabry suspected that the doctor had a crush on Trudy. It didn't surprise Gabry. Most men who met Trudy did the same.

Nick couldn't believe his mom was working so hard at the diner and enjoying it. She seemed to like getting up and putting on her apron every morning before she left for the diner. "Everyone is so friendly and concerned about Trudy. I can't get over the love for her in this community."

Nick's father was working even harder at the general store helping Nick and Vincent. The painting was complete. Andy had installed the new tables and shelves. They were in the process of restocking the aisles with supplies. New supplies kept arriving each day. Nick felt they would be ready for the grand reopening. Nick really appreciated his parents' help and realized how fortunate he was. His mom might be a bit on the pushy side, but her heart was always the reason for it. Melissa had not been mentioned during their visit so far.

~

As for Melissa, she was back in Chicago staying in a motel in a rundown part of town. She couldn't believe what was happening to her and had a harder time accepting it. Adam had made her leave after she found out about the other women in his life and had given him an ultimatum—them or her. She had started throwing things and destroying his expensive condo overlooking Lake Michigan. He'd kicked her out and told her not to come back.

Adam had always had drugs handy for his guests and friends. He only used them occasionally, but Melissa liked the taste of cocaine and had become addicted quickly. She still held her job but spent most of her paychecks buying coke from street dealers. She wasn't sure how many more times she could miss work or come in late without being fired. She knew she needed to quit using, get her life together, and start over. But she couldn't, she needed Nick. Every lonely minute brought back the taste and escape the cocaine offered.

Nick had seemed so hurt when she left him she figured he would be happy to take her back. Melissa couldn't believe the way he talked to her. She had hoped that maybe going to find Nick would bring some relief. She hated Nick for rejecting her and sending her back to the drugs. She blamed him for the fact that she continued to use the stuff. It was his fault and, the two bimbos. Her mind told her they were brainwashing him into rejecting her. *How dare they! She knew she could get Nick back, and she knew how.*

~

On that Tennessee Friday evening Nick picked up Josh and took him out to eat. They went to Friendly's in Pineville. They ate burgers and fries and ordered ice-cream for desert. Nick got a sundae. Josh ordered a banana split and it came topped with a mountain of whipped cream. Josh asked, "When can we go fishing again?"

"How about next Saturday morning? I'm very busy helping a good friend stock his store and we need to be done by Wednesday. I hope you understand. "

Josh looked down at his ice-cream and said softly, "Okay." He took a big bite of the strawberry scoop of ice-cream and then asked, "How is Miss Flynn doing?"

"She's doing great, Josh. Her operation was a success and she should be back teaching the class in a couple of weeks. I'll tell her you asked about her. That will make her happy."

They sat in silence for a few minutes and then Josh asked, "Could I help stock the store?"

Nick smiled and knew that Josh just wanted to spend time with him. "Sure. We could use your help. How about I pick you up first thing in the morning?"

Josh smiled to himself and said, "Okay."

Nick arrived home after dropping Josh off and watched TV with his mom and dad until they decided to turn in early. They were both tired from a busy day. Neither was used to working as they had been. Nick said goodnight and went to the phone and called Gabriella. It was only nine thirty. Gabriella answered the phone.

"Hi, sexy," Nick said.

"Is this an obscene phone call?" Gabry answered.

"Yes."

"Good. I was hoping I'd get one tonight."

"Would you like some company?"

"How soon can you be here, big boy?" Gabry teased.

"Two minutes," and he hung up the phone and hurried to his car.

Two minutes later Gabry was so happy to see Nick coming up her steps. It excited her. She opened the door before he could ring the bell and she jumped into his arms and kissed him. "That's quite a welcome."

"I welcome all my men like that."

"Do you?"

They settled onto the couch and Gabry snuggled close to him. They kissed and talked and kissed and talked. It seemed like they had not had much of a chance to see each other lately with all that was going on. Gabry told him how great Trudy was doing and about Dr. Green. Nick told Gabry how the work at the store was going and about how happy he was about Josh.

"I knew he would find you irresistible. I did," Gabry smiled.

"You're the one that's irresistible." Nick kicked off his shoes and reclined on the couch and pulled Gabry onto him and they kissed.

He loved the feeling of her body lying on him and he gently caressed her back and neck as she relaxed with her face nestled at his neck. He carefully moved his hand inside her cotton pullover and touched the small of her back. She melted in his touch. His hand moved up to gently rub her back. Gabriella moved her body down Nicks and unbuttoned the top three buttons of his shirt. She began kissing his chest and touching the hair gently. She wanted this moment to last forever. It had been so long since she felt like this, if she ever did. She moved back up and kissed his lips. She playfully took his lips one at a time and caressed them with her lips. It was driving Nick crazy.

They both knew it was too soon. She asked, "You want something to drink?"

"Yeah, how about a cold shower?"

She laughed.

"Very funny to you, huh?" Nick said laughing.

"It's good to know that I excite you," she said from the kitchen.

"You definitely excite me. Just looking at you excites me." He moved back up to a sitting position and buttoned his shirt.

When she came back with drinks, she asked Nick about Melissa. They had not talked about her visit since it had happened.

"I don't know what she was up to. She looked awful. She and Adam must have split or been having trouble. He's a real player, one of those smooth talkers. She never could see it. You know the type I mean."

"You mean the type that sits at the bar in a lounge looking for their next prey."

"Yeah. Something along that line," he laughed.

"Do you think she's using drugs?" Gabry asked.

"I don't know. I don't think so. Maybe. She always thought drugs were used by morons. But something was happening with her. I'd never seen her look so bad."

"Do you worry about her?" Gabriella asked.

"No."

Gabry didn't believe him. She knew Nick didn't want to worry about her, and maybe he was telling himself he didn't, but if she knew Nick at all she thought he couldn't help but worry about Melissa. How could he not?

"Let's talk about something different or get back in that same position we were in earlier."

"You couldn't take it again," Gabry smiled.

"You're probably right. But they say the pain makes you stronger."

"I don't want to hurt you."

Nick laughed and started singing Mellencamp, "It hurts so good."

~

SATURDAY, MAY 12

The next morning Nick picked Josh up early. He was waiting on the porch when Nick pulled up. "Let's get some breakfast."

"Trudy's Place?" Josh asked.

"Sure, but she won't be there."

Nick noticed Josh's face pout up.

"There'll be plenty of people to wait on us, though." Nick's father and Vincent were meeting them there at eight. Nick's mother was already pouring coffee when they arrived. Nick introduced Josh to his mom when they walked in.

Mike said, "This is the best service she's given me in years."

Everyone laughed and she whacked him on the head. Josh laughed at that. Nick introduced everyone else to Josh. "He's going to help us today."

Vincent said, "I sure appreciate it, Josh." Josh nodded.

Stella came by to say hello. Nick winked at her and said, "How's the bacon sizzling, sweetheart?" in his best Bogart impression.

"Okay, Nick. That one goes on the list with the other. That might even go to the top."

"I know you really loved it," Nick said as she walked away.

Tom was in a battle of words with Nick's mother. "I don't know how Mike has lived with you so long."

Sue cracked back, "And what's the name of the favorite person who lives with you?"

Andy laughed and said, "Frank, his dog." Everyone laughed. "And Frank leaves him every once in a while. Just wanders off."

"Who could blame good old Frank?" Sue added.

Tom said, "He's just looking for a good woman."

Stella walked by and said, "Like dog, like owner." Laughter erupted.

Nick could tell that Josh was enjoying the banter in the restaurant. They ate and then went to the store and got to work. Josh began helping by carrying things. Nick then showed him how to hang objects and place them on the shelves. Josh did everything perfectly.

~

Gabry woke and went to Trudy's to look in on her. Trudy said she felt so much better. Gabry told her about the evening with Nick and all the conversations.

"Nick would surely have to worry about Melissa after all the years together," Trudy agreed.

Gabry didn't go into great detail about the time spent on the couch. She decided to keep it to herself. Gabry was falling in love with Nick more every day.

"Monday, I go to see Dr. Green for my checkup. I think he really likes me," Trudy said.

"I think he does also. But Trudy, don't do anything you'll be sorry for later. Let him make the first move."

"Of course I will."

"Of course."

"You can take me, can't you?" Trudy asked. She already knew Gabry would take her.

Stella decided she was going to drop off food from the restaurant each day. Trudy was told she would not be able to go back to the diner for at least three weeks and then only to manage, not waitress. It would be five to six weeks before she could resume normal activities. Gabry advised her to enjoy the time by reading books and catching up on watching a lot of good movies. Trudy knew she needed to hire a waitress until she could return and had asked Stella to put a sign in the window. She couldn't ask Sue to help any longer. She was so indebted to her for her kindness already.

~

The general store was really taking shape. It looked like a different place but somehow maintained its charm. Nick felt the store needed to keep some of the old attraction so he made a section for odds and ends and placed the items haphazardly in the aisle. He had plenty of odds and ends to fill the section for months to come. Josh had worked hard all day. Vincent took a liking to Josh and bought him a burger and fries at the diner for lunch. He let Josh pick out a baseball glove at the end of the day for helping. Josh thanked Nick for letting him help as he was getting out of the car.

"You were a big help, Josh. I know Vincent appreciated it."

~

Nick had called Gabry and asked her to come over for the evening with him and his parents. They grilled out steaks for dinner.

During dinner Mike asked, "How is Trudy doing?"

"She's really doing well. She goes back for a checkup on Monday."

"That's good news," Mike said.

"I hate to say so, but I'm very upset with Trudy," Sue told everyone.

"Why?" Nick asked surprised.

"She's trying to replace me at the diner."

"What?" Nick didn't understand what she was getting at.

"Trudy had Stella put a 'help wanted' sign in the window to take my place."

"But mother, you're going home soon, aren't you?"

"Trudy said she couldn't impose on you any longer. She is so grateful for your help. She said she didn't know what she would have done without you," Gabry tried to explain.

"Well, that's a fine way to show your gratitude, by replacing me."

"What are you saying, Sue?" Mike asked.

"I'm not ready to go home. I'm enjoying being here and working at the café. I want to stay and help until she's ready to come back."

Nick looked at his mother in amazement. "Mom, you have never worked outside the home."

"I know, and I like it. Especially working at Trudy's Eating Place."

Mike said, "I don't mind staying for a few weeks. I would like to fish some of the ponds and streams, and I saw that there are a few poker tournaments coming up in Knoxville."

Nick just shook his head as he gave Chester small pieces of his steak, "You two are always full of surprises. You know you are welcome to stay as long as you want…within reason."

After dinner was cleaned up, Nick put in one of his favorite movies, *The Untouchables*. He and Gabriella sat on the couch together. Nick kept his arm around Gabry, or they held hands. After the movie was over Sue and Mike decided to turn in. Nick and Gabry were happy to have some alone time.

"Your parents are so sweet."

"They are good people, aren't they?"

Nick and Gabry decided to take Chester outside for a short walk in the yard. They stopped and held each other tight and kissed under the stars. Chester spotted something and took off after it.

Gabry turned and Nick held her from behind and kissed her neck. Nick put his mouth to her ear and said, "I love you."

Gabry turned back around and kissed Nick again and again. "I love you too, Nick. I never thought I would feel like this again."

"Me either," Nick said.

"Are you sure it's not too soon? I don't want to be your rebound girl. I want you to be sure."

"I don't want that either, and I've thought about it. I didn't come here looking for love. But I found it. Let's take it slow and make sure for both our sakes. We don't have to rush it. There's no hurry. Neither of us are going anywhere," Nick suggested.

Gabry hugged him knowing she would always love Nick.

Chester returned and they went back into the living room and lay together on the couch. Chester lay on the small pillow Nick had bought for him. Nick knew his parents always went to sleep quickly. They kissed and touched each other's arms and necks and faces. Nick was making his way to second base with his hand under Gabry's blouse when suddenly Mike said, "Excuse me."

Nick jumped up and Gabry tried to straighten her clothing. "What, Dad?"

"I'm sorry to interrupt, but do you have any antacid? I need something."

Nick directed him to where he could find the medicine cabinet. Mike smiled and said, "You two can go back to whatever you were doing." Mike turned and walked away smiling.

"I feel like I'm in high school again," Nick said.

Gabry laughed and said, "No luck then either, huh?" Nick laughed.

Gabry turned serious, "I know this is a self-fulfilling question. But why me, why did you fall in love with me? Trudy is such a grea—"

Nick stopped her by putting his finger to her mouth and answered, "Because I see the goodness in you, I see the kindness in your eyes. You are not only the most beautiful woman I've ever seen, but you have the best soul. You have something hard to describe, a deep love, a lasting love. It's like I can see the love inside you. I want it. I want your love."

"That's the sweetest thing anyone has ever said to me," Gabry said as tears filled her eyes.

"Besides," Nick began.

"What?"

"I love your sexy legs." Gabry jumped on him and hugged him and laughed and cried at the same time.

"I found the antacid," Mike announced, standing inside the room. "Thought you might want to know… in case you were worried about me."

Nick and Gabry cracked up laughing.

15

Nick, Gabry, and his parents went to church the next morning. They arrived early so Nick could say hello to Josh. He smiled when he saw Nick.

Later in the day, Nick went with Gabry to check on Trudy. She had just begun watching *In Her Shoes*. They stayed and watched it with her. After the movie Trudy looked at them and said, "You two look so happy. What's up?"

Gabry smiled and said, "We confessed our love for each other."

"The big three words. The best three words ever put together in the English language."

Nick said, "The three words *I love you?*"

"No, Nick. The three words *shake your booty*. Of course I mean *I love you*."

It was good to see Trudy telling jokes and laughing. She seemed like herself.

"You two are so cute together." She looked toward the window and said, "The rain is really coming down hard now."

The rain had started right after church and was predicted to last all night. Nick liked hearing the rain fall. It was comforting. Nick told Trudy about his mom wanting to work at the restaurant until she could return.

"That's great," Trudy said. "Won't having your parents here that long cramp your style?"

"I have no style," Nick confessed.

Gabry went on to retell the story of Nick's father walking in on them twice. Trudy could hardly contain the laughter.

~

Wednesday's grand reopening of the general store was a great success. Vincent, Nick, and Mike waited on customers. Vincent said it was his biggest day of sales ever. Customers congratulated Vincent on the changes made to the store. Vincent was all smiles; he even played his violin as entertainment during the day. Vincent knew business would slow because the village was so small, but Vincent didn't want a lot of customers anyway. They kind of got in the way. He did like the store a lot better now though.

~

During the week Gabry took Trudy for her checkup and continued her painting while stopping in every day to check on Trudy and spend time with her. Trudy asked all sorts of questions about the romance. Gabry would answer her while blushing.

"I'm so happy for you two," Trudy told her.

"Are you really?" Gabry asked.

"Yes. I really am. Besides, I have a doctor after me. He asked me Monday if he could take me out on a date when I was up to it."

"You're kidding."

"No, I'm not. I told him I was ready now." Gabry laughed at Trudy's reply.

Trudy continued, "He is so nice. He's a Christian. He even prayed before he did the surgery. He's forty-five and has been divorced eleven years. Walker Green," Trudy looked to heaven as she said his name.

~

SATURDAY, MAY 19

Nick took Josh out for breakfast and then to Virgil's pond to fish. They had a great time. As a surprise Nick took Josh by Trudy's house to see her. He called the night before to tell her they would stop by. Josh was embarrassed by all the fuss Trudy made over him.

Trudy had made a pie and had Nick cut them all a piece. Josh wolfed it down like it was the best thing he had ever eaten.

Nick finally said it was time to go. Josh got up and headed for the door.

"We'll see you later, Trudy," Nick said.

Josh hesitated, turned and ran to Trudy and hugged her. "I'm happy you're going to be okay. I miss you."

Tears welled up as they left and Trudy had a good happy cry when they were gone.

~

When Melissa was forced to leave Adam she headed to Tennessee to find Nick. After she was turned away she spent the next two nights in Knoxville in a cheap hotel snorting cocaine until she ran out. She was hoping to die. When she awoke and didn't know where to find coke in Knoxville she headed back to Chicago. The drive was long and painful. Her head spun in the I-75 traffic and she stopped often with dry heaves, aches and pain, needing nap breaks. She spent a miserable night at a rest stop outside Cincinnati and drove on to Chicago the next day.

She had nowhere to go once she got to Chicago. She went back to Adam's apartment hoping he would let her back in. He refused her request for a place to stay and for more cocaine. She ended up checking into a seedy motel in a rundown part of Chicago and took to the streets looking for the drug. She found it. She spent the next three weeks going to work, late most days, and she filled her evenings of loneliness with coke. Her nosebleeds became more frequent and the headaches became worse. When she began having chest pains and trouble breathing she checked into the rehab center—telling them she had tried to kill herself.

Late that afternoon Nick received a phone call from a treatment center in Chicago. They informed him of Melissa's condition and attempted suicide. She'd told the staff that she would talk to no one until she could talk to Nick face-to-face. They asked if he would come. Nick was stunned and said he would call them back. He called Pastor Hill for advice and then called Gabry, "I need to come over and talk to you about something." "What's wrong?" She knew something was wrong by the tone of his voice.

"I'll be right there." Nick hung up quickly.

Nick kissed Gabriella as he entered the door to assure her it wasn't something between them. They went out to the porch and he explained everything to her. Gabry wondered if this was the card that was up Melissa's sleeve. She also knew that she needed to be supportive and let this work itself out. She trusted Nick to do the right thing. She hated the thought of Nick having to go to Melissa in Chicago, but she knew she couldn't tell Nick that. She wanted to have a life with Nick, a life with Nick without any regrets. Nick could resent her if she told him not to go, if Melissa died when he might have helped.

Gabry could tell that Nick was struggling with the decision. She saw that he truly didn't want to go. She saw the anger he had toward Melissa when she showed up at his home. They went inside and he called the Knoxville airport and made reservations to fly to Chicago Sunday evening. He made no return reservations. He then called Vincent and told him of the development. Vincent wished him well.

They decided to go to Pineville for dinner and a movie. Nick wanted to try to get his mind off Melissa and spend the evening with the woman he loved. Nick was quiet most of the evening but loving toward Gabry. She understood and didn't push anything. She enjoyed his loving touches and holding his hand in the theater. She kissed him every so often during the movie to remind him she was there.

~

Sunday morning Nick told his parents about the situation and his decision. They said they would take care of Chester while he was gone and look after the house. They gave him the keys to their house so he would have a place to stay while he was in Chicago.

Gabry went to church with Nick and his parents, and Nick and Gabry spent the early afternoon visiting Trudy.

Trudy warned Nick, "She said she had another card to play. Be careful, Nick. You do realize you don't have any responsibility in this, don't you?"

This was what Gabry wanted to tell him, but couldn't.

"Don't take any blame for her mistakes. She's a big girl and apparently a stupid one."

"Trudy," Gabry said as she gave Trudy a look that said *you're crossing the line.*

"Gabry, it's okay. I know that what Trudy is saying is true. All I want to do is to see why she wants to talk to me and if I can help her. I think I made a mistake by not talking to her when she came asking me to. I might have prevented having to make this trip."

"Remember, Nick, we love you. A whole bunch of people in this community need you," Trudy warned. Those words surprised Nick.

Nick dropped Gabriella off at her house. It pained him to leave her. Knowing he wouldn't be two minutes from her. Knowing he couldn't hold her in his arms and kiss her lips. He still wanted to get to second base. He drove to Knoxville alone; afraid of what was to come in Chicago. He began second guessing his decision. How was this getting away from Melissa and Chicago? What kind of peace and seclusion was this? He drove on to the airport, checked his bags, and boarded the flight. He had bought Larry McMurtry's book *The Sin Killer* at the airport bookstore to read on the trip.

While sitting on the plane, he couldn't concentrate enough to read, so Nick thought about Melissa. He realized that Melissa had an addictive personality. He thought about how she always overdid things she liked. On their honeymoon, a bottle of champagne was delivered to their room on the first night. She loved the taste, which she had never had before, and ended up drinking the entire bottle. After their first expensive vacation, she then wanted a couple every year. If she found shoes or blouses she liked she bought multiple ones in different colors. Something about her needed to overdo everything. And when she began making more money, she wanted more and Nick then became the wrong man for her.

He listened to the older couple sitting beside him talk about how much they enjoyed their week in the Smoky Mountains. It saddened him even more to be heading back to Chicago. He wished he had been able to ask Gabriella to come with him, but he knew Trudy needed her. He thought about the statement Trudy made, "People in this community need you." It was kind of Trudy to say, but he wondered if it was true. He figured everyone was doing great before he arrived. No one person makes that much difference in a community, at least not an ordinary person like himself. His thoughts turned to people who did make a difference; Lincoln, Martin Luther King, Mother Teresa, Hitler, and Churchill.

But Trudy's statement was true. People did need Nick and counted on him. Gabry loved him. Josh needed him. He was a son to Vincent. Trudy never felt as alive as she did when Nick was around. Chester owed his happy life to Nick. They all had melded together because of Nick's arrival.

Nick was tired from a restless night and finally fell asleep and woke when the pilot announced for everyone to buckle up for the landing.

~

Back in Sleepy Valley, Gabry told Trudy, "I miss him. He's only been gone hours and just knowing he's not in Sleepy Valley is awful."

"You have got it bad, girl."

"I do, don't I?"

"Nick will be back soon, even if it might seem like forever to you. He loves you."

Gabry worried, "I wonder if our love is strong enough."

"The good thing is; you're going to find out how strong it is. I fear it's going to be tested by Melissa."

"Why did you have to say that, Trudy?"

"I just said what you were thinking. If Nick is the man we think he is, he will do his best to help Melissa and then come back to the person he loves… you. Besides, I've been thinking, we're partially to blame for this mess."

"How?" Gabry asked.

"Nick was right, he should have talked to Melissa when she came to see him, and we had a big part in scaring her off."

Gabry thought about it and said, "We did, didn't we?"

"A big part," Trudy confirmed, "Especially me!"

"I hope Nick knows how much I love him."

"He does. Now, let's talk about Dr. Walker Green."

~

Nick arrived by cab at his parents' home outside Chicago at ten-thirty. He was going to use his mother's Cutlass while he was there. His appointment at the rehab center was for nine the next morning. He would have to leave by eight to get there. He walked in and picked up the phone and called Gabriella. There was no answer, so he hung up and decided to try a little later. He went to the fridge and got himself a diet Pepsi. As he watched the Chicago news anchor tell about another murder he fell asleep on the couch to the dim light of the TV.

~

Gabriella returned from Trudy's and walked into her home a minute after the phone stopped ringing. She hoped to hear from Nick since he had promised to call when he got to his parents' home. She checked the recorder… no messages. She went to bed and worried.

She woke when the phone rang. Daylight was coming through her bedroom window. She answered, "Hello."

"Good morning, sweetheart. Did I wake you?"

"Nick, I'm so glad to hear your voice."

Nick explained what had happened the night before and told her that he loved her and that he already missed her. He gave her his parents' phone number in case she wanted to call. He promised to call back that evening.

16

Nick drove to his appointment at the rehab center. He thought as he drove. Memories of his past marriage came back to his mind. The worst ones were images of Melissa telling him she wanted a divorce and telling him about Adam. Trying to justify it by saying they were now different people from when they first married. Nick had to agree. Melissa hadn't been a slut and adulterer when he married her, and he told her as much.

He remembered the words that hurt so. "You can't give me what I need, Nick. You never will." So here he was driving to a rehab center to help her because she said she needed him. *How ironic,* he thought. He remembered the day they married, a bright, beautiful, sun-filled day at the church. They had promised to take care of each other through sickness and health, to stay together through the good and bad. At the time they meant it. They loved their Chicago apartment, shopping Michigan Avenue, and going to Wrigley Field. They rooted for "Da Bears" and Michael Jordan. Life was good.

Nick pulled into the parking lot of the rehab center. Nick walked slowly and entered the large, gray, stone building that used to house a large Chicago public library. He went to the front desk and told them he was there. He was told to be seated.

A lady in white soon arrived and led Nick to the office of Dr. Al Matheny. Nick shook his hand and flopped into a very oversized soft leather chair in front of the doctor's desk. Nick sat in silence while the doctor read the contents of a manila file, which he held in front of his face.

Dr. Matheny finally spoke, "Mr. Stewart, we have a strange case here. Your wife checked herself in while under the influence of cocaine."

"Ex," Nick interrupted. "She's my ex-wife."

"Your ex-wife, huh?"

"Yes, for almost five months now."

"In this report she claimed you two were still married. She never mentioned the divorce. Why would she claim that?"

"Well, just off the top of my head…cocaine. But you're the doc." Nick suddenly didn't feel comfortable with the situation.

The doc looked over his reading glasses at Nick and continued, "She told us she tried to kill herself by overdosing because of the loss of your love."

"Doc, I think this was just a ploy to get me to talk to her." Nick went on and told the doctor the story of their divorce and Melissa's trip to Tennessee and how he had sent her away without talking.

Dr. Matheny scratched his chin and said, "Well, she is indeed an addicted lady in need of help. She may or may not have tried to kill herself. We need to treat her as though she is suicidal. She will no longer talk to us until she talks to you. Are you willing?"

"Yes. I wouldn't have come all this way to say no."

"We would like to watch the conversation. We have a room where we can record everything. Do we have your permission?"

"Yes. Did Melissa agree to it?"

"She's our patient. We don't need her permission. During your conversation with her, try to get her to acknowledge that the two of you are divorced."

"Why?"

"To see if she's delusional or lying to us. Either way is bad, but then we'll know where we stand."

"If I may ask, what will keep her here to get treatment?"

"Nothing, unless she'll listen to you. She has to want to be here to stay. She can walk out the front door anytime she wants." He hesitated and added, "In that case, she might die. She has all the signs of a strong addiction and is not that strong. The next usage could be her last. She needs you."

Nick put his hands to his eyes and rubbed.

"Are you ready?" Nick was asked.

Nick breathed hard and rose from the chair. He nodded yes.

"Please follow Nurse Miller to your meeting with Melissa." Nick followed the burly woman down a quiet hallway. He paused to get a drink out of an old-fashioned, porcelain water cooler. His mouth was dry, his hands were wet from nerves, and his stomach churned from hunger. He realized he hadn't eaten since lunch yesterday with his parents and... Suddenly he couldn't think of Gabriella's name.

"She's waiting inside here, Mr. Stewart."

"Thank you."

Nurse Miller stood looking at Nick as he stared at the door. He finally figured out that he had to open the door and go in. Maybe that was the first test of his willingness to get involved. As he reached for the doorknob he tried to tell himself to turn around and leave. *Get out, now! Don't get involved!* He wanted to listen to himself, but he couldn't. He couldn't leave Melissa to possibly die.

He slowly turned the knob and pushed the door open. Melissa sat on a plain tan couch. He walked toward her and lowered himself onto the other end of the couch. "Hello, Melissa."

"Hello, Nick. Thanks for coming. It's so good to have you come back to Chicago. This is where you belong."

"Why did you want to see me, Melissa?"

"I love you and I need you, Nick. My life is awful without you."

"How did you start using cocaine?" Nick asked. Melissa began crying and shaking. She couldn't control herself. She pulled her arms around herself and placed her head between her knees. Nick watched, not knowing what to say or do. Ten minutes passed as she cried and rocked herself up and down.

"Did Adam give you the drugs?"

"Yes!" she yelled. Nick jumped at the loudness of her answer. "He always has drugs in his apartment for his friends. I tried the blow and liked it. It felt good. It made me forget about you leaving me."

"Melissa, you know that's not true. I didn't leave you. You asked for the divorce, you cheated on me with another man, Adam."

"Only because you wouldn't give me what I wanted. You made the decision to force me to find someone that would."

"What, cocaine? Is that what you wanted?" Nick had already heard enough nonsense. "What do you want me to do?"

Melissa scooted over to Nick and said, "Take me back, Nick. Love me again. I was wrong. I admit it." She waited to continue. She wanted her apology to sink in. "Nick, you know that in God's eyes we're still married."

"No, we're not, Melissa. Is that why you told the doctor we were married?"

"Yes. Because we are. Remember "forever and always till death do us part" and all the other stuff we promised during our wedding?"

"Melissa, you probably also remember the part about being faithful to each other. You committed adultery."

"But it was your fault."

Nick stood and looked down at this person he barely recognized and said, "No, it wasn't." He stood, turned around and began to walk toward the door.

"Nick, if you don't help me, I'll die. I know I will."

Nick stopped and turned to face her.

"You need to stay here and get healed. You need help. The cocaine is killing you."

"I know, but I won't stay unless you help me. I need your help. I have no one else. You know that." She looked at Nick with pleading eyes.

"Melissa, I'll stay for a few days."

She rose and ran to Nick and threw her arms around him,

"Thank you, Nick. You won't regret it. You'll see. We'll be happy again."

Nick turned and walked out the door. Nurse Miller led Nick back to the doctor's office. The doc thanked Nick and said they would call him for another meeting the next day.

"It's important for you to give her hope while she rehabbing."

"I don't want it to be false hope, Dr. Matheny," Nick said.

"Right now, Nick, she needs any kind of hope."

Nick left and felt numb as he walked to the car. He called his sister Laura and asked her to go to lunch with him. She was happy to hear his voice and readily agreed. Nick picked her up and he drove them to their favorite neighborhood Chicago-style pizza joint and ate. Laura spent the entire two hours asking about Tennessee and Melissa's condition. Nick told her how happy he was in Sleepy Valley and how in love he was with Gabriella. He told Laura about their parents. Laura couldn't believe her mother was a waitress in a little café.

"She's enjoying it?"

"That's what she says. It shocked me," Nick proclaimed.

As Nick drove Laura home she said, "Gabriella sounds wonderful."

"She is, Laura. You will like her."

~

In Sleepy Valley the rain came down. Vincent missed having Nick in the store with him. Trudy prayed for Nick's situation, and she even prayed for Melissa. Gabriella spent time painting a sad face of a woman she had photographed in Italy. The face ached of torment. Josh sat in his classroom at school and wondered if Nick would never return like his father hadn't. Chester whimpered in his cage; missing his companion.

~

Nick arrived back at his parents' home and called Gabriella. She answered on the first ring. They talked for an hour, going over the day's events. She was disappointed to find out that he was going to stay a few more days to help Melissa even though Gabry knew it was a possibility when he left. Her hope was that he would be back that day. He told her that the doctors felt Melissa could die if she continued. He didn't tell her that Melissa begged him to take her back. Nick didn't want to worry Gabriella. He knew there was no chance of it happening.

The next three days were much the same. He visited with Melissa in the mornings, his sister during the afternoons, and watched baseball and *American Idol* on Tuesday and Wednesday nights. He had long conversations on the phone with Gabriella. Each day they had less to talk about, rehashing the same things about Melissa. They told each other of their unwavering love for each other. It became clear to Gabry that Nick would not be coming back at the end of the week. She thought of flying to Chicago for the weekend, but she had an important client arriving on Saturday and Trudy still, though better, wanted Gabriella to visit every day. Boredom was driving Trudy bonkers.

On Friday morning Nick met Melissa outside in the rehab's garden area. Melissa looked better for the first time. Nick thought maybe it was just the sunshine. Melissa even seemed happier and talked of pleasant things. She spoke of what she wanted to do when she got out. Melissa had asked for a medical leave of absence from her work. By filing for the FMLA leave the company couldn't use her time away from work against her. Her company, by law, had no right to ask why she was off work as long as the doctors signed the papers, which they did.

"What do you do all day?" Nick asked.

"I have lectures to attend, individuals sessions with two different doctors, we eat three meals a day, and there's snacks all day. We have a social time with the other patients. We talk, play games, relax, or watch TV. There're a lot of really messed up people in here. It scares me to think I could have turned out like them."

"You don't think you *are* like them?"

"No, of course not." Nick knew she needed a lot more treatment. She was still in denial.

~

SATURDAY, MAY 26

Nick arrived at the rehab center and was told Melissa was in the garden again waiting for him. When he entered the garden she greeted him with the singing of "Happy Birthday" and a chocolate cake. It was the first time his birth date had crossed his mind since last year when his mom made a big cake for his birthday. Melissa missed that party because she said she had to work late. He later found out Melissa celebrated his birthday with Adam at his apartment. He remembered thinking, when Melissa finally admitted where she was, that Adam's headboard was probably keeping rhythm as his family sung "Happy Birthday" to him.

This time, though, he smiled and thanked her. "That was nice of you. I'm surprised you remembered."

"Nick, I know you better than anyone. Come on, let's have some cake." She had plastic plates, forks, and knives. They sat on a garden bench and ate.

"Where did you get the cake?"

"I made it. The center's cooks were forced to watch over me as a made it. Guess they didn't trust me to not put my head in the oven. I don't guess I can blame them after all the stuff I told them when I checked in."

"Are you feeling better? You're looking a lot better, getting some color back in your cheeks." She still looked bad, but Nick wanted to encourage her.

"I am a lot better. Nick, I appreciate you coming back to Chicago for me. I promise that we're going to be so happy from now on. I'll be out soon, and we'll start over."

Nick knew what Melissa meant, but tried ignoring the comment. Then he mistakenly said, "I hope you do find happiness, Melissa. Everyone should be happy. You can start over. Get back to church. Find a nice guy who will love you."

Melissa's face changed colors. "I meant with you. Me and you, Nick, together again. Are you just leading me along? Do you not have any plans for us?"

She was yelling by then, and the male nurses quickly came running. She picked up the cake and threw it, hitting Nick in the chest and knocking his plate to the ground. "You ungrateful bastard!" she screamed. I made you that cake and look what you did to it!"

The nurses grabbed her by the arms and forced her toward the door.

"You will. You will love me again. You have to!"

Nick couldn't believe how quickly things went wrong as he tried to clean up the mess. *Melissa had seemed to be doing so much better,* he thought. He felt as if he did make a mess of things. He knew he should have just nodded.

Melissa went to her room, knowing it was a great performance. She had to keep Nick in Chicago and away from the *southern bimbos.* She had to pretend to have relapses so that he knew she still needed his help and support.

She actually did hope to gain strength through the rehab and recapture Nick to survive. She didn't want to die. She did want to kick the cocaine addiction. She knew it was ruining her life, and Nick was her only support. Melissa's parents had died when she was young, and she had been reared by her aunt, who had passed away three years ago. She had some friends, but had broken ties with them when she'd left Nick for Adam. Her friends she had made through Adam cared nothing about her. She really needed Nick badly.

~

Saturday in Sleepy Valley was warm. The summer weather had arrived. Gabry was showing the client from New York her art. He saw the painting that she had completed before Nick left, the one that was special to her.

"Miss Morelli, this is a masterpiece. It is the best work I've seen this year by anyone. I want it. How much are you going to take from me?" he teased.

"Mr. Saunders, I'm sorry, this one is not for sale," Gabry informed him.

"You drive a hard bargain. I'll give you $25,000 for it."

Gabry couldn't believe the generous offer. "I'm truly sorry, I can't. It's for someone special. I'm in love, and I painted it for him."

"Then, my dear, love becomes you. It's your greatest painting and your others are marvelous. This guy of yours is a very lucky man."

"I'm the lucky one, Mr. Saunders."

He spent $15,000 on four other paintings and left happy. Gabry enjoyed the compliments, but it didn't help her sadness from missing Nick. Even though they talked every day it was not the same. Nick seemed stressed, and Gabry worried about him. It seemed like Nick wasn't telling her everything. He seemed evasive with some of his answers.

~

Trudy's diner was quiet without her and everyone went about their business. Meals were cooked and served without much banter. Trudy was sorely missed. Tom even missed two breakfasts during the past week. The first time since Trudy opened the diner. Sue was still doing a good job, and Stella tried her best to keep things lively, but it wasn't the same.

~

Mike walked Chester daily, but didn't pay a lot of attention to him otherwise. He played in a no-limit hold'em poker tournament in Knoxville and placed in the money. Not a lot.

~

Josh had nothing to look forward to and was slipping back into his quiet place, convinced that Nick didn't really care about him. The phone rang and Josh answered it. Nick was on the line.

"Hi, Josh."

"Hi, Nick."

"I've really missed our time together this week," Nick said seriously.

"Me too." Nick asked him about school and Sunday school. He promised Josh that they would go wading and fishing in a stream when he got back. He promised him they would have a great time. When he hung up, Josh smiled.

Nick called Vincent next and talked for a few minutes. He assured Vincent that he was doing well, but missed everyone. He called Trudy next to see how she was doing. Trudy told him how much Gabry missed him and that he needed to get home soon. He promised he would.

"I couldn't stay away from your sexiness for long."

"You smooth talker, wait 'til I tell Gabry."

His call to Gabriella was hard. He told her he needed to stay a little longer and tried to explain the best he could. He didn't want to hide things from Gabry, but he didn't want to tell her the details of how much Melissa wanted him back.

"I love you, and I miss you so much, Gabriella."

"Nick, I had no idea how much I would miss you. Take care of yourself and know how much I love you." Nick hung up, remembering the words that Trudy told him before he left: "People in this community need you."

~

After talking to Nick, Vincent missed him even more and had an idea. He knew he would miss their Saturday evening together so he called Gabriella to see if they could visit Trudy that evening together. Gabry agreed that it would be good for all three of them and called Trudy to let her know.

Vincent picked Gabry up and they arrived at seven. Trudy had fixed herself up and even made a dessert for later. Gabry brought a store-bought, ready-made pizza and they placed it in the oven to bake. Vincent said, "Trudy, you look great. How are you doing?"

"I'm hanging in there, for being bored out of my mind. Another few days, and the doc said I could go to the restaurant to pester my customers if I have any left."

"Stella and Sue are doing a good job. It's not as lively, but the food is still great."

They chitchatted for a while, and then Vincent told them he had talked to Nick that afternoon. "So did I," Trudy said.

They looked at Gabry and she nodded that she had also. Vincent held his hand out for Gabry's hand and said, "You poor dear, you must miss him a lot."

"It's only been a week, but it feels like months. I didn't see him much at all the week that you guys worked on the store, but it was different. I knew he was near."

"That's a sign of true love," Vincent comforted her. "He'll be back soon."

"Honey, he couldn't stay away from you if he tried. If he picked you over me then you must be pretty special," Trudy teased. They all laughed.

"Nick was so sweet when he called. He was worried about how I was doing and if I was being taken care of."

Scone wandered into the room and rubbed up against Trudy's leg.

"Who is this?" Vincent asked.

"That's my boy, Scone. That's right. He hid all evening the last time everyone was here." Scone was a beautiful, large, fat cat. He soon wandered over to Vincent and took residence in Vincent's lap.

During the evening they ate pizza, talked, laughed, and told each other how much Nick meant to them. Vincent confessed that Nick was like a son to him. Trudy said Nick had brought joy to her weekends and she would always have a crush on him despite Gabry.

Gabry spoke of her love for Nick and how he had opened her heart again to the hope of romance and love and faith. "I love him so much."

~

In Chicago, Nick spent the evening alone in front of the TV, flipping stations trying to find something worth watching. He gave up and picked up *The Sin Killer* and read. He wanted to be in Tennessee with Gabry, Vincent, Trudy, and Chester.

Nick went to bed early and read some more until his eyes began to drift shut.

~

Gabry hugged her pillow wishing she had magical powers to transform it into Nick.

~

Melissa debated with herself about whether to stay or leave the facility. She was depressed and needed something to kill the feeling of loneliness and hatred. She wanted relief.

~

Sunday morning came. Nick wanted to go to church but didn't know where to attend. He couldn't walk back into his old church. He picked up the Bible and opened it. He read of Christ's crucifixion and remembered how he had been so moved when he saw *The Passion of the Christ*. He knew he would do anything for Christ. Staying to help Melissa recover was one of those things he felt he had to do. She was one of God's lambs gone astray. He, with God's help, was the only person able to help her pull through the lie Satan was presenting her.

He knelt and prayed that God would lead him during this difficult time and that Melissa would improve. Nick had prayed this same type of prayer before, but this felt different to him. He was more focused and dire in his need. There were no visiting hours on Sundays, so Nick had the day to himself.

~

Melissa woke with a better attitude and felt stronger after defeating the urge to leave and find drugs. She thought she was improving.

~

Gabry was lonely when she woke and didn't feel like going to church alone. She called Nick's house and asked Sue if she could have Chester for the day. She picked Chester up and took him hiking all day. Seeing Chester limp happily along made her feel better. It made her think of how kind Nick was. He had taken in an unwanted crippled puppy and loved it, he had loved her despite her anger at God and helped change her outlook, he had brought happiness to everyone he came in contact with. She realized because of his goodness he was in Chicago trying to help another who needed him.

She wondered how much love could one man have and... would he save enough for her?

17

Nick made it through the week by thinking of returning to Sleepy Valley and Gabriella. He went through the same routine as the week before. He had met Monday morning with Dr. Matheny. They discussed the previous week's ups and downs. Dr. Matheny said it was a great sign that Melissa lasted more than a week. He said most in her condition didn't.

On Thursday they had Nick attend a class with Melissa. He was to be there for support due to the subject of the class. It was a class that was especially for advanced recoveries and it was difficult for them to listen to. A film was even more difficult to watch. It was not easy for Nick to see. Melissa held his hand during the hour. Her mood had begun to change during the week. She talked to him less about them and more about her recovery and what got her to this place in her life. Nick was pleased with the progress.

~

Gabry had planned to fly to Chicago on Friday and spend a few days with Nick. Nick looked forward to it. On Thursday she got a call from her dad that he was coming to see her Saturday. Disappointed, she canceled her flight. She hadn't seen her father in a year. She loved her father and was glad she would see him, but why this weekend? Was it fate keeping her and Nick apart?

He arrived that afternoon and they went to dinner at the Oak Club that evening. She told him about her love for Nick. He said he was sorry he couldn't meet the lucky man. He informed Gabry that he was retiring and moving to California. They had family in Sacramento, and he wanted to be near them. He was going to stay with his brother until he found a place of his own. "I might learn to surf," he said and laughed.

Gabry was happy for him and told him so.

~

The Cubs were home and Nick's sister, Laura, with her Chicago cap on backwards, went with him to the afternoon game at Wrigley Field. The Cubs were playing the Atlanta Braves. Laura was a big baseball fan. She and Nick had attended many games together and had often sat in the bleachers and worked on their tans when they were younger. She enjoyed the afternoon ballgame with Nick. Even though the Cubbies lost again 5–3, Nick and Laura got to watch Lou Pinella kick dirt all over the ump and get thrown out of the game.

Nick took her home after the game and played with his niece and nephew, Molly and Sam the rest of the afternoon. He teased Sam about his broken arm. Laura's husband John came to the backyard and announced that dinner had arrived. They gathered in the kitchen for a Chinese take out meal.

As they were eating Molly said, "Uncle Nick?"

"Yes, Molly?"

"I miss you not living here anymore."

"Me too," Sam echoed.

"Well," Nick started, "you two will have to fly down every few days and visit me in Tennessee."

Molly said, "How can we do that?"

Sam glanced at Nick and said, "We can't do that."

"Just jump on your Mom's broomstick and fly on down."

The kids began laughing and Laura threw noodles at Nick.

"Jerk," she yelled at him. Nick did miss his sister and the kids. John was stiff and business-like most of the time, and what he wasn't as a brother-in-law he made up for as a good father, husband, and provider.

~

Back in Sleepy Valley, Vincent spent the evening at the Oak Club also, not knowing Gabriella and her father were there. He spent most of the evening with the small orchestra playing classical tunes. Gabry spotted him on stage and during a break introduced him to her father.

Dr. Walker Green told Trudy she could begin to go out and therefore invited her to dinner. They arrived at the Oak Club later in the evening and ran into Gabry, her father, and Vincent. They all spent the evening together and had a good time. Gabriella thought of Nick most of the evening, wishing he were there.

~

The next week was long, and Nick was so tired of the routine. He longed to return to Sleepy Valley and those he cared about and missed. Melissa was gaining weight and doing very well with her rehab. Dr. Matheny thought Nick could leave soon, but not quite yet.

On Thursday, Nick visited Melissa and was surprised by her request.

Through tears she begged, "Nick, I'm sorry. Forgive me, please. I made you come to Chicago to help me through this, thinking I could get you back. I knew I needed help and figured I could use it to keep you away from where you wanted to be. I thought you would forget about her and begin loving me again." She sobbed for a while and gathered herself as Nick put his arms around her.

"You can leave whenever you want. I can make it now. I'm thinking better, and I'm stronger than I've been in months. I love you, Nick. But I know I blew it, and I don't blame you for not taking me back. I'm so sorry for using God to try to get you back. I hope God will forgive me." She began crying again. "I wish you nothing but happiness. Thank you for helping me, Nick."

Nick had tears of his own. Hearing Melissa apologize and sound better than she had for a couple of years tore him up. He wanted Melissa to be happy and knew she could be if she kept herself clean.

After a couple of minutes Nick said, "I had to help you. You didn't have to trick me. I care about you, and I'll stay another week to help you through the final stages. You're going to make it. You are going to make it. God will forgive you for everything if you ask him. He's faithful and true." He hesitated to say it but did, "One thing though, Melissa. If this happens again, I won't be here. You have to make it work this time."

"That's only fair, Nick. Thank you."

~

SUNDAY, JUNE 10

Nick decided to stay till Friday. Melissa was doing well and the doctors felt she could leave by then, exactly four weeks from the day she entered. Her doctor wanted her to come back for a meeting each week. She would have a sponsor assigned to her so she would have someone to talk to and help her in her continued recovery.

~

The faces of the customers at Trudy's Eating Place lit up when Trudy returned to manage the diner. She just walked around and fussed at people and yelled at Tom. One day she filled his cap with whipped cream and placed it back on his head. He loved it. She was back and everyone was delighted. The kids were also thrilled when Trudy walked into the Sunday school class. Just having her there brightened the room. Josh's face lit up when he saw her.

Gabriella had not been to Victory Road Community Church the last two weeks and realized she missed it. She met Trudy after Sunday school and they sat together in the sanctuary for the service. In Pastor Hill's message, he talked about the mercy and grace of God. Pastor Hill preached that in return, God expected his children to show mercy and grace to others and also to Himself. He gave the example of Horatio G. Spafford, a lawyer from Chicago in 1873, who lost his home in the great Chicago fire in 1871, and then his four daughters when an Ocean liner crashed into another and immediately went down crossing from America to England. He later crossed the ocean, going to his wife on the same path, and when the vessel got to the spot that his daughters drowned, he prayed for strength and God inspired him to write the words to the great hymn, "It Is Well With My Soul," despite his great loss.

Gabriella knew then that she was wrong in blaming God for Jimmy's death and she wanted the same savior Nick and Trudy had, the Jesus that had died for her also. She asked Trudy to go forward with her, and quietly and humbly she accepted God's grace and mercy.

~

That afternoon she called Nick and said she was catching the first flight to Chicago and asked if she could stay with him till he came back.

"Of course, I would love that. I've missed you so much." He explained that he was coming home the next Friday and that they could enjoy the week together in Chicago. Trudy and Vincent drove Gabriella to the airport. "Bring him home," Trudy shouted as Gabry walked away toward her terminal.

That evening Nick watched for her at the airport arrival area. Gabry saw him standing there waving to her. She ran into his arms and they kissed fervently, not caring that everyone was watching them. An eleven-year-old boy walked past them and matter-of-factly said, "Get a room." Nick and Gabriella laughed.

Nick thought how wonderful and comforting it felt to have Gabriella in his arms. He didn't want to release her there in the airport. He did, and they headed to the baggage claim and to his car. "You look fantastic," Nick told her as they walked. She wore a sleeveless blue top and jeans, and her eyes glowed with love as she looked up at him.

"Thanks. I've missed you, Nick."

"Hungry?"

"I'm starving, I haven't eaten all day."

"There's a terrific Italian restaurant on the way."

"Sounds great," Gabry agreed.

They had so much to tell each other, but they drove in silence and held hands.

Gabriella placed her head on Nick's shoulder to relax and enjoy the scent of her guy. She wasn't sure she should come to Chicago, but now it felt right. She played with his fingers and stroked his arms and Nick smiled. "I think you did miss me."

"Don't get a big head."

She told Nick about taking Chester on their day-long hike. She then began telling him about Dr. Walker Green and Trudy and about her father's visit. They had discussed the same things over the phone, but Nick just wanted to hear the sound of Gabry's voice. She seemed excited and anxious to talk. Nick loved the feel of her presence next to him.

He pulled into the lot of the restaurant and they were able to get seated quickly. They got a booth in a quiet corner and sat opposite each other. After the waitress took their order Gabriella said, "I have news." She began to well up and Nick suddenly was concerned.

"I went to church this morning with Trudy." Nick held her hand as Gabry dabbed her eyes with her cloth napkin. "I went forward and accepted Christ. I felt God's urging, and I knew I had to." Nick moved around to sit beside her and she threw her arms around him. Nick hugged her and drew her close.

"I am so happy for you, Gabriella." She explained how his comments about Jimmy's death being an accident made her think. She told him about Pastor Hill's message hitting home.

"I don't want to live my life in anger with a God that loves me and loved Jimmy." She looked at Nick and said, "Thank you, Nick. You are a special man that's brought such happiness and contentment to my life. I have so much because of you."

"There's nothing special about me, Gabry. I serve a special God."

They ate and talked about Sleepy Valley and Melissa. Nick confessed that he hadn't told her everything about Melissa and her demands and wants.

"Nick, I knew there was more. I'm a woman. I could tell you weren't telling me everything. I didn't think I should press it. What is she saying now?"

"She seems to have her clear thinking back. She's thankful I stayed and she realizes I'm in love with someone else. She's accepted it."

"Me?" Gabry teased.

"No, Chester," Nick teased back. "Of course, I meant you."

They snuggled in the booth side by side like lovers and tried each other's food. They ordered a slice of strawberry cheesecake and shared it. While good, it didn't compare to Trudy's desserts.

They drove to Nick's parents' house in the dark. It was the same house Nick had lived in all his life growing up. He pointed out spots where events had happened in his past.

"My first spin-the-bottle game was in the basement of that house. It was my first kiss."

"What was her name?"

"Lynn Fisherman."

"What is Lynn doing now?"

"I think she's doing hard time in prison. Never got over me," Nick kidded. Gabry socked him in the arm.

He pulled into the driveway and carried in Gabry's suitcases from the car. They spent the night cuddled on the couch talking and touching. They fell asleep in each other's arms.

~

The next morning Nick went back to see the doctor at the rehab center. He found Melissa happy and glad to see him. She had called her employer and they'd assured her that she still had a job to return to. She even had a month's pay coming. Nick was able to pick up her paychecks and Melissa signed them over to him.

Nick told Melissa that Gabry had come to town.

"Do you mind if Gabry helps me find you an apartment?"

Nick wasn't sure how she would react to his request. He was pleased when she agreed and she said, "Maybe this way it will have a nice woman's touch." Nick and Gabry secured a pleasant, small apartment for Melissa in a nice neighborhood near her work.

Nick and Gabriella ate lunch at a quiet little café and then went shopping on Michigan Avenue. That evening they went to his sister's house for dinner. Laura and Gabry hit it off right away. Gabry had a terrific time with Laura and the kids. John was quiet and pleasant as always, but Nick could see that John was impressed with Gabry. Work was ahead for them all the next day so they said their goodbyes.

Melissa's belongings and furniture were in a storage unit. Nick rented a U-Haul on Wednesday and he and Gabry moved Melissa's belongings to her new home. They unpacked all the boxes, put things away, and made the place look like home. Melissa would be able to move in and relax. Gabry even did her laundry and put her clothes away in the dresser and closet. They spent the evening grocery shopping and stocking the fridge and pantry.

Thursday morning Nick told Melissa about all the work Gabry had done and Melissa cried. "That's so sweet. I don't deserve this kind of love and kindness."

Melissa asked if Gabry would come with him the next day when she was to leave the rehab center so she could personally thank her.

"I'm sure she would."

~

That afternoon Nick took Gabriella to Wrigley Field for the Cubs game against the Seattle Mariners. The Cubs scored two runs in the bottom of the eighth and held on for a five to four win. Nick bought her a Cubs cap and he thought she looked sexier than ever when she put it on and stuck her ponytail through the back hole. Chicago-style pizza for dinner completed Gabry's Chicago experience. This was their last night in Chicago. They had reservations to fly back late Friday afternoon.

The next morning they loaded their suitcases, locked the place up, and left to get Melissa. Gabry was nervous as they drove to pick up Melissa. Melissa was nervous to be getting out. She thought she was strong enough to resist the drugs' temptation, but she wasn't sure. Everything was in place. She had formed a good relationship with her sponsor and she looked forward to returning to work. She looked pretty for the first time in months. The hollowness of her face had gone away and she wore make-up when Nick and Gabry arrived.

Nick and Gabry walked into Dr. Matheny's office and Gabry shook his hand. He turned to Nick and said, "I can't explain how much you have meant to Melissa's recovery. I commend you for your patience and caring in difficult circumstances."

"Thank you. Your facility has done a remarkable job. It's now up to Melissa, I guess."

"It is. Are you ready? I'm sure *she* is."

They walked to a waiting room where Melissa was sitting with her sponsor. Melissa jumped up and hugged Nick and then hugged Gabry. "You are so sweet to help with my apartment. Nick told me what all you did."

"You're welcome. It was my pleasure. I want to apologize for the time we met before."

"It was a bad time for me. Let's forget it," Melissa asked.

"You look great. How do you feel?" Nick asked.

"Nervous... but ready."

"Let's go then." Nick drove Melissa's car and Gabriella followed in his mom's car.

Melissa began talking. "I couldn't have done this without you, Nick. You are the greatest. I don't know what I was thinking."

"It's all in the past," Nick pleaded. "Just focus on your future. One day at a time. You're going to be okay."

"I wish I was that sure," Melissa said.

Nick parked in front of the two-story apartment and Gabry pulled in beside him. They got out and looked up at Melissa's new home. "I like it." Nick handed her the keys and asked her to open the door. She glowed as they went from room to room. She couldn't believe there was nothing for her to do. Everything was in its place. She loved it. She checked out the kitchen and the fridge that was full of necessities. They hugged Melissa good-bye and left her to discover her new home.

When they closed the door and left, Melissa sat down at the kitchen table and cried with her head burrowed in her arms. It all hit her. The love shown by a husband she cheated on and left for another man. The care shown to her by a woman she had called a bimbo and hated. The thought that her work was willing to take her back was overwhelming. She was grateful to the rehab center and the doctors that helped her. She had been so close to death, but the feeling of not knowing if that lifestyle would come back into her life was scary. As she cried, the need for relief filled her mind. She shook it off, stood, and walked to the fridge and found a crisp apple.

Nick and Gabriella headed to his sister's house. They were going to lunch with Laura before heading back to Sleepy Valley. They went to a small café that had seating on a side patio.

"How is Melissa?"

Gabry answered, "She looks great. She's a very attractive woman. She seemed thrilled with the apartment."

Nick said, "It will be a long battle for her. All we can do now is pray God gives her the strength to resist."

They turned their attention to family matters. Laura had talked to her mother that morning. "Mom said they were anxious to come home. She said Trudy was back to work and she was unemployed again. She said Dad had been fishing with Vincent and Josh."

Hearing Laura talk about happenings in Sleepy Valley made Nick long for home.

Laura shocked Nick when she asked him, "When are you going to pop the question?"

Nick almost choked on his bite of salad. When he regained his composure he smiled and said, "Sis, we're taking it slow."

"Okay, you can try that line on others, but I'm your sister. I know you. I can tell you two are crazy about each other. You've fallen head-over-heels for this beautiful, wonderful angel."

"I'm glad you have this all figured out," Nick responded.

Gabry stayed quiet and smiled at the two of them discussing her and Nick's future. She could imagine Nick and Laura growing up as children together, battling through the years, but loving each other. Finally Laura asked, "Gabry, what do you think?"

"I agree with Nick, we're taking it slow, to be sure," Gabry answered.

"You two, I can't believe it. You've been rehearsing your answers. See, you're like two peas in a pod, perfect for each other."

Nick reached for Gabry's hand and looked at Laura and said, "I hope you're right." They finished lunch, dropped off the car at his parents' house, and Laura drove them to the airport.

When Laura hugged Gabriella good-bye she whispered in Gabry's ear. "I can't wait for the wedding."

Gabry whispered back, "Me either."

They waved as Laura pulled away from the curb.

18

Nick knew it would be fun flying back to Knoxville together. He remembered how much he had dreaded the flight to Chicago four weeks earlier. Everything was better now with Gabriella next to him. Their row had three seats. Gabriella sat by the window and Nick in the middle with a small seven-year-old girl with pigtails on the other side. Her parents and smaller brother were seated behind them.

"Hi, I'm Trena," the girl looked at Nick and Gabriella.

"Hello, Trena, I'm Nick. This is Gabriella."

"Are you married?" she quizzed.

"No. We're dating."

"We're going to Tennessee to visit my mamaw and papaw. Where are you going?"

Nick smiled and said, "I'm going home."

"You live in Tennessee?"

"Yes."

"Do you live near my mamaw and papaw?"

"I don't know. Where do they live?"

"Tennessee, I already told you that."

"What are their names?" Nick asked, hoping to end the conversation soon.

"I already told you, Mamaw and Papaw. Do you have a hearing problem?"

"What?"

"Yep, you must. What were you and your girlfriend doing in Chicago?"

"Visiting."

"Who?" Trena asked.

"My family."

"Are you and Gabriella living in sin?"

Nick was shocked. All he could say was, "What?"

Trena figured he couldn't hear her again so she raised her voice and asked again, "Are you two living in sin?" Gabry looked up from her magazine and everyone around their section stared at Nick and Gabry.

Nick waved his arms and said, "It's all right. Everything is okay."

Trena's mom and dad both had on headphones listening to music and didn't hear the encounter. "What do you mean, *it's all right?* Mommy says people shouldn't sin."

"We are not living in sin. Well, I should say, no one is perfect."

"Mom says I am."

Nick turned to Gabriella, she smiled and said, "Don't look at me. I have no experience with kids. She's all yours. And no, I'm not switching seats with you."

"Thanks. You're a big help."

Nick stayed turned toward Gabriella hoping Trena would decide to occupy herself in a different way. Soon he felt a small hand tugging at his shirtsleeve.

He looked down at her and she asked, "Why don't you two get married?" Nick was reminded of his sister.

"We haven't known each other very long."

"How long have you known Gabriella?"

"Only a couple of months."

Trena studied the situation and said, "Then why are you visiting family together?"

"It's a long story, Trena."

"We've got the whole flight, Nick," Trena stated.

Nick decided to give up and tell Trena a story about visiting his family. He told a long story about witches and dragons and boys with long ugly noses. He weaved the story with blue geese and cows that talked. He told how a Capricorn unicorn galloped with a mockingbird on its back to warn everyone of the pending doom if someone didn't find the magic lizard with great powers.

A stewardess brought drinks and a snack to them, but Trena made Nick continue as he ate and drank. Gabriella gave up on reading and listened to Nick's story.

"What was the lizard's name?" Gabry asked.

Nick shot a look at Gabry and grinned.

"Just so happens that her name was Trena, Trena Banana."

Trena laughed and listened intently as Nick continued the story as Trena Banana was found by a lemon raccoon named Meadowlark. Trena saved the Kingdom from the witch's destruction and all were saved to enjoy the best pudding at a great feast. The King named the treat Trena Banana pudding.

Just as Nick finished the story, the pilot informed everyone they would soon be landing. "I hoped you enjoyed the flight."

Trena yelled out, "I did."

When the plane stopped and everyone stood to disembark, Trena's mom said to Nick and Gabry, "I hoped Trena didn't bother you two."

Nick looked down at Trena and smiled as he answered, "Not at all, she's perfect."

Trena hugged Nick and Gabry and waved good-bye. As she walked away with her family she turned around and yelled, "You two are nice!"

Nick and Gabry laughed as they talked about Trena on the drive home. Gabry mentioned how much she liked Nick's sister and family.

"It makes me miss not having sisters and brothers and loved ones. And now my dad's moving to California to surf."

"I wish I could have met him," Nick said.

They drove straight to Nick's house. Nick wanted to see Chester. His parents were in the porch swing and Chester was roaming the yard when he pulled down the lane. Chester spotted the vehicle and ran at full speed to Nick's door. Nick jumped out and picked Chester up.

"You've grown so much, boy. Dad, what have you been feeding this puppy?" Nick said laughing as the pup whimpered and whined and licked Nick all over his face. Nick placed him down, and Chester kept excitedly jumping up on Nick's leg.

"That's the happiest I've seen Chester since you left," Nick's father called out.

Nick's mom walked out and hugged Nick. "It's good to see you, Nicky."

"It's great to be home."

For the next two hours they all sat on the porch and talked about the past four weeks. Nick told them about Melissa's recovery, their house, and his sister and family.

"Did you make it to any Cub games?" Mike asked.

"I went with Laura one day and took Gabry yesterday."

"How did you like Wrigley Field?" Mike asked Gabry.

"I loved it. The ivy walls are remarkable."

Sue informed them that it was her last day as a waitress. "I gave up my apron this afternoon. Trudy is back, and Mike and I are heading home in the morning. I miss my own home."

"I know you two have been a blessing to everyone, including me," Gabry told them.

Sue continued, "We've enjoyed the entire time that we've been here. We now know that Nick is among friends, and I understand why he loves it here so much." Sue then changed the subject. "Trudy sent a pie home with me. She said you would want a dessert after your trip."

Nick said, "Sounds great. I can't pass up Trudy's pie."

Sue got up and headed to the kitchen. Gabry followed. "I'll help, Sue."

"Thank you."

They walked into the kitchen and Gabry said, "I know everyone will miss you and Mike so much."

"I'm glad we were able to help out." She faced Gabriella and said, "Gabry, I'm also glad Nick has found someone he really cares about. I wish we could have gotten to know each other better."

"Me too. I really do love Nick."

"I know you do, and I know Nick loves you. I can see it in his eyes. I hated it when Nick and Melissa divorced. A mother only wants her kids to be happy. They were so happy a few years ago. I knew Melissa had made life awful for Nick, but I still hoped they would get back together. That's why I told Melissa how to find Nick. I was wrong for doing that."

"It worked out for the best though."

"You think so?" Sue asked.

"Melissa may have died if Nick hadn't gone back to Chicago to help her."

"Oh, dear."

"You raised an angel. Thank you." She walked over to Sue and placed her arms around her. "Nick is a great person, and Laura is fantastic."

"Thank you. You'll take good care of him," Sue said with tears in her eyes. It thrilled Sue to hear Gabry say she had done a good job rearing Nick and Laura.

"If he'll let me, I will," Gabry promised.

They had cut the coconut cream pie and placed pieces onto the plates. They each picked up two and took them to the porch.

It was getting late when they finished the pie and conversation. Gabry hugged Mike and Sue good-bye and Nick took her home. Nick walked her to the door and kissed her passionately. "I'll miss you."

"Not as much as I'll miss you," Gabriella teased.

"No. I'll miss you more."

"Okay. You probably will," she laughed.

"Let's have a cookout tomorrow evening at my place. I'll call Vincent and Trudy."

"Okay. I'm sure they will be excited."

Nick kissed her goodnight.

19

The next morning he called Josh and Vincent. Mike and Sue left early for home and Nick went to pick Josh up for breakfast. They were meeting Vincent at Trudy's Eating Place. Nick and Josh walked in and Trudy yelled, "There's a sight for sore eyes." She hurried over and hugged Nick and then hugged Josh. Josh beamed. "I've really missed you around here. Wasn't sure if you would come back," Trudy said.

"I had to. Nowhere in Chicago do they serve French toast like you do."

"I'm sure of that. But I thought if you came back it would be to see me."

"They got hundreds like you in Chicago," he teased.

Tom yelled out, "I'm moving to Chicago then."

Trudy looked at Tom and said, "Finally, my boobs can take a rest."

Tom followed with, "Trudy, I'm not the only one that keeps close tabs on them. Who else comes in to check Trudy out? Let's see some hands. C'mon, don't be bashful." Hands shot up all over the restaurant.

The crowded restaurant erupted in laughter. Even the women had raised their hands.

"You people are sick," Trudy insulted them.

They laughed and Andy said, "You have a lot of admirers."

"I've got a lot of lusting sickos, is what I have."

The door opened and Vincent walked in. Nick rose from the

table and greeted Vincent with a firm handshake and hug. Trudy announced, "Here's the only gentleman in Sleepy Valley. Good morning, Vincent."

"Good morning, my dear."

Nick invited them both to his house for the cookout. They quickly accepted his invitation, and Trudy took their orders. Stella stopped by to welcome Nick back.

"Have you been working on your lines, Nick?"

"I pretty much still have the same ones. But they love them in Chicago."

"Do they now? The women in Chicago must be easy, or trying for big tips."

"I think that's it, Stella. I missed you, if that helps."

"Now that means a lot."

Trudy came back and sat at the table and said, "What're my boys up to this morning?"

"Josh and I are going fishing for a while this morning," Nick answered.

"I'm opening the store in a few minutes. Big fun," Vincent said. "I rather go fishing. Nick fixed up the store and now I get too many customers. It's too much like running a store now." Everyone laughed.

"I'll be in Monday morning to help you."

"Can I help?" Josh asked. "You don't have to pay me."

Vincent asked, "You're out of school for the summer now?"

"Yeah."

"You did do a great job when you helped before. I think I could use another helper. Okay. You've got a job." Josh smiled and dug into his pancakes. They finished their meals and drove to the pond.

Nick and Josh fished side-by-side at the pond. "How were your final grades for the year?"

"I passed." Josh jerked when his floater disappeared, but missed. He looked up at Nick and asked, "Why were you gone so long?"

Nick decided it would be a good opportunity to talk to Josh

about the evils of drugs so he told Josh the story about Melissa, and how it had almost ended her life. Josh listened intently and told Nick, "I ain't ever using drugs."

"I'm happy to hear it," Nick said and tousled Josh's hair.

The weather had warmed up during the month he had been away from Sleepy Valley, Tennessee, and the fishing had slowed. They caught a few largemouth bass and some bluegills but turned them loose. Nick said for their next fishing excursion they would try one of the streams. Nick took Josh home after they fished for a couple of hours. He had a lot to do to get ready for the evening cookout. He went to the market in town and spent the afternoon with Chester outside doing yard work.

After the grass was mowed, he had time to take a walk through his woods with Chester. They started down the trail that he had begun. He had cut the trail back to just past the creek. He hoped he would now have time to work on it and complete it. Nick and Chester made their way toward the creek. When they got there he was shocked to see a beautiful, small wooden bridge with railings built over the creek. It rose to a couple of feet above the stream and then back down to the other side. He wondered who had built it and why. Nick thought that it could have been his dad, but doubted it. He was very thankful, though, however it had gotten done.

He continued until he was at the back edge of his property. As he walked he realized how much he had missed his home and the nature that surrounded it. The birds again followed him as he walked. Chester spotted a chipmunk and chased it into a forest floor hole. Chester stood with his nose pressed into the hole with a look of bewilderment on his face.

Nick decided to take the path on around following the markers for the trail. When he arrived again at the creek on the south side of his property another bridge had been built over the water just like the first one. The only difference was that it only had one railing and a person could sit on the bridge and their feet would reach the cool water. So Nick did just that. He removed his shoes and socks and soaked his feet. He was grateful to whoever built the bridges.

Small minnows swam about his feet, and bugs flitted on top of the water. He noticed a crawdad creeping from rock to rock against the gentle current of the stream. Chester ran off the bridge to lap up a drink and then laid down beside Nick, wanting to be petted. This was the life Nick wanted here in Tennessee. This was the scene he was looking for. This was far from what he had experienced in the last month. Nick wondered if life was meant to be enjoyed in this way. Or was it meant to be hard and difficult?

Nick did understand that life was meant to be lived serving others. He always knew helping folks was one of God's true blessings to his people. He believed in the saying; *to give is better than to receive*. He always enjoyed seeing the happiness his gifts brought to someone else a lot more than receiving a gift himself. He realized it was selfish for him to ever think that he should seclude himself from people because he was disappointed in the human race. He thought of how Christ must have been disappointed in those that shouted out to crucify him. But still he gave his life for them.

~

Gabriella spent the day thinking about her week in Chicago with Nick. She had enjoyed it a lot more than she thought she would. She had been reluctant to go, but now she was glad she decided to. She loved Nick's sister Laura. She had a better feeling about Melissa and what kind of person she once was. She now could see what Nick had seen in her at one time. Hearing Dr. Matheny telling Nick what a sacrifice he had made to be there for Melissa made her love Nick more. She knew Nick didn't want to be there at all, but still he did it.

Gabriella wondered if she would do what Nick did. Did she deserve a guy like Nick? Why did Nick choose her? Did she have something special about her that drew Nick to her? She worried that maybe she could never live up to Nick's expectations. She thought that maybe Melissa had the same problem. Trying to be what Nick was, but finding out she couldn't.

~

Nick looked at his watch and found that his guests would be arriving within a half hour and he still needed to walk back to the house, shower, and start dinner. He would never be ready. As he walked, he thought of Gabriella again as he did most of the day. Could he ever replace Jimmy? He knew how long Gabriella had grieved after his death. Nick knew he didn't have much to offer. All he had was love. He was unemployed, and had run to a troubled ex-wife when she needed him. What did Gabry think of that? Was it possible to be the man she needed?

He jumped into the shower, finished quickly, and put on a pair of khaki shorts and a red golf shirt, slipped on a pair of sandals and headed for the kitchen. He threw potatoes in a large pot to boil for potato salad and began forming hamburger patties. He hoped Trudy would bring dessert. He glanced at the clock on the microwave and noticed it was six thirty.

He heard the front door open and then Gabry's voice, "Nick."

"I'm in the kitchen, sweetheart."

Gabry's heart skipped at the sound of Nick's voice calling her sweetheart. She followed his voice to the kitchen. "There's my type of man, behind an apron cooking my dinner."

Nick turned his head to kiss her and said, "I'm running late."

"Something happen?"

"Yeah, I put my feet in the creek back in the woods and didn't remove them until I was late."

"Sounds like a great reason." Chester was at Gabry's feet waiting for her attention. She asked Chester, "Do you enjoy having your pack leader back?"

"He hasn't left my side since I got home. He plopped down by the shower and watched me."

"I understand why that might be fun."

"You naughty girl, I kinda like that."

"Anyone here?" Trudy called out from the porch.

"In the kitchen," Gabry called out.

Trudy walked into the kitchen wearing a knockout sleeveless orange top with coconut designs that showed off her figure and dark blue shorts. "What's up, lovers?"

Nick teased, "Gabry was just saying how she would like to watch me take a shower." Gabry threw a dishtowel at him.

"Well, she's more of a watcher. I'd jump in and help you wash that gorgeous body."

"Trudy!" Gabry screamed with surprise. The three of them laughed.

"I'd have to admit, that does sound like fun." Gabry punched him in the arm. Nick tried rectifying the situation. "I meant with you, Gabry."

"Yeah, right," Gabry and Trudy said at the same time, and laughter filled the kitchen.

"Sounds like the party has started without me," Vincent called out as he walked into the kitchen. Trudy and Gabry both greeted him with hugs and kisses on the cheek.

Vincent looked at Trudy's top and complimented, "Nice coconuts." They all laughed.

Trudy told him, "You've been hanging around Tom entirely too long."

Trudy did bring a blackberry cobbler and a lemon meringue pie. Gabry had made coleslaw and a large fruit salad. Vincent brought a bottle of wine, flowers for the table, and a six pack of diet Pepsi for Nick.

"Thank you, Vincent."

During dinner they caught up on everything that happened over the last four weeks. They talked about the church, Melissa, Mike and Sue, Dr. Walker Green, and Josh. Gabry told Vincent and Trudy about Nick's sister and family and their time in Chicago. She told them about Trena on the plane and how Nick had spent the entire flight making up a story for the little girl. Trudy about rolled off her chair when they told about how Trena had yelled out about them *living in sin*. "One of those embarrassing moments we talked about a few weeks ago," Nick said.

"You should have thrown the little brat out the window," Trudy said.

"Actually, she kind of reminded me of you, Trudy," Gabry said.

"Me?"

"Say what's on your mind. Nothing-is-off-limits kind of girl," Gabry explained.

Trudy thought about it and said, "You're right. I think I like the little angel."

Nick then asked, "I have to know. Who built the bridges over my creek?" He looked at everyone. "I love them. I've got a big kiss for whoever did it," Nick said trying to find the answer.

Trudy, of course, raised her hand quickly and said, "Me. Me. I'm the carpenter."

Gabry answered, "I guess you owe Andy a big kiss."

Vincent laughed, "That wouldn't be good."

"Andy built them. Why would Andy build them?"

"I asked him to," Gabry said. "A birthday present to you from me."

Nick hugged Gabry and kissed her and asked, "How did you know it was my birthday?"

"Your mom told Trudy, and Trudy told me. I asked Andy if he had time to build them. He really enjoyed doing it. Your dad helped him some, or at least watched him. I paid for the supplies and Andy did the work for free."

"You're kidding. Why would he do that?"

"He said you were special and what you were doing was special. Plus, he's always liked me."

"Thank you. It really surprised me when I walked back there today. I'll have to personally thank Andy."

Trudy and Vincent didn't know anything about the bridges. Gabry and Andy had kept it between them and Nick's parents. After eating dinner Trudy and Gabriella got up to get the pie. They put a candle in the middle and lit it. After singing happy birthday to Nick they all ate dessert.

They decided to play Euchre after the lemon pie. Trudy changed the subject to the Smoky Mountain National Park. "When are you going to take us?"

"I'll go any day everyone can go." Nick looked at Gabry and continued, "It's kind of whenever you two can take off work," glancing toward Vincent and Trudy.

"I can close the general store for a few days. I deserve a vacation."

"Stella can run things for me. I've hired a new waitress part-time. I've decided to take it a little easier for a while."

Nick suggested, "Let's pick a date. Do we want to go for more than a day? There's a lot to see."

Nick left the table to get a calendar. After returning and looking at the calendar they settled on a week. They were going to go for five days and make the most of it. Leave on Monday the twenty-fifth of June and come back on Friday. They figured they would beat the Fourth of July crowd and only be there during the weekdays. Nick recommended a hotel and Gabry said she would make the reservations the next day. She also invited everyone to her home the next Saturday evening.

They were full of excitement to be taking a trip together. Nick wanted them to love the park as much as he did and was anxious to show it to them. They settled into a game of bid Euchre and Vincent and Nick beat the girls badly. Trudy and Gabry accused them of cheating. Around midnight both Vincent and Trudy decided it was time to go home. Gabry stayed behind with Nick. They made their way to the couch and snuggled close.

"It was a wonderful evening. I've missed our Saturday evenings with Vincent and Trudy. Trudy may be the funniest person I've met. Are you looking forward to the trip?"

Gabry didn't answer but said, "Can we not talk? I just need for you to hold me and kiss me and touch me."

"I can do that." And he did. They ended up lying on the couch with their bodies pressed against each other. Nick slowly kissed her eyelids and lips. He ran his hands through her dark hair and moved his head down to kiss her neck. She rolled him over onto the cushions and positioned herself on top on him. She began sliding his shirt up and kissing his chest as she went. She slid his shirt over his head and laid her head on his chest. She slowly moved her hand along his sides sending chills up his body. His hands found the bottom of her pullover and with one quick motion he removed it over her head. She gave no resistance to the move. He slowly moved his hands up and down her back with his fingertips. He loved running his hands along the small of her back. She loved the touching.

"I love you, Nick."

"Shh. No talking, remember? I love you." He reached for the lamp and turned off the light.

Second base was as nice he thought it would be. Nick halfway expected his father to walk into the room. Later they rolled unto their sides and fell asleep.

Chester woke them the next morning whining from his cage. He needed to go out. Nick got up to let him out. Gabriella grabbed her bra and top from the floor and ran to the bathroom. She came out on the porch where Nick was watching Chester and said she was going home to get ready. "Pick me up around a quarter till ten?" she asked.

"I'll see you then. Love you."

She gave him a light kiss and headed for the car, "I love you. I enjoyed last night, especially the last two hours."

It was hard not making love to Gabry. He knew that in a way they were making love. Maybe, even in a more caring way. They wanted to wait. He really wanted to wait until they were married, if they married, he knew that was what God expected. So for the time being, second base would suffice. It fact, he loved second base, especially Gabriella's second bases.

After church the next morning, Pastor Hill invited Nick and Gabriella to go to lunch with him and his family. He saw Trudy and invited her also.

"Sorry, but I can't. Dr. Walker Green is taking me out for the afternoon." She was off in a hurry.

They spent a nice lunch together. Pastor Hill said the church had decided to start a Sunday morning second service. The crowds were overwhelming and something had to be done. Gabriella enjoyed Teresa's company. Teresa explained that she had liked art class in school but never had the opportunity to pursue it further. Gabry offered to help her start again if she'd like.

Nick wanted to work on his trail after lunch and Gabry asked if she could help. He said he would love her help so they spent the afternoon cutting tree limbs and bushes. Gabry fed them into the machine and they raked the mulch unto the new path. They were able to get the new path a hundred feet past the creek. They quit and walked back to the creek.

Nick removed his shoes and socks and Gabriella followed his lead. Soon they both were resting on the new bridge with their feet in the coolness of the stream.

"Now you see why I was late yesterday."

"It is nice. This was a great idea to make the path. We could put benches every so often," Gabry suggested.

"We could, huh?"

She laughed. "I made the reservations for Gatlinburg after you dropped me off from church. The Bearskin Lodge only had two rooms left. They had just had a cancellation. We got two rooms with two double beds."

"We were lucky."

"Listen, Nick, I want to pay the cost for the rooms for everyone."

"You don't have to do that."

"I know. But I want to. Everyone means so much to me. My business is doing great, and I'm rolling in the cash. I don't know what to do with it."

"You are kidding, aren't you?"

"No."

"Great, because you may have to loan me some if I don't find a job soon."

"Do you want to teach again?" Gabry asked.

"Yes. Would that bother you?"

"No. Why would it? I know you're a great teacher. They always need teachers around here."

"It doesn't pay a lot," Nick said, quizzing.

"Nick, I'm not Melissa. I think everyone should do what they love. I love painting. Just so happens, it's paying very well right now."

Nick leaned over to kiss her. "I know you're not Melissa. I didn't mean to suggest you were anything like her."

"Nick, I've never cared about money. I've always wanted to do what I love, which is creating art by painting and throwing clay. I would want the same for you."

It was true. When Gabry had begun painting she'd realized she might not make anything, might not be able to pay the rent. She'd felt bad and worked as a waitress part time to help make ends meet. Jimmy had hated it, but had known they needed the extra money. Pay hadn't been great starting out in the fire department. They'd survived long enough for her work to catch the eyes of collectors. Not long after, Jimmy's tragedy had struck.

As they sat with their feet in the stream, thunder sounded in the distance. They both turned to see black clouds rolling in from the northwest. "We'd better head to the house," Nick suggested. "It looks bad." Lightning was getting closer. They quickly slipped on their socks and shoes and started back up the path toward the house. Chester ran ahead of them. They made it to the house just as the rain starting falling on the tin roof.

They spent the rest of the evening snuggled on the couch watching a couple of DVD's, *The Missing* and *Cold Mountain,* and eating popcorn. The wind blew hard all evening and the rain soaked the entire area. Nick had built a cozy fire in the fireplace and the rain pinged musically off the tin roof while they touched each other and kissed during the movies. It was late before Gabry reluctantly left for home, after the rain let up a little.

~

Nick spent the following week helping Josh and Vincent at the store in the mornings and working on his trail in the afternoons and evenings. He really enjoyed his time alone with Chester in the woods creating the path. One day as he rested on a log, two coyotes walked within fifty feet of Nick and Chester. Nick grabbed Chester before he could take off after them. The coyotes stood and stared at Nick, and then sheepishly snuck away. They were beautiful, but at the same time Nick worried about Chester roaming around the woods. There were stories of cats and dogs coming up missing. The speculation was the increase in the coyote population was the reason. Farmers had also lost livestock to the coyotes. Nick decided he needed to watch Chester more closely.

Gabriella spent a couple hours with Nick almost every evening. They would eat dinner together or take a walk, or she would help him on the trail. They decided to try and stay away from the intimacy they had Saturday evening. Knowing they were so physically attracted to each other, they wondered how long they could resist the temptation if they continued going halfway around the bases.

Gabry enjoyed talking to Nick about her new faith and asked him lots of questions about the Bible and what Nick thought about different topics. They talked about politics and music and their favorite writers. As their friendship and love deepened their physical attraction for each other grew, and they came to love the small things about each other. Gabry loved the way Nick's cheeks swelled when he grinned. Nick loved the way Gabriella's left eyebrow arched when she was in deep thought. They were getting to know each other more every day. Something they each needed more than their physical needs.

20

Nick picked up Josh early to go fishing. Nick had promised to take Josh wading in Little Rocky creek. He talked to some guys at Trudy's one day, trying to find out where the best stretches of fishing were in the creek. He was told of a section that was only two to four feet deep with some deeper pools. He was told the creek had a few different types of fish.

Chester played in the creek and on the shorelines while Nick and Josh waded and fished. Nick could tell Josh was having the time of his life from the grin on his face. They caught a few smallmouth bass and sunfish and some rock bass. It was nearly ten when Josh heard something on the bank above him. Nick was fishing on the other side of the creek. Suddenly three fury animals slid down the bank and plopped into the water at Josh's feet. Josh began screaming. Nick looked around quickly when he heard the splashes.

Nick yelled out, "What was it, Josh?"

"I don't know! I didn't see them, but they scared me to death!" Just then, they jumped up in the air right in front of Josh. He stepped quickly backward and slipped on a rock and went under the water. Nick knew what they were; river otters. After Josh managed to stand back up, the otters climbed the bank and turned as if they were laughing at Josh.

"What are they?"

"They're river otters. They're not dangerous, just mischievous. They enjoy playing and fooling around with humans."

"Yeah, they're real funny," Josh said while wiping water from his face and hair. The otters jumped back into the water near Josh and splashed him at the same time. They came up on top of the water surrounding him and floated on their backs, snickering at Josh. Josh began splashing them back. Chester saw the otters from the opposite bank and was barking with all he had. He jumped into the water and began swimming toward them as if he was going to save Josh. When he got fairly close the otters dove and disappeared. A minute later they climbed the bank farther down the creek.

As Nick was driving Josh home Josh said, "The otters were really fun. I had never seen otters before. I loved fishing in the creek. I want to do that again."

Nick smiled and simply said, "Okay." Josh knew they would.

When Nick got home there was a message on the phone from Melissa. She said she was doing great and just wanted to let him know. She said she loved her apartment and her work was keeping her busy after her being off so long. Nick hoped things continued to go well for Melissa.

Nick spent Saturday afternoon watching baseball and taking a nap beside Chester. Chester was worn out from his time at the creek and swimming after the otters.

Time for the party at Gabriella's came quickly. Gabriella decided to prepare something other than another Italian meal and had cooked a large roast with mashed potatoes and plenty of vegetables. She even made a loaf of bread for the meal. Trudy came early to tell her all about Dr. Walker Green. She spent the half hour before Nick and Vincent came telling Gabry that she thought Walker was getting serious.

"Do you like him?" Gabry asked.

"Yes. And it worries me. We have hit it off so well. He's all serious all the time, you know, like a doctor at a hospital, until I loosen him up and then he becomes so much fun."

"If anyone can loosen a person up, it's you."

"He's just so busy. He's constantly at work, and we haven't had a lot of time together. He promised to take me to the Grand Old Opry in Nashville when he finds time. That would be so much fun."

"It would be. I'm sure he's crazy about you, Trudy."

Trudy went on and on about what a gentleman he was and what she knew about his first marriage. Finally she asked, "How are you and Nick doing?"

"I love him so much, Trudy. Everything is going well. It almost scares me, it's been so perfect. I'm really looking forward to our trip this week."

"Me too. But you're going to have me and Vincent tagging along."

"That's what I'm looking forward to. It's going to be so much fun," Gabry assured Trudy.

Vincent and Nick both arrived at six thirty and walked through the door together, Vincent with his flowers and bottle of wine and Nick empty handed.

"Vincent, is it your intent to make me look bad every week?"

"Yes, you are what you are, son," Vincent teased.

"Thanks. What I am is a poor country boy who bareth no gifts, but an appetite for good food and love."

"I've heard everything now," Trudy laughed. "Try that one out on Stella."

Gabry walked in grinning and said, "Kind sir, I have food to whet your feeling of hunger, and the love in my heart I offer to you to do with what you will."

Vincent sighed and said, "My stomach, it does turneth in turmoil at the poor Shakespeare I heareth. I am sickened at this display."

"I am going to taketh my pies and goeth home if this doesn't stopeth," Trudy joined in.

"Okay, we're done. Please! Don't take your pies," Nick begged.

"Dinner is ready," Gabriella announced.

Nick said grace and everyone dug in. The meal was scrumptious. Everyone ate like they hadn't eaten in days. Gabry loved having her three friends to dinner. She had been lonely and angry for so long that she treasured the change of having friends and a love and a relationship with God. She hoped the anger was gone for good. "There's plenty, eat all you want."

During dinner Trudy looked at Nick and said, "I propose that we leave the itinerary of the trip totally up to Nick. I don't want to make one decision during the trip."

Vincent agreed, "Yes, this is Nick's territory. We're at your command, Nick."

"I've already been planning a few things to do. Vincent, how much can you hike?" Nick asked.

"I'm glad you asked. I've been going out after work and hiking every evening this week. I'm up to five miles on mountain trails, no problem."

"That's great, Vincent," Gabry said. "You can probably out-hike us."

"I don't think so, dear, and after a couple of days I'll probably need a rest and you three can take a long hike if you want without me," Vincent suggested.

Nick continued, "Most of the trails I have in mind are less than five miles. We should be fine. But any time you need to rest, just let us know. Also, to get this out of the way so we don't have any arguments during the trip, Gabry wants to pay for the rooms herself."

"That's awfully kind of you," Vincent said.

Trudy said, "Why would you do that?"

"Because I'm so happy, and I'm able to. My business has been very good, and I want to do something kind for my best friends."

Trudy said, "This vacation is getting better all the time."

"That's very sweet of you, Gabriella. Thank you," Vincent echoed again.

"It's my pleasure."

After dinner they went into the family room and relaxed. Trudy suggested they play another question-and-answer game. They all had enjoyed the game the first time they had played. The laughter was plentiful and they had learned so much about each other before. It seemed like forever since that night, but in another way it seemed like only yesterday.

Trudy asked who wanted to provide the first question. Vincent said he would go first. "What is your favorite holiday of all time and why? Trudy, you have to go first."

"This is hard, because I love all holidays. When I remember back, I always think of the Easter when I was ten. Our family was all together and we were going to Easter services at our church. I awoke that morning and there was an Easter basket beside my bed filled with fake green grass and candy, including Peeps, a Pez dispenser, and a large chocolate bunny. The Easter bunny of course, had arrived during the night. But beside the basket was a large package wrapped in colorful spring paper. I looked at the tag and saw that it was for me from Mom and Dad. I tore it open to find the most beautiful Easter dress I had ever seen. It was yellow and blue with a big green ribbon for a belt that tied in the back into a big bow. Also in the box were new white socks and a new pair of shoes. We were a poor family, and I had never had anything like that dress before. I felt so different when I put it on. To this day, I think that dress has influenced the clothes I wear. I liked that feeling, like I was special."

"You are special," Nick said. Everyone agreed with him.

Nick and Gabry were snuggled on the couch and it was Gabriella's turn to answer. "One Fourth of July I remember sitting in my mom's arms on a blanket in a park and watching the fireworks high in the sky. We oohed and aahed at them all. We began laughing as we listened to others around us doing the same thing. But we couldn't help doing it ourselves. We went on *oohing* and *aahing* till the last explosion went off. My mother died a month later. The memory of that night is so special to me. So I always think of that evening when I see fireworks."

"That's too sad," Trudy said. Nick hugged Gabry tighter and kissed her on the cheek.

Nick knew it was his turn and began, "Christmas 1984 was my favorite. Laura woke me early that morning, and we ran to the tree before Mom and Dad could get there. A new doll was under the tree for Laura and a new bicycle. I also had a new bike and an Ernie Banks baseball glove. I still have the glove. There were wrapped presents under the tree also. I opened a long skinny box to find a Billy Williams baseball bat. That was the Christmas I'll never forget."

Trudy asked, "Who are Ernie Williams and Billy Banks?"

Vincent teased, "You are quite the baseball fan."

"It always bored me," she answered.

It was Vincent's turn. "I always loved Thanksgivings with Maria. She always prepared all the traditional dishes. Well, musicians can be a strange bunch—a lot of lonely single folks in the philharmonic. Maria wanted to invite everyone who didn't have plans for the holiday, so we did. It was a fantastic idea, many attended our feast. I learned so much about my fellow musicians in that one day. I had been playing among strangers, but they all became lasting friends because of Maria's kindness."

"I love that story," Gabry told Vincent.

Gabry decided to ask a question next because Trudy was still trying to come up with one. "Who has been the biggest influence on your life? It can't be your parents or a past husband or wife. Someone that's been in your life at some point that you knew."

Nick was first. "It had to be a coach I had in high school, 'Foxy' Hopper. He was such a good coach. I could tell he really cared about each player. I felt I was special to him. But I'm sure all the kids that played for him thought the same way. Even the students in his history classes probably felt that way. He's the reason I wanted to be a teacher and coach."

"Foxy?" Gabry questioned.

"He had a pointy nose and red hair and kinda looked like a fox. What can I say?"

Vincent was next to go and explained, "Of course, it would have been my Maria, but due to the strict restrictions that have been placed upon our answers I would say the friend I had in high school that introduced me to Maria. It was the best day of my life."

"Okay, okay, we get it. Your answer is really Maria," Nick said.

"I wish we could have met her," Gabriella said.

Trudy was next. "My grandmother Flynn. She was the most loving person. Although I was pretty wild and very disobedient while growing up, she never judged me. She just kept pouring on the love. She was the one I didn't want to disappoint the most. When I visited her, which was often, she made cookies and pies and cakes and had me help. We spent hours in the kitchen cooking and talking about everything. She never told me to change my ways... even though she knew I was headed down the wrong path. I think she knew each person had to find their own passageway. I truly loved her."

"I take it that she was the one who taught you to make your famous desserts at the restaurant," Nick asked.

"Yes. Most of the recipes are from her."

"Thank God for your grandma Flynn," Vincent said, and everyone laughed.

Gabriella was next to answer her question. She hesitated while choosing her words carefully and then began, "My answer is simple... Nick." She turned to look at him and continued, "I was buried in sadness. I was stuck in a place where blaming God for Jimmy's death was my main reason for getting up. A few words from Nick started uncovering the truth that I had been running from. And Trudy, Vincent; you have been part of that healing process. Thank you."

Nick pulled Gabry to him and hugged her. She kissed him on the cheek.

"Gag me with a spoon," Trudy said. Vincent almost fell out of his chair with laughter.

"I know. I know. But I can't help it," Gabry explained.

It was Nick's turn to ask a question. "What's your favorite sport to either go to or watch on TV?"

Vincent was first. "I've never been much of a sports watcher, but I do enjoy March Madness every year. I usually catch a few of the games on TV. It's quite exciting."

Trudy answered next, "Football. All those men running around in tight pants, and they all have such big shoulders. I really like watching those men play football."

Nick teased, "I can see you're a big fan of the sport. I take it your favorite player is probably the tight end."

"Yes. I like any of them with tight ends." They laughed.

Gabry quickly answered, "Baseball. I lived in Boston near Fenway Park, and Nick took me to Wrigley Field. It's a great sport to watch while working on your tan."

Nick was next. "I love all sports, except soccer, so this is a hard one to answer. On TV it has to be NFL football and in person, it's baseball, but I love coaching basketball."

"You never did answer the question," Trudy told him.

"Football," Nick answered.

They next looked at Trudy for her probing question. She said, "I would like for you to tell something about yourself that none of us know about, and I want to go first."

"This could be interesting," Gabry stated.

"I'm really very shy," Trudy relayed to everyone. They waited for her to continue. When she didn't, everyone laughed.

"That's it... you're shy? I don't buy it," Gabry said.

"No way. You're the furthest thing from being shy," Nick exclaimed.

"I wonder what she would be like if she wasn't shy," Vincent commented. Everyone laughed again and they all put their hands up to acknowledge that they didn't accept it.

"Well, anyway, I feel like I am. It's your turn, Gabry."

She laughed and began, "I love Hershey's kisses. If I had a large bag right here in front of me I would eat them until they were completely gone."

"I've never seen you eat one," Nick said.

"That's because I don't want to blow up to be two hundred pounds. I don't buy them for that reason. I'm a chocoholic."

"I don't think so. If you don't believe I'm bashful, I don't believe you would eat that much chocolate." Everyone found it hard to believe looking at Gabry. Gabry looked like the person who hardly ever ate anything that was fattening.

"I guess it's my turn," Nick began. "It's hard for me to admit. But I'm a shy chocoholic who used to hide in my room eating candy kisses."

Gabry yelled, "Real funny." Vincent and Trudy laughed as Gabry began hitting him with a pillow from the couch.

"Okay, I'll be serious." Nick took a breath and started again, "When I moved here all I wanted was to be alone. I didn't want friends, and I definitely didn't want a relationship. I was looking for peace and seclusion from everyone. You guys made that impossible. Thank you. I've never been happier."

Gabry raised her hand, "I already knew that."

"How?" Nick asked.

"Why do you think I moved here?"

Trudy echoed, "Same reason I moved here. I wanted the same isolation."

Vincent seriously chimed in, "We all moved here to Sleepy Valley for the same reason. But there was one thing we didn't realize; people need love. We need relationships and friendship. I think we all could say we agree with that."

Heads nodded yes around the room.

"I've learned that my relationships and community with others are the most important things in my life. We don't have to go through sorrow by ourselves. We have each other to comfort and help us. It took a long time to realize that. I love all of you," Gabry said.

"This is getting mushy," Trudy finally said after a moment of silence. "Vincent, it's your turn. What don't we know about you?"

Vincent looked as though he was carefully deciding what to say. "I guess it's time to tell you. I didn't think I ever would." He took a drink of wine and looked around the room at each of his friends he had learned to love and trust. "I told you that Maria died a few years ago, but I never said how. I believe I led you to believe it was by sickness. Well, she was healthier than I am today. I went to a rehearsal early that morning and was going to go downtown to take some information to an investment firm. Maria made arrangements for us to meet friends for brunch after I was done as we did many times. So my sweet Maria said she would take the papers to the firm and meet me afterwards.

"I kissed her good-bye and told her I loved her as I always did when we parted. I went to our rehearsal." Tears began welling up in Vincent's eyes. "We were interrupted when someone ran in to tell us about one of the twin towers being hit."

"Oh no," Gabriella gasped. Trudy began to cry softly.

"It was where Maria was going instead of me. I ran out and called home. I tried her cell phone and got nothing. We all stood before a TV and watched the towers come down. I prayed Maria hadn't arrived there yet. There was nothing else I could do. I then rushed to the restaurant where we were to meet. No one was there. I waited for an hour. I kept calling and calling."

Gabriella was holding on to Nick, and Trudy had slipped over to Vincent and held his hand.

"I never saw her again. Her body was never recovered. I moved here not long after. I had to get away." Tears fell from his cheeks.

"Maria would have loved my new friends. I should have moved away long before that day. She even wanted to, but I told her that we would miss our friends, so we stayed."

"I'm so sorry, Vincent," Nick said.

"I'm just one of the thousands of lives that were changed on 9–11."

Nick asked, "Vincent, if I may ask, what about the urn you keep?"

"I had some connections and was allowed days later to go to ground zero. I walked among the ruins, and I brought home a sack of ashes, and that's what is in the urn. It's my only hope of having something of Maria."

"You have the memories of your love and all the years you were together and happy." Nick tried to think of assurances, but that was all he could come up with.

Gabriella quietly said, "Someday in heaven, you will be reunited."

"We may, my dear, we may."

The rest of the evening was spent talking about 9–11 and different stories they had heard. They ate Trudy's dessert and then talked about what time they were leaving Monday morning for vacation. The vacation couldn't be coming at a better time.

"I would like to attend the church service in the morning if you don't mind." Vincent looked to Nick.

"Gabry and I will pick you up around nine forty-five. We would love for you to go with us."

21

Nick rose early Monday morning and took Chester for a walk. Josh had asked his mom if they could keep Chester for the week while Nick was gone. She said it would be fine. She was so happy with the change in Josh since Nick had come into his life, it was the least she could do. Nick placed Chester's cage in the back, and Chester rode shotgun to Josh's house.

"Next Saturday we'll fish another section of the creek," Nick said to Josh.

"I don't think we should, Nick. I think Vincent will need my help Saturday at the store after being gone all week."

"You're probably right. Maybe one day next week." Nick was so proud of Josh.

"Sounds great."

When Nick drove away he saw Josh and Chester playing in the side yard. It thrilled Nick to realize how caring Josh was toward Vincent. Besides not having a father, Josh also didn't have a grandfather that he ever saw, so the bonding was predictable.

Nick went back home and loaded a small bag with hiking shorts, T-shirts, underwear, and hiking boots. He took his binoculars and camera. His next stop was to pick up Gabriella. He saw a small suitcase on the front porch and loaded it in the back with his bag. He opened the front door and called out, "Good morning, sweetheart."

Gabry entered the family room and said, "I like having a handsome man come into my house first thing in the morning and call me sweetheart."

"You do, huh?" Nick said as Gabry slipped her arms around his neck.

"Yes. I never grow tired of it, even though it happens every day."

"It does, huh?"

"Well, maybe not every day."

"How often does it happen?" Nick teased.

As she kissed him she answered, "Actually, this was the first time, but I loved it."

Nick caressed her back as they kissed, and he lowered his hands to her butt.

"Are we feeling frisky this morning?" Gabry asked.

"Are we?"

"I guess we are, but too bad. It's time to go."

Nick sighed, "Just when it was getting interesting."

Gabry picked up her makeup bag and also brought her binoculars and a camera. She locked the front door and they headed to Trudy's.

Nick told her on the way, "I'd like for you to sit up front with me on the way. Okay?"

"Okay, love." Doing her best Sandra Bullock impression she flirted, "You like me, don't you? You *love* me."

"That's funny."

They pulled into Trudy's driveway. Gabry jumped out and ran to the door and opened it. As Nick made it to the porch, Gabriella came out with a suitcase. "Here, I'll take it."

Gabry smiled and said, "I got it. You can get the other ones inside."

"What? What do you mean the other ones?" Nick walked through the door and saw another large suitcase and an oversized makeup bag. "Trudy!" Nick yelled.

She walked into the room carrying another small bag and said, "What, dear?"

"I think maybe you've over packed for our trip."

"A girl can never have too much."

"We're only taking one vehicle. I could go rent a U-Haul if you would like."

"You're a doll, Nick. Hurry back."

"I was kidding," Nick said as he dragged the case to the vehicle. After loading her cases he had one small space left for Vincent's stuff. Trudy did look beautiful though. She wore a bright Hawaiian sleeveless top and white shorts, and had her hair in a full ponytail.

As Nick drove to Vincent's, Trudy said, "This is exciting. I feel like a kid again going on vacation. Are we there yet, Daddy?"

Vincent was standing on the sidewalk talking to Tom when they pulled up. They all piled out of the SUV to greet Vincent.

"Is there room for one more?" Tom begged, as he looked Trudy up and down.

"On top of the roof, you old fool," Trudy said.

Tom answered, "I'd let you drag me at the end of a chain if I could spend the week with you."

"That's the only way you could get me to go with you, tied to a chain."

Tom laughed and said, "I may have to try that." Everyone laughed. "Well, if I can't go, you all have fun. I've got to get to the bank."

"Thanks, Tom," Nick said as he grabbed Vincent's suitcase.

Vincent then said, "There's another one in the house."

"See, I'm not the only one with more than one suitcase," Trudy stated.

"You had four. Vincent, we need bungee cords," Nick said. Vincent and Nick walked down the block and unlocked the store. They went inside and found some large ones. When they returned, Nick hoisted the suitcase up to the luggage rack and secured it with the cords.

Everyone began to load themselves into the vehicle. "Vincent, you're in the back with me."

"Goody."

Trudy winked and said, "We can make out in the backseat."

Vincent rubbed his hands. "This is going to be a fun trip."

"The bank isn't open yet, is it," asked Nick.

"No," Trudy answered.

"Tom said he had to get to the bank. But it's not open."

Everyone looked at Nick with surprise and he asked, "What?"

Trudy leaned forward and said, "He's the president of the bank. You didn't know that?"

"No," Nick said with surprise. "I had no idea what Tom did."

Trudy said, "He's like a multi-millionaire. He is really a brilliant guy."

"And you're not chasing him?"

"He's also happily married to the sweetest lady."

"Unbelievable," Nick said. Never in a million years would Nick have thought Tom was president of the bank, a millionaire, or married, especially happily married. He realized then that he still had a lot to learn about living in the community of Sleepy Valley. For some reason it pleased him to know about Tom. He figured it was because people here were just people, no pretense, put-on, or act. They lived the way they wanted and didn't care what others thought of them, each person an individual.

"Apparently you didn't know that," Vincent noted.

"No. Had no idea what he did for a living."

"Are we there yet?" Trudy asked again.

Nick laughed and told Vincent, "You need to entertain little Trudy so she's not bored."

"I could tell her a story about the young gangly Walker Green."

"Yes. Yes. Tell me the story," Trudy giggled.

It was a beautiful summer morning. A light breeze rustled the leaves in the tall trees that lined the country roads as they drove away from Sleepy Valley toward Gatlinburg. Light wispy clouds looked lost in the massive blue sky. Gabriella reached for Nick's hand and she gently touched his fingers as he drove. Shivers ran up his arms at her touch. He thought of the wonderful day they spent in Cades Cove. The day he was sure of his love for Gabriella.

Gabry was thinking of the same day as she looked at the side of his strong, yet gentle face. She thought of how different her life was now than just three months ago. She had faith and love and hope for a future filled with happiness. She didn't wonder *if* Nick would ask her to marry him, she wondered *when* he would. She would say yes that moment. She would let Nick drive her to one of the lovely small chapels she had heard about in Gatlinburg and marry him today without any hesitation. Her mind thought of marriage as Nick drove.

Trudy leaned forward and put her arms on the front seats. "You guys are awfully quiet. What are you thinking about?"

Gabry snapped out of her dream and answered, "I was wondering what my darling has planned for us."

"By saying *us,* do you mean us four or you two?"

"The four of us," Gabry half lied.

"What do you have planned, big boy?" Trudy asked.

"We can't check in until two, so I thought I might drive us through the park to show you the mountains and maybe take some small walks till then. Eat lunch at the Pancake Pantry and then check into our rooms. Then we'll play it by ear this evening. Maybe someone will see something they would like to do."

"Are we going to Dollywood this week?" Trudy asked.

"I've never been to Dollywood. I've eaten her chocolate boobs though."

Gabry yelled, "What?"

Vincent perked up and said, "Tell us more."

Nick laughed and explained, "A candy store makes solid chocolate shaped to look like Dolly Parton's breasts—big seller with men."

Vincent laughed and commented, "I don't eat a lot of chocolate, but I will try Dolly's boobs."

Gabry cried out, "You men are unbelievable."

Trudy admitted, "Gabry, I actually think I'll have to try a pair myself."

Gabry laughed and said, "Don't get me wrong. I'm going have a set, but only because they're chocolate, not because they're boobs."

Nick suggested, "Trudy, maybe you could sell them in your restaurant and rename them Trudy's boobs."

"They wouldn't last long. Tom would buy up every one of them for himself," Trudy said laughing.

Everyone in the car imagined Tom sitting at the counter licking on the chocolate boobs while making comments to Trudy and all the patrons. Simultaneously they all four burst out laughing.

Nick loved driving the country roads. After driving in the Chicago traffic for so many years and wasting so many hours sitting in jams and backups this seemed like heaven. A two-lane, country road with farms and woods and an occasional road kill to look at instead of angry motorists honking horns and flipping each other off. Foothills rose in the distance before rising into the Great Smoky Mountains.

The road followed the valleys between the mountains where early settlers had made their way to this region, knowing it was home as soon as they saw the beauty. Over a century ago families escaped unhappy lives to begin new ones in this area. Not unlike what the four travelers in Nick's SUV had done as they made their way to Sleepy Valley. Each of them had left sorrow and heartache to find a serene privacy and a new beginning. Nick and Trudy suffered failed marriages due to unfaithful mates, and Gabry and Vincent felt the lasting pain of their mate's unexpected deaths.

When Nick arrived in Sleepy Valley, the other three were still in their state of mourning and unhappiness. Trudy filled her life with the restaurant and her church, but she still ached for companionship that was meaningful and lasting. Gabry had carved a little corner for herself where she created and painted and hid her pain within the mournful eyes in the faces of her paintings. Vincent hid in the general store letting the store run down more and more every day. He placed all his energy in the only thing that still made him happy; his music, whether playing or teaching, it was his only escape from the memory of the day Maria died. He asked himself why he had not insisted on taking the papers to the tower later after their brunch or another day. Why did he selfishly let her do it for him, thus saving him, the all-important musician, from having to do it? He blamed himself. If only he could undo that day and have those days with Maria back again.

For some reason though, Nick had arrived, just in the nick of time they all thought. Something about Nick gave them all hope and happiness. Nick was just another man full of hurt himself. But he cared. In his eyes, a person could see the caring and thoughtful expressions that poured from his heart. He was a person who cared about others and their hurts and unhappiness. His smile brightened up a room. His simple way of nodding or saying good morning warmed the surroundings. Nick had weaved, unknowingly, the four of them together into a friendship of love.

It seemed as though everything he touched turned to happy. He found Chester in a barn ready to be destroyed, but Nick saw a dog that needed love. He saw the dog the puppy could become. He took Josh and paid attention to him and talked to him and showered him with a father's warmth and love that Josh was missing in his life. He left the peacefulness of Sleepy Valley to help Melissa who had abandoned him and caused his heartache. But he went because he cared and knew he could help her.

Pastor Hill could see the goodness in Nick the first time he laid eyes on him. The gifts that God had bestowed on Nick covered him without Nick even knowing. Nick had no idea how much he meant to others. He knew they liked him and he knew that Gabry had fallen in love with him, but he had no idea the influence that his arrival had meant to everyone.

"Maybe I could create suckers," Trudy said.

"What are you talking about?" Nick asked.

"I could create suckers shaped like my boobs and sell them in the store. Sell them for say five dollars."

They laughed and Vincent said, "You are on your way to being a millionaire, my dear."

Nick suggested, "You could make it like a tootsie roll pop; put a treat in the middle."

"Like what?" Trudy asked.

"Silicone." Everyone cracked up at Nick's suggestion.

Trudy, insulted, cried out, "You know there's nothing fake about these things, Nicky."

"No, but I wish I did." Gabry reached over and grabbed Nick's leg and began pinching. "I mean, I'm sure they're not, and it doesn't matter to me, because I love Gabry, and her beautiful breasts."

"That's my man," Gabry said, slowly letting go of his leg.

Trudy teased, "Nice try, Nick."

"Yeah, real smooth," Vincent chipped in. Everyone laughed. Nick was nearing Townsend and would soon be in the Smokies. When they arrived in Townsend, Gabry pointed out the hole-in-the-wall where she and Nick had eaten pulled-pork sandwiches.

"Charming," Trudy said sarcastically. "I'm kidding. That's usually where you find the best food."

A few minutes later, Nick stopped at the *Welcome to the Great Smoky Mountain National Park* sign. They all piled out and Gabry got out her tripod and camera and set it on the delay timer and ran to get in the picture of the four of them standing in front of the sign.

When Nick stopped at the dead end, instead of turning right

to Cades Cove he went left toward Gatlinburg. As Nick drove the winding road along the rock filled creek, everyone took in the beauty of the stream and the stunning, blooming mountain laurel and green hemlocks on the overhanging walls along the opposite side of the road.

Comments continued about the beauty and landscape before them. A camper crept along in front of Nick going under the twenty-five miles per hour speed limit. But this was the type of traffic jam Nick could tolerate. Nick had driven this section of road many times and each time it still humbled him seeing the splendor around him. Nick came to a pull-off where the river crossed under the road called The Sinks, where the water's elevation dipped, creating rolling cascades of waterfalls and a fishing hole at the bottom. Nick parked in the small lot and they grabbed cameras and walked around taking in the sight.

Nick and Gabry found their way to a large rock looking down at the rolling water. Trudy and Vincent made their way up to the couple and they relaxed to the quiet roaring of the falls. "Is the entire park this lovely?" Vincent asked.

"Pretty much," Nick answered, "but different. There are different trees, flowers, and animals as the elevation changes. No matter where you are in the park though, it's beautiful."

"I can't wait to see it all," Trudy offered.

"You'll never see it all. But we'll do our best," Nick promised. Gabry knew how special the park was to Nick, and it was fast becoming that way to her. Nick had promised to take her to see some of his favorite artist's studios while they were there. Artists were all around in the area. Endless subjects to paint and draw inspiration from. "Everyone feel up to a hike? Up the road a little ways is the trail to Laurel Falls."

When Nick stopped at the pull-off for Laurel Falls, Gabry and Trudy changed into hiking boots, and they were off. The trail was six to ten feet wide and flat or slightly upward for a mile and a quarter to the falls. They walked at a steady clip, stopping every so often for pictures and rest. Nick knew this would be a good test to see how Vincent would do on harder trails later in the week. Vincent was doing fine and even wanting to pick up the pace.

"Easy, Vincent, we have five days of this. Let's not wear ourselves out the first morning," Nick warned.

They worked up a sweat on the trail even though the day was cool for the end of June. Nick passed around his canteen to everyone as they hiked. The sound of the falls was welcoming as they passed the last bend to see the cascading water fall the eighty feet or so to the pool below. They rested while taking in the surroundings. They watched couples and families that were playing and picnicking around the waterfall. Some kids were playing in the water below the falls. Gabry took a seat on a flat stone and Nick laid his head on her lap to rest. Vincent began a conversation with another elderly gentleman near the top of the falls.

After a little while, Gabry looked around for Trudy and spotted her, "Look, Nick."

He raised his head and Gabriella pointed to the bottom of the falls toward Trudy. She had taken off her boots and socks and was wading in the pool splashing the kids. The kids began splashing back, and Trudy ended up running out before she got soaked. The kids laughed at her. She had all the older men's attention as she tiptoed around the pool to her footwear.

This beautiful woman, taking time to have fun like a kid again, gave Nick a glimpse of the child that still lived in Trudy. He wondered how much she suffered in her marriage. He knew something had been taken away from her by the abuse she had endured. It thrilled Nick and Gabry to see her having so much fun, which was strange, because Trudy was probably the most fun person they knew. But it was always so forthcoming that it seemed like a cover-up for the heartache underneath. Today, Trudy seemed truly happy and carefree.

Trudy looked up to see her friends waving. Trudy made her way up the path to Nick and Gabry. She smiled at them and said, "I almost made a big mistake."

"Looked like you were having fun," Nick countered.

"If those kids would have soaked me in these white shorts it would have given all the men here something to stare at."

Nick said, "Trudy, all the men were staring at you anyway. I don't think you really realize how beautiful you are."

"Really?"

"Really," Gabry agreed.

"Thanks, guys. Must be the company I keep." Trudy hugged Nick and Gabry.

After resting for thirty minutes, Nick suggested, "Let's head back. By the time we get to Gatlinburg and eat lunch we should be able to check into our rooms."

They went over to gather Vincent, and he introduced them to Mr. Fred Fields. "I'll see you on Wednesday," Vincent told Mr. Fields, and they headed back down the trail.

When asked about Mr. Fields, Vincent explained, Mr. Fields was seventy-nine and there for the week with his son and grandchildren and that he wasn't able to hike like they wanted.

"His son and grandchildren are hiking to what they call the Chimney Tops Wednesday, and we decided to spend the day together. Give you young folks a chance to do some real hiking."

"You sure you want to abandon us?" Trudy asked.

"It will give Fred and me a chance to pick up young women. He says the streets are filled with women in their seventies."

"Better watch yourself with those young whippersnappers," Trudy warned.

It took just short of forty minutes to get back to the SUV. They arrived in Gatlinburg around one. "We still have time to eat lunch before checking in," Nick recommended.

"I'm starving," Trudy commented.

"Hiking builds an appetite, for sure," Gabry agreed.

Nick found a parking lot near the restaurant that was his favorite spot for lunch. They walked through an alley to the main street. The street was filled with restaurants, candy stores, souvenir shops, T-shirt and quilt stores, and artist galleries. Not a blade of grass could be seen on the parkway. It definitely was a tourist attraction or trap, whichever way you looked at it.

Nick led them across the street inside a crosswalk as cars stopped for pedestrians to cross in front of them. They entered the Pancake Pantry. As usual, the restaurant was nearly filled with patrons. The building had high ceilings in the front covered with light-colored woodwork, and there were tall timbers rising from the floor to the ceiling holding it in place. They were seated by the large front bay windows from where they could view the herd of people walking from store to store. You could also watch a gentleman in the window next door work with taffy, placing it on a large machine that twisted it and fed it into a chute that wrapped it and spit it out into a large basket.

"The hamburgers and fries are the best you can get other than Trudy's, of course."

"Of course," Trudy agreed with Nick.

"Everything is good, though. They bring out crocks of marinated cucumbers and onions with the meal. Wait till you taste them."

A waitress appeared beside them and took their orders. As they waited on the food they watched throngs of people walk past. It was enjoyable watching newlyweds and families and large groups walk by the window smiling and laughing. It seemed as though everyone was enjoying being in Gatlinburg on vacation.

Soon the food arrived and everyone loved what they ordered and the cucumbers and onions were a hit. Gabry and Nick had the hamburgers, Vincent ordered the Reuben sandwich and Trudy got a melted ham and Swiss creation. They paid and Nick took them into the candy shop next door. Vincent bought some jellybeans.

Nick bought vanilla taffy. Trudy found coconut haystacks that she wanted and Gabry stared at the chunks of milk chocolate. "Are you debating which to get?" Nick asked her.

"No, I'm drooling and salivating over all this fantastic chocolate," she explained.

"This is vacation. Have some chocolate."

She ordered a quarter pound of milk chocolate chunks and a half pound of chocolate turtles. "Will you still love me if I blow up to twice my size?"

"Yes, we'll go there together."

"No, I want you staying just like you are."

"Okay, so that's the way it's going to be, huh?" Nick exclaimed.

Fifteen minutes later they were checking into the Bearskin Lodge at the edge of town. Their rooms were next to each other on the third floor. Nick found a carrying rack and loaded all the suitcases and delivered them to the rooms overlooking a mountain stream.

"What are our plans for this evening, Nick?" Trudy asked.

"How about we take a drive later and then maybe walk around the town this evening?"

Vincent took a shower and then took a nap. Trudy took a shower and wanted to relax and read on the balcony overlooking the river below. She watched the mallards swim back and forth in the gentle stream. Fly fishermen were casting for trout just upstream from the hotel.

Nick and Gabriella went for a walk along the river toward the Sugarland Visitor Center. They walked hand in hand until they found a spot to sit along the stream. They kissed softly and held each other as they watched the ravens land on branches near the water.

"Nick, I'm very happy."

"I'm glad you are. I am too. Why are you so happy?"

Gabry turned her head toward the water and explained, "I'm in love with you, for one, and I see life so differently since I accepted Christ. It feels like a heavy weight was removed from my shoulders. I see how wonderful His creation is, from the mountains to the ravens and the smallest flowers. I have great friends, and it's nice to see everyone so happy."

A family of ducks floated by as they sat and talked. The babies bobbed up and down as they tried to stay close to their mother while they searched for food. A gentle breeze blew down the river stirring the leaves and giving a cool relief to the warm afternoon. Mountain laurel hung from the banks filled with flowering blooms. Nick and Gabry fell deeper in love during the time spent together at the river.

"We had better head back," Nick suggested.

When they returned they gathered Trudy and Vincent and went for a drive. Nick wanted to take them for a drive around the one-way, scenic Roaring Fork Road Motor Nature Trail.

"So where did you two roam off to?" Trudy asked.

"We took a walk along the river toward the park. It was very relaxing," Gabry answered. Nick turned onto the one-way road and the town disappeared. It was like turning off a switch. In one turn they went from hustle and bustle of hotels and shops to a quiet forest canopy. The mountain laurel perfumed the air from the open windows and they slowly drove along the narrow road past primitive homesteads and small waterfalls. They got out at one of the old farms and walked around.

Vincent stated after walking around, "Can you imagine how hard life was back then, farming and clearing and raising children and breeding stock? No wonder people died so young. They were worn out."

Nick was pleased with everyone's excitement and joy for the trip so far. The Smokies were the reason he had chosen to move to Tennessee, and he was glad his friends loved them also. The rest of the evening was spent walking around the downtown area, buying t-shirts and souvenirs and eating ice cream. Gatlinburg was very much a family destination, but it didn't stop men from turning to watch Gabriella and Trudy walk by. *Beautiful women have that effect anywhere in the world,* Nick thought.

Around ten they headed back to the lodge and up to their rooms. Everyone was tired, especially Vincent. "I have a hike planned for the morning. Let's be ready for breakfast around eight and then head into the park."

When Nick and Vincent walked into their room they turned on the TV and switched the station to ESPN for the day's highlights.

Trudy and Gabriella talked about the wonderful day. Gabry told Trudy how romantic it was sitting by the stream and holding hands. She told Trudy how Nick put his arms around her. "This time it gave me gigantic goose bumps for some reason."

Vincent fell asleep quickly, worn out from the hiking and traveling. Nick wondered how Vincent would do on the more strenuous hike he had planned the next day.

The girls giggled and talked about how it felt like a slumber party. They talked about Nick and Walker until one in the morning. They finally drifted off to sleep.

22

The morning came quickly. They ate breakfast at the Pancake Pantry and they just beat the crowd. By the time they left the line stretched out the restaurant and down the sidewalk fifty feet. Nick drove out of town and headed toward Newfound Gap. After about a half hour drive, he pulled into the parking lot for the Alum Cave Bluff trail head. They all had walking sticks, and Gabry and Trudy took cameras. Nick had a backpack with water, snacks, and a first aid kit. A sign was posted at the trails beginning, warning of bear sightings on the trail and gave instructions on how to be safe while hiking.

One was to constantly make noise, such as talking. Nick commented over his shoulder to the group, "That's why we brought Trudy." She goosed him with her walking stick. For the first mile the trail followed a mountain stream. They constantly stopped for pictures. Nick figured it might help Vincent by giving him frequent rests. The trail then turned into a tunnel stairway blasted through a large boulder, and then the trail grew steeper.

They climbed higher and higher, resting occasionally, the girls pretending they needed the rest. But Vincent seemed to being doing well. When they got near the bluffs they came out on a point that overlooked the mountains. They were breathless, not because of the hike, but the view. The morning was clear and the view was spectacular. It was easy to see how the mountains got their name. The smoke lay in the valleys with the mountain peaks rising above the cloudlike layers. It seemed they could see all the way to North Carolina and Kentucky and Georgia.

"This is absolutely breathtaking, Nick," Gabriella said.

"I think it's the best view in the Smokies for the hike you have to take," Nick explained. "Mt. LeConte is a better view, but the hike is very difficult and long."

"You've been there?" Vincent asked.

"Yes, once. There's a lodge up there, and they have cabins you can reserve."

"How do they get supplies up there?" Trudy asked.

"Llamas," Nick answered. "They use them to carry everything up."

"Amazing," Gabry stated.

They all were seated on a large rock looking out at the scene before them, when Nick removed the backpack and handed out water. He then opened a small pack of peanuts and placed some on the trail near his feet.

"What are you doing?"

"Just watch."

Soon little ground squirrels came out from under the evergreen bushes along the trail. They scurried to the nuts, stole them and hurried back to their hiding spots. Everyone laughed, and Trudy said, "They are so cute."

Nick placed some nuts on the toe of Trudy's hiking boot. A minute later a squirrel appeared and cautiously sneaked up on to her foot and stuffed the nuts into his mouth and scooted away. They fed the squirrels for the next twenty minutes and had them eating out of their hands before they ran out of peanuts.

"Let's go. We're almost there."

Trudy asked, "You mean this wasn't it? I thought we were there."

They followed Nick on a narrow trail through tall pines. The trail fell steeply off on the left side. Ten minutes later the trail opened up to a large overhang. The view again was outstanding.

A few other hikers had beaten them to the bluffs and they greeted them.

The overhang was nearly a hundred feet above them. Under the overhang was loose rock and dirt. A few large rocks were scattered about creating seats for weary hikers. To the left as they looked out from the cavern there was a slender rock formation that jutted out into the vast openness in front of them. It looked like a mountain had split and fallen in both directions leaving a fraction of it behind. It was only a few feet wide, and a young man had made his way onto it.

Gabry asked Nick, "How did he get out there?"

Nick explained to everyone that they had passed a trail that went down to the forest floor. "You can follow the trail to a spot where you can climb up to the ridge. I've been up there once. It was actually very scary. It was something I'm glad I did even though my heart felt like it was trying to escape my chest."

Vincent surprised everyone when he said, "It looks like a great spot to spread Maria's ashes. I'll never find a better spot."

"You can't go out there, Vincent," Trudy told him.

"No, no. Nick could do it for me. Would you, Nick?"

"I don't think Nick should go back out there," Gabriella stated.

Nick looked at Gabry and said, "Yes, I would do that for you, Vincent. Next time we come if you want." Gabry understood that Nick had to say yes, but it still didn't make her feel any better about it.

They rested another forty minutes, taking pictures, eating snacks, and enjoying the scene. Gabry thought of the paintings she might do. The rock ledge with no sides was her number-one candidate. She took many pictures of it. On the way back down the trail Nick stopped to show them a view of the slender wall that showed there was a large hole that went through the middle of the rock wall. Gabry took pictures. When they made it to the parking lot they could tell Vincent was tuckered out. Nick drove them to

Newfound Gap where there was a large parking lot with restrooms and another great view of the mountains.

Nick explained that the Tennessee-North Carolina state line ran through Newfound Gap. Instead of driving on across the mountains they decided to head back to Gatlinburg. Nick wanted to take them to the Sugarland Visitor Center. They took in all the animal displays, bought maps and T-shirts, and then watched a twenty-minute movie about the park. The visitor center was a treat for everyone. "I enjoy it every time I walk in," Nick told them.

They ate lunch at the Cherokee Grill and went back to the hotel. Vincent decided to take an afternoon nap. Trudy wanted to take a walk along the river by herself. She really just wanted to give Nick and Gabry time alone. They decided to check out the local artists. Nick told them he wanted to drive them to Cades Cove for the evening and to be ready at five thirty. Dinner would be at the "hole-in-the-wall" in Townsend.

Nick and Gabry changed and headed out of town to the artist loop outside Gatlinburg on Buckhorn Road. The artist's studios were scattered along the country road. Trudy changed into a beautiful, yellow sundress and strolled along River Road toward the center of town. She stopped and watched the mallards and the fishermen. She walked across the street to get fresh-squeezed lemonade from an outside refreshment stand. She turned away quickly and bumped into a man. "Excuse me. I'm sorry. Did I spill on you?" She said looking to see if anything spilled on the person she ran into.

"No," the gentleman said. "I'm fine." Trudy looked up to his face. She saw a handsome man with a shaved head and pleasant smile.

She smiled back and said, "Sometimes, I can be so clumsy."

"Its okay, no harm," he said. But he thought, *this gorgeous lady can run over me, and I wouldn't care.* "Have a nice day," he said.

Trudy crossed the street and glanced back to see the gentleman buying a cup of lemonade also. He crossed the street and walked behind her. He was glad he was going in the same direction. Of course it wasn't the direction he had planned to go. Trudy stopped to watch a fisherman casting a fly into the stream. She wondered if the man would say anything as he walked by.

He didn't want to seem forward, but he didn't want to pass up the chance to meet this beautiful lady. He stopped five feet short of Trudy and pretended to watch the same fisherman.

"Do you think they catch anything?" he asked her, trying to make conversation.

"I saw a guy catch one yesterday from my balcony. It wasn't very big. Looks like fun though."

"Yes, it does." He fumbled with his next words. "Th—the lemonade was a good choice."

"It's hard to beat good lemonade. My name is Trudy Flynn." Trudy liked this man and how awkward he seemed to be attempting to talk to her. It was a good sign.

He held out his hand and said, "I'm Wade Morgan. It's my pleasure to meet you."

"Would you like to walk a ways with me, Wade?"

"Yes. I have nothing planned." They began strolling down the walk. "What brings you to Gatlinburg?"

"I came with friends. They're off doing other things. I decided to take a walk along the river. It's very relaxing," Trudy explained. "What brings you here?"

"This is going to sound a bit strange. I came with my mom and aunts."

"Big time swinger, huh?"

"I deserve the humiliation. Go ahead and pile it on. I live outside Knoxville and they ask me to bring them here a couple of times every year. They shop, and I hike and look for beautiful women to bug."

"I'm the lucky one today."

"If you want to call it lucky," he laughed. Trudy thought he had a very nice laugh. Not forced, very genuine and kind. She was going to enjoy their walk.

~

Nick took Gabry to the Hippensteal Inn. It was Nick's favorite Bed & Breakfast and was owned by a local artist whose family also ran the Inn. Each room was named for one of his paintings and a print was prominently displayed in that room. The hallways were filled with his wonderful prints. The view of the mountains from the balcony was stunning. The wilderness stretched out before them and the Great Smoky Mountains marched into the distance.

Next, he took her to see the artwork of his favorite artist at the G. Webb Gallery. They walked in and were greeted by a nice lady that Nick said had worked there for years. Gabry studied the paintings and talked about techniques that Nick knew nothing about. Gabry bought a small painting and they spent the rest of the afternoon browsing through craft stores and snacking on sweets.

~

Meanwhile, Trudy told Wade where she lived and about her diner. She told him she was divorced with no kids. She, of course, didn't mention Dr. Walker Green. Wade told Trudy he owned a company that sold and built Timberframe homes and that he also was divorced with no kids. He didn't mention Sally Trigg who he dated off and on. He said he knew exactly where Sleepy Valley was and that he had built a home on Mountain Road for Jerry and Betty Carter. Trudy said, "Small world. They gave my friend Nick his dog, Chester."

"I think I might have eaten in your diner when we built the house. Great pie!"

"That's it."

They walked along the water till the river turned and then they continued in front of stores without paying attention to what was inside them. "So, why the shaved head, Wade?"

"I was going bald anyway. I tried the comb-over for a while."

"You didn't."

"I hated the wind though. Made it look like I had a piece of pine bark stuck in my head. I decided to try this and liked it better."

"You did not have a comb-over! Well, the Mister Clean appearance does look good on you. You have a nice face."

"Thank you. So do you."

Wade took Trudy into a shop that was his favorite, named Beneath the Smoke. The store sold photographer Ken Jenkins' wildlife pictures. They were amazing. A lot of the pictures were taken in the Smokies. Other photographs of buffalo, pumas, giraffes, and other animals were from all around the world. Trudy bought a picture of bear cubs.

When they exited the store, they walked a little farther and Trudy turned to him and asked, "Where can we find chocolate boobs?"

When they returned from finding the Dolly Parton look-a-likes in Pigeon Forge, Wade parked his car at his hotel and walked Trudy back to the Bearskin Hotel. "I'm meeting Mom and my aunts for dinner soon. Would you like to join us? I should have asked you sooner."

"I'm sorry, I can't. We're going to Cades Cove this evening."

"May I call you sometime?"

"What are your plans for tomorrow?" Trudy thought, *what am I doing?*

"I was going to hike to Andrews Bald. Would you like to join me?" Wade so much wanted to hear a yes from Trudy. "You'll love the flowers."

"Yes. I can do that. What time should I be ready?" *Why am I doing this?*

"I'll pick you up at eight. We'll have breakfast and go."

"Sounds like a plan. I enjoyed the afternoon. You're a good escort."

"Thank you. You'll love Cades Cove. I'm jealous."

He turned to leave and Trudy called out, "What could beat dinner with mom and your aunts?" Trudy watched him walk away. She could tell that he grinned when his cheeks swelled. He turned to see her watching him and he waved good-bye. She smiled and ran into the lobby. Vincent was sitting there reading the paper.

"How was your afternoon, dear?"

Trudy leaned over and kissed him on the cheek and said, "Very nice."

"Nick and Gabry just got back also. They're upstairs getting ready."

Trudy took the stairs instead of taking the elevator. She burst into the room and screamed with delight. "Trudy, what's wrong?" Gabry asked her.

"Absolutely nothing. I have a date for tomorrow."

"What?"

Trudy explained while she quickly changed into different shorts and a top.

"You just met him, and you're taking a day-long hike with him into the wilderness. You think that's real smart?"

"Yes, I do, Mother Morelli. I'll tell you all about him on the way to Cades Cove."

They knocked on Nick's door, and the three of them left to meet Vincent in the lobby. Trudy talked almost the entire way to Cades Cove. She had Vincent sit up front with Nick so she could watch Gabry's expressions as she talked.

After she told them all about Wade she asked what they thought.

Vincent said, "I'd like to meet him before I comment. You know he has to meet my approval."

Nick said, "The Carter house is really nice. He must do a good job."

"That's all you can say," Gabry thumped him on the back on the head.

"I hate to bring this up, Trudy, but—what about Walker?"

"I'm just going on a hike with him that's all, friends out hiking, very innocent. Vincent has a play date, and now I have one. You two love birds will have the day all to yourselves."

"I have a play date?" Vincent moaned.

"Well, you know what I mean. We'll all go to breakfast together so you can meet him. Perhaps that will make you feel better about it. He's picking me up at eight."

Gabry worried about this new adventure in Trudy's life. She knew nothing about this Wade character other than he was cute and built things. Still, she realized that Trudy was a big girl and definitely could protect herself from harm, but maybe not heartbreak. Gabry was always the cautious one, looking out for Trudy. She felt better about Trudy's hike knowing she would get a chance to meet the guy the next morning. She felt as though she was good at judging people right away, after all, she knew right away about Nick.

Nick thought the guy sounded like a good fellow, hard worker, cared about his mother and family. He loved the mountains and hiking. Sounded like a perfect match for Trudy. Better than a doctor. He had nothing at all against Walker, but simply put, he thought Trudy and the doc didn't go together. But that was a man's way of thinking. Also, a man's way of thinking was to stay out of it.

Vincent's thought was, "I'm really looking forward to this pulled pork sandwich and coleslaw I've heard so much about."

As Nick drove around the bends and sharp curves Trudy stared out the window at the river on the right side on the car. She hoped to see a black bear taking a bath as she thought about what she was doing. She questioned herself big time. Walker was such a good catch. A surgeon that was sweet, nice looking, had money, and seemed smitten by her. Why was she then spending the day with another man she had just met? It was crazy. She started to cry. She wasn't sure why she was crying. Gabry reached over and held her hand.

"Everything will work out. Follow your heart and not your mind," she whispered to Trudy. "And don't listen to me, I worry too much."

At the intersection to Townsend they saw plenty of folks playing in the water even though it was now evening. Yellow and black tire tubes carried kids in the current toward Townsend. A couple of minutes later Nick pulled into the gravel parking lot of "Little River Bar-B-Que." They could smell the barbeque as they walked toward the door. Smoke rolled from under the smoker beside the restaurant. A waitress seated them on the back deck overlooking the river. Kids and parents were getting out of the water and carrying their inner tubes to the rental shop next door. The diners were surrounded by laughter.

"What can I get y'all to drink?" the teenage waitress named Betty Joe asked.

They ordered drinks and the Mason jars were delivered in a jiffy. "I'd be happy to take y'all's order now if y'all are ready."

Everyone ordered pulled pork sandwiches and coleslaw except for Trudy, she ordered two.

"Two," Gabry gasped.

"You must'a worked up an apptite today hikin' 'em mountains," Betty Joe said.

"Yes, I did, dear," Trudy said.

"You two ladies are so purty," Betty Joe told them as she looked at them.

"Thank you, you're very sweet," Gabry said. "You're awfully cute yourself."

She was cute. Her face was young and covered with freckles and she had strawberry blond hair cut short. She was a doll.

"Thank ya. I'll gather your food right up for y'all."

Trudy managed to eat both large sandwiches and coleslaw and

had room for blackberry cobbler. "The cobbler was not nearly as good as yours," Nick told her. They left Betty Joe a big tip and left for Cades Cove full and happy.

It was seven forty-five before they got to the cove. Trudy and Vincent marveled at the beauty. Gabry couldn't believe how different it looked in the evening light. An even deeper calm fell over the area with the sun making its way toward the mountaintops. Herds of deer grazed in almost every field. Evening shadows crept across the meadows, covering the groundhogs as they munched on the clover. Rabbits chased each other around and around. Squirrels sat on fence posts looking for handouts of nuts from passing motorists who ignored the "Do Not Feed the Animals" sign posted as they entered the cove.

They stopped to look at an old Methodist country church and walked among the tombstones that stood beside the church. Most carried dates from the 1800's. Infant graves told tales without speaking a word. Trudy walked with her hands tucked inside Vincent's arm. She watched Nick and Gabry walk hand in hand laughing and caring for each other. She longed for that in her life. She then knew what she had to do. She knew what her heart was telling her.

They stopped at the visitors' center to visit the restrooms and then walked to the farmhouse at the rear of the property. Dusk was quickly coming as they circled the house. Most folks were heading for their cars. Trudy saw something move in the tall weeds next to an outbuilding behind the house. "Nick, something is over by that building."

The four watched as a bear lumbered from the cover of the weeds and was followed by two cubs. Nick slowly motioned for everyone to climb up on the back porch of the house. They watched the bears from that viewpoint. One of the cubs turned and smelled the ground in their direction. He left his mom's side and walked toward the porch with his head down. Nick whispered to Gabry, "This isn't good."

Right at that time the cub looked up and saw the four humans watching him. He stopped dead in his tracks, not knowing what to do. The mother and other cub were scratching the bark of an old apple tree unaware of the cub's discovery. Nick tried waving the cub away. But he stood on his back legs and roared. The sound would have been hilarious, if the mother hadn't looked over and seen her baby in danger. She turned and ran toward the porch at them. Nick knew there was no escaping the mother if she wanted them. He quickly put Gabry and Trudy behind him and Vincent backed up against the porch wall.

He whispered to everyone, "Stay still and quiet."

The black bear growled at the cub as though she told him, "Go to your brother." The cub turned and ran. The mother bear pawed the ground and roared much louder than the cub had. To Nick's extreme unbelief a little six-year-old girl came running around the side of the house screaming, "You can't catch me."

Nick instinctively jumped the porch railing and grabbed the laughing girl as she unknowingly ran directly toward the bear with her head turned. The young girl's mother wasn't far behind. When she saw Nick tightly holding her daughter she screamed. Vincent picked up an old bucket that was standing next to him on the porch and ran to the railing and threw it at the enormous bear. With a bucket falling at his paws and all the commotion and screaming, the bear decided it was time to lead her cubs out of the area. She ran out of the yard and into the dark woods behind the old house.

Nick handed the frightened crying girl to her young mother. Gabry and Trudy hurried off the porch and attempted to calm the mother and daughter. Gabry carefully explained what had happened to the crying mom. The mother soon realized that her daughter was heading straight into the arms of an angry black bear. She hugged Nick and Vincent and thanked them over and over. They walked to the visitors' center and reported the incident. She told the ranger how Nick had saved her daughter's life with Vincent's help.

The ranger had them fill out a report and sign it. Everyone laughed and hugged before they separated. Gabry told the mother, "Nick's our guardian angel."

"I'm so happy he was there," the mother agreed.

They drove slowly on around the cove talking about how unbelievable the event was that had just happened. "I think I got a good picture of the bear," Gabriella told them. "That was something we'll remember the rest of our lives."

"I didn't think the rest of our lives were going to last much longer," Trudy added.

Darkness was taking over as they passed by the field where Gabry and Nick had fallen in love. Nick told them that he would drive back through Cades Cove Friday on their way home.

In the darkness the others didn't notice his tears as he drove. He knew God had placed him in that spot to save the young girl. The event could have easily become tragic. Nick was humbled by the experience. He realized that God was using him here in Tennessee, but he didn't know why. He was no one special. He figured he was just a man doing his best to make the world a little better. He only wanted to treat others as he would want them to treat him. What was so special in that? Wasn't that the Golden Rule? Still, he knew God was leading him. The thought of how God was using him scared him as much as pleased him.

I came to Tennessee to get away from people, but God keeps putting more and more people in my path, he thought as he wiped the tears. Gabry saw them finally and held his hand.

23

Wednesday morning they went downstairs at eight to meet Wade. He was waiting in the lobby for Trudy when they exited the elevator. Trudy introduced everyone.

"It…it's a real pleasure meeting everyone. Trudy told me so much about each of you yesterday."

"Wade, do you mind if we join the group for breakfast? They insist on checking you out. I have to get their approval, especially Vincent's, before I can spend the day with you."

"I would love to."

Nick laughed and said, "You make it sound like we want to check out the inside of his mouth. Open up! Let's see those teeth." They all laughed and then drove to the Pancake Pantry and were seated near the back.

"This is my favorite restaurant also," Wade told them.

The breakfast went well. Gabry thought Wade was charming and genuine. Nick liked his candor and relaxed demeanor. Nick told him how much he liked the Carter house. "My dream house is a Timberframe," Nick told him.

"You'll have to come see mine sometime. It's not real big, but I built it right. A large stone fireplace, open oak staircase and wide hickory planks for the flooring."

Nick told him he would love to. "It sounds like a great place."

Nick and Gabry decided to drive to Cataloochee, on the eastern side of the Smokies, to see the elk herds that had been introduced to the park a few years earlier, something Nick had always wanted to do. He invited Wade and Trudy to join them.

"Thank you, I'd love to, except I've always wanted to see the flame azaleas on Andrew Bald. They're supposed to be perfect right now," Wade explained. "You could join us."

They decided to go their separate ways but were going to meet at the Park Grill for dinner at six thirty. Wade and Trudy dropped Vincent off at the hotel so he could meet Fred at nine. Vincent told Wade that he had his permission to take Trudy, "But take care of her. She's special to us all."

"Thank you, Vincent. I can understand why." Wade drove away toward Clingmans Dome where the trail started for Andrew's Bald. He was looking forward to getting to know Trudy. Wade asked Trudy, "Tell me about Trudy Flynn."

"I told you just about everything yesterday."

"There's got to be more. I want to know everything."

"I don't think I know you well enough for all that."

"Tell me what you're comfortable telling me."

"Okay. I'm a simple girl trying to make a difference in life. I love to have fun. My first marriage wasn't fun, so I left."

"Do you ever regret that decision?"

Trudy looked at Wade and he continued, "I mean, I know you said he was abusive. But do you ever think maybe you should have stayed and tried longer?"

"No, not at all. He had chance after chance to change. I had taken too much abuse."

"Good," Wade said.

"I regret not listening to my parents. They tried telling me he was trouble. I was young and wanted out of the house. He was my escape. But, I'm happier now than I've ever been. I have really great friends."

"Yes, you do."

"I love teaching my Sunday school class and running the restaurant. Life is good now."

"Have you been dating anyone?"

Trudy had failed to tell Wade about Dr. Walker Green. So she began telling Wade about the operation and about meeting Dr. Green. She knew her feelings for the doctor weren't very strong or she wouldn't have been on a date with Wade. She explained that they had dated a couple of times but nothing was serious. She went on and told Wade about Nick's arrival and the effect he'd had on the community.

They arrived at the Clingman's Dome parking lot and found the trailhead for Andrew's Bald. Wade had bought lunch and placed it in a backpack for when they arrived at the bald. They walked and talked all the way while getting to know each other better. Wade ended up having to answer all of Trudy's questions, which were many.

~

Fred arrived at the hotel at nine, and he and Vincent decided to go to the new Ripley's aquarium to see the sharks. Next they went to the Mysterious Mansion and were scared out of their wits with all the ghosts, monsters, and goblins. They ate lunch and then went to the Guinness World Records Museum and then to the Ripley's Believe It or Not Museum. The day was tremendous fun for the two men acting like children again. Nick and Gabriella drove to Cataloochee. The drive took well over an hour to get there. It gave Nick and Gabry a chance to talk. Gabriella said, "It seems I've known you for years, Nick. Why is that?"

"I don't know. It does seem a lot longer than it's been."

"Do you think it's because we're so comfortable around each other?"

Nick smiled and said, "Are you really comfortable around me?"

"Of course. Don't you feel like that around me?"

"Are you kidding? I'm as nervous as a hen in a fox den when I'm with you."

"You are not," Gabry said as she hit Nick on the arm.

"I'm scared that you'll look at me and wonder why you're with me. You'll see my insecurities and faults and decide to find someone else."

She squeezed his hand. "You are kidding, right?"

"When a wife decides to find someone else and then divorces him, it doesn't leave a guy with a lot of confidence. I'm unemployed and almost broke. Not a lot to offer a beautiful successful woman such as you."

"You're serious. Nick, you are the most wonderful man. You are kind, generous, loving, handsome, and a great kisser."

"So you think I'm a good kisser, huh?"

"I do. I love you so much, Nick."

"I love you." Nick wanted to ask Gabriella to marry him, but he would not do it without having a job. When he got back home he was going to make that his main priority.

They arrived at Cataloochee and marveled at the beauty. At the edge of a field they saw elk grazing on the grasses. Gabriella pulled out the binoculars and they sat and watched the magnificent animals. They spent the rest of the day taking short walks and studying the history of the area. They walked arm in arm acting like the couple in love that they were. They kissed often and Gabriella took plenty of pictures for possible future paintings.

They came across wild turkeys in a field and followed them for an hour until they were almost lost.

~

Trudy and Wade, after walking for nearly ninety minutes, arrived at Andrew's Bald. Trudy knew she had never seen such beauty as the orange-flamed azaleas. The bald was full of large azalea bushes stretching to over ten feet high and wide. The view was astonishing on top of the mountain. She posed by the orange blooms and had Wade take her picture. She had worn tan cargo shorts and an orange tank top.

Wade cried out, "Where did you go? I can't find you in the flowers." Her top matched the flowers almost perfectly.

"Come over here, and you can touch all the flowers until you find me."

"Oh, yeah?" Wade walked over and began fondling the blooms until he touched the bottom on her top. "This feels different," he teased. He then pulled Trudy close to him and kissed her.

Trudy felt as though she was going to faint. The kiss was superb. Wade felt the same way. Then she did faint. Wade was holding her when she passed out. He carefully lowered her to the ground and placed her head gently on the grass. Wade knew Trudy had undergone surgery not long ago, but didn't know if this was from that. Wade took his shirt off and poured water on it and placed it on her forehead. He was beginning to get frantic.

A couple of minutes later Trudy came to. She asked, "What happened?"

"You either passed out or fainted—if there's a difference."

"So you decided to take off your clothes and take advantage of me," she said as she stared at Wade's strong chest.

He answered, "I do that to all the women who faint after I kiss them."

"You did kiss me, didn't you? It must have been quite the kiss. I don't really remember it very well. Maybe you should try it again."

"Perhaps, after we get to a lower elevation."

"I've got a good-looking, half-naked man bent over me and I can't lure him into kissing me again. I must be losing it."

"I don't think you've lost anything, beautiful," Wade promised.

Trudy tried to rise. "Why don't we rest here for a while? I've got some lunch for us." They spent the next thirty minutes eating lunch and teasing each other about the fainting episode.

Wade told her, "I could have taken off your top to use on your forehead."

"You're a good man, Wade Morgan."

~

That evening, everyone met for dinner at the Park Grill, a restaurant that was made with large timbers brought in from Utah. The place was wonderful with a large mural staring patrons in the face when they walked through the door. Real stuffed animals stood on the naked beams and a piano adorned the lobby. Trudy had talked Wade into calling his mom and aunts and asking them to come join the dinner party. They gladly accepted.

Trudy asked for a table for eight when they walked in. Nick and Gabriella arrived a few minutes later, and Vincent soon made his way to the restaurant. Wade introduced everyone and they were seated. Vincent sat between the two aunts, Grace and Faith. Wade's mother was named Pearl. It was easy to see that the three women were sisters. They all had the same eyes and round facial features. Pearl was the youngest at sixty-eight, Grace was seventy-three, and Faith was two years older and still hadn't lost her motherly tendencies toward her younger sisters.

After the park-ranger uniformed waitress took their drink order Nick asked, "How long have you three been sisters?"

They all three looked at Nick, either not knowing how to answer or trying to figure out the answer. He laughed and answered for them, "Probably all your lives, huh?"

Everyone laughed except for the three sisters. Faith then said, "No. I've only been a sister for seventy-three years of my life. The first two were spent quietly alone."

Grace spoke up and said, "You haven't ever done anything quietly in your life. You'll be telling God in heaven how he made this mistake and that mistake, on and on, over and over… if you get in."

Wade, embarrassed, said, "Ladies, we have guests."

Grace continued, "Well, just because her marriage was the most perfect in all history, I have to hear about why my marriages went kaput again and again."

"Well, if you would have put out every once in a while, you might have kept a husband longer than five years," Faith said for at least the hundredth time to Grace.

The waitress returned just in time with their drinks. Vincent was the only one that had ordered alcohol, having a glass of wine. He looked at the waitress and said, "Keep them coming. I'm going to need them."

Nick was so sorry after asking the question. Little did he know that the aunts could find anything to argue about.

"Are you an alcoholic, Mr. Marconi?"

"No. I haven't been."

"Alcohol is the devil's workshop." Faith said as she and Grace stared at him.

"Yes ma'am, but I'm not the devil." Trudy and Gabriella rolled their eyes at each other, wondering where this evening was going.

When the waitress returned, Gabriella asked loudly, "Bring us a bottle of wine, whatever Vincent is drinking. We can't let Vincent drink alone."

You could hear Faith and Grace huff out loud. "Well, I never."

The waitress soon brought the bottle and glasses. Trudy, Nick, Wade, and Gabry all accepted glasses. After a moment's pause Pearl said, "I would like a glass, dear."

Faith looked like someone had stuck a corncob in the wrong place. Her face puckered up and her wiry eyebrows lifted above her forehead.

"Don't you say a word," Pearl demanded as she shot a look toward Faith.

The waitress poured the wine into each glass. Nick had her stop filling his when it was only half full. Nick never drank, but he couldn't let his best friend, Vincent feel like a sinning alcoholic. Nick appreciated Gabry's love for Vincent and the gesture.

Gabry looked at Wade and Trudy sitting across from her and asked. "Please tell us about your hike."

Trudy laughed and said, "It was great until I fainted."

"You fainted?"

Trudy and Wade took turns explaining what had happened and

how he had kissed her, and then she passed out. Nick exclaimed to Wade, "Must have been quite a kiss!"

Trudy winked and said, "Yes, it was!" Everyone laughed, even the aunts.

Gabry was concerned about Trudy actually passing out. It had been seven weeks since her surgery and she wondered if the strenuous hike was too much, too soon.

Trudy sensed the worry from Gabry and said, "I'm fine now. I had no problem hiking back or anything. I think it really was the kiss." Trudy knew she was fine. She had been given great care from her doctor—Dr. Walker Green. She had not thought of Walker much since meeting Wade. It was strange how she had thought so much about Walker just two days before and now thirty-six hours later she only thought about him because of her health. Walker didn't give her the same spark, the excitement that she wanted and felt with Wade.

Kissing Wade was an adventure that she wanted to take over and over. Kissing Walker was just that and nothing more—a kiss. She felt it was great that a doctor had interest in a country girl like herself. She liked the thought of being a doctor's wife, but she knew it was not something that she could grow accustomed to. She already knew it would get old, always waiting for your husband to come home and him leaving at odd times, emergencies coming up and so many long hours. Not the life she thought she could get used to.

Nick asked Vincent, "How did your day go with Fred?"

Vincent explained all the things they did. The group was astounded at the places they'd gone. Then Vincent said, "It went very well until the end of the day. As we were leaving and saying good-bye, he kissed me."

Everyone stared at Vincent and finally Trudy yelled out, "He did what?" Others began asking questions and laughing and talking over each other. The table was abuzz.   Vincent held his hands up and then said, "And then I fainted."

Everyone including the aunts began laughing after realizing that Vincent was making it up. He continued, mocking Trudy, "I guess it was the kiss that made me pass out. He was such a great kisser." Trudy was laughing so hard wine came up out of her nose and she grabbed her napkin and covered her face. The crowded restaurant stopped to see where the laughter was coming from. Gabriella got up and walked over behind Vincent and bent down to kiss him on the cheek. "That was so funny," she told him.

"So did you and Fred pick up those whippersnappers you were looking for?" Nick asked.

Vincent smiled and said, "Well, we saw these two lovely ladies, Faith and Grace, across the street and thought about picking them up."

"And what stopped you?" Wade asked.

"Fred said he had heard that Grace didn't put out." That did it. The table erupted in laughter again. Wade's mother Pearl was holding her sides. They hurt so badly from the laughter. The aunts took it all very well.

Grace put her arm around Vincent and said, "A gal might just change for the right man."

Faith joined in, "It's been so long, she's technically a virgin again."

Pearl said over the laughter, "What do you mean—again?"

The evening turned out to be tremendous fun. Everyone told stories, drank wine, and laughed. Nick's wine sat in front of him. He sipped it a time or two and drank his diet Pepsi. The aunts turned out to be great fun to listen to. As they left the restaurant Trudy and Wade said their good-byes. He was taking his aunts and mother home the following morning. Wade kissed her again, and Trudy was able to keep her feet under her this time. Wade promised to call Trudy when she got home Friday. They were going to spend the evening together Saturday.

The four friends walked across the street toward their hotel after a long day. They had stayed at the Park Grill so long that it was dark out. As they walked they laughed about the evening's fun. Nick had decided to drive them across the park to Cherokee, North Carolina, the next morning and had something special planned for Thursday evening. Nick and Gabry took a walk along the river talking about the day and evening and kissed goodnight before going to their rooms. Trudy lay on her bed in the hotel room and was already missing Wade.

~

The following morning they walked to Bennett's for breakfast. The restaurant had a good breakfast buffet and fruit bar. Sausage and bacon, biscuits, gravy, and eggs were a few of the items. It was really a feast. Nick then drove them across the mountain range to Cherokee. They spent the morning exploring the different shops. Lots of Indian crafts were for sale. It turned into a very relaxing day. They returned to Gatlinburg in time to take a late afternoon hike to Grotto falls along the Roaring Motor nature trail. The hike was a little over a mile up to the falls.

The beautiful trail traveled through large gullies filled with tall trees and soft grasses as they made their way up the sides of the mountain. When they arrived at the falls they saw that they could actually walk behind the twenty-five-foot falls and have the water drop in front of them. The spray from the water felt good in the late afternoon warmth.

When they returned to the vehicle from the hike they headed off to dinner. As they ate Nick said, "I have something planned for later. We can go back and freshen up, and we need to leave by eight."

"What are we doing?" Trudy asked.

"Can't tell you, but I will tell you that you won't believe what you see."

"You've piqued my interest," Vincent stated. They had an hour before they had to leave so Nick jumped in the shower. Vincent laid

253

down for a catnap. Trudy and Gabry both showered but left their hair alone. Nick knocked on their door at eight and Trudy came to the door in her bra and no top. "Come in," she offered.

"I'll wait."

"You've never seen a woman in a bra? It's just like a bathing suit bikini."

Gabry came to the door ready and said, "Trudy, will you please put your top on? You're making me feel very inadequate."

"Okay. But I had to answer the door."

Nick whispered to Gabry, "You will never be inadequate. You're perfect." She kissed him lightly.

Nick drove them past the Sugarlands visitor center to the Elkmont campgrounds where he parked. There were lots of other people parking and walking down a wide trail. The four of them followed. Trudy asked, "What are all these people doing here? Why are we following them?" Just as the words left her mouth she saw Wade standing in front of her. She ran to him and threw her arms around him and kissed him. "What are you doing here?"

"I came for the show."

"What show? Are they playing a movie out here?"

Wade looked at Nick and asked, "You haven't told them yet?"

"No. Not yet. Go ahead."

Wade began explaining, "We're here to see the fireflies."

"What?" the other three asked in unison.

Nick took over, "The lightning bugs are a big attraction in these woods. They're called synchronized fireflies. They all light up at the same time. You have to see it to appreciate how wonderful it is."

Wade explained, "They've only been discovered in three or four places in the world and this is one of the places. Nick told me he was bringing you here tonight and I couldn't miss it. I came back to see it with you."

Vincent asked, "Seems like I read about this once. Have you guys seen it?"

They both answered yes. "Earlier in the month they bring bus loads of people in here and you're not allowed to drive in," Wade said.

Trudy asked, "Let me get this right. Everyone just sits in the woods waiting for it to get dark and they watch the fireflies."

"That's all. But it's very romantic. It's like being serenaded by candlelight," Nick explained.

Trudy looked at Wade and said, "So, you want to sit in the dark woods with me and be serenaded by fireflies."

"I can't wait."

"So, you're a big romantic."

"You got a problem with that?" Wade smiled.

"Not at all," Trudy smiled back.

They arrived at a small glen where people were scattered about in groups. Some standing, others sitting in lawn chairs, on blankets and fallen logs. A few cameras were in place on tall tripods to take pictures of the phenomenon. Children were excited, but asking their parents questions about why they were there, much like Trudy and Gabry did. It was understandable, since it wasn't often people wandered into the forest and waited for it to get dark, especially parents with children.

As it got darker, the anticipation grew. They could feel the excitement all round them. The first lone lightning bug was spotted and people pointed it out to others as though a falling star had streaked across the sky.

Nick had brought blankets from his SUV for everyone to settle down on. Gabry and Trudy were sitting back in the arms of Nick and Wade. Vincent met an older couple, Bill and Pat Ramsey who had come up from Nashville to see the spectacle and he had taken residence on their log with them. Anticipation rippled through the crowd.

Nick was kissing the back of Gabriella's neck when the show began in earnest. At first a few fireflies were spotted rising from the grasses. Then the woods quickly filled with flashes of light hovering above the forest floor. In unison they flashed on and off five times. There was a long moment's hesitation and then they flashed on and off five times again in perfect harmony. At each beginning the numbers grew greatly until the woods lit up like stars on the smooth surface of a lake

Gabry told the group that it looked like someone had put out small twinkling Christmas lights throughout the woods. As far as their eyes could see, lights went on and off, on and off. Gabry and Trudy quickly realized that this was one of the most magnificent and beautiful sights they had ever seen. Nature doing something totally unexpected, and it left you wondering why. What made these fireflies do this? This question entered most of their minds. The fireflies weren't different in any way from others except for blinking in unison, but it made them so special and unique.

People sat all over the glen, stood on the path, and even wandered into the woods. The show continued for some time until the fireflies finally rose up into the trees. The meadow emptied of most of the watchers, leaving couples sitting in the dark.

"It was romantic," Gabry told Nick.

"You make everything I do romantic," Nick answered as he kissed her. Trudy and Wade slipped off the blanket and walked toward the path arm in arm.

"This has been a wonderful week," Gabriella told him.

"It has. What do you think of Wade and Trudy?"

"They seem great for each other. You're a guy. What do you think about Wade?"

"Thanks for noticing. I think he's the real thing. He's very respectful when talking about Trudy. He was genuinely excited about coming back this evening to see the fireflies with Trudy. I think he's a great guy. What you really want to know is; are his intentions honorable?"

"Yes. Exactly."

"In my judgment, they are. It's my intentions on this blanket here in the dark that you need to worry about!"

"Oh, yeah."

24

The next morning, Nick took the suitcases down to the parking garage and loaded them. Two more of them ended up on top due to all the purchases on the trip. They had decided to drive back to Cades Cove after breakfast on their way home. Everyone wanted to go around the eleven-mile loop again. They stopped at the overlook on the west end of the cove and spent an hour just watching the deer in the meadows and fields.

While there, Nick explained his love for the cove. "Each time I come here I'm treated to something new. The sighting of a different animal, or the way the mountains are covered by sunshine, or clouds, or smoky haze. A person could even find love here. This is a very special place to me." Gabry leaned over and kissed Nick on the cheek.

As they were returning to the vehicle Nick saw a rare Pileated woodpecker at the edge of the woods hopping from stump to log to tree. "There's an example of what I was talking about."

Trudy did her best Woody Woodpecker imitation, which wasn't very good. They all laughed.

On the way through Townsend they stopped at a small drive-up, hamburger shop that Nick knew served great burgers. For some reason there were bluebirds flying all around the joint. When the sun hit their backs as they flew the blue of their feathers were brilliant in color. They were enormous entertainment while they ate.

When they continued toward home Trudy pulled out a bag. "I'm always the one to bring dessert. Today is no different. Here you go." She pulled out chocolate replicas of Dolly Parton's boobs and passed them out to everyone. The gang laughed and ate chocolate boobs all the way home.

"Best gift I've ever been given," Vincent joked.

"Amen," Nick agreed.

"Great chocolate," Gabry said.

As they neared home Vincent thanked everyone for including him. "I had a wonderful time. The mountains are amazing. It won't be my last trip there."

Nick answered, "Vincent, it wouldn't be the same without you. I'm glad you enjoyed it."

Vincent laughed and said, "I'd like to thank you for placing me between Faith and Grace at dinner."

Trudy said, "It took a strong person. We knew you could withstand it."

After Vincent and Trudy were dropped off, Nick and Gabriella went to her house to unload her bags. "Can I go with you to pick up Chester?"

"Sure." They hopped back into the car and headed for Josh's.

Halfway there, Gabry asked Nick, "Will you always love me?"

Nick looked over at her. She appeared to be very serious. "Sweetheart, to stop loving you would be like trying to hold back the wind. I'd never be able to hold it back, and I'll never be able to stop loving you."

Gabry lifted his hand and kissed it.

Gabry surprised herself by asking him the question. She wasn't sure why she did other than wanting Nick to know that she wanted his love forever. His answer surprised her. It was so natural, with no hesitation, as if from his heart. It was as though he was certain about his love for her. It pleased her greatly. "I'll love you forever, Nick."

When Nick drove into Josh's driveway they saw Chester and Josh in the side yard playing. Chester looked up and saw Nick opening the door and ran straight to him. He whined and whimpered and barked as Nick petted and rubbed his ears. He then ran to Gabry and jumped up on her leg to get petted. Josh was close behind, and Nick and Gabry gave him a hug.

"How was your trip?"

"Wonderful. I'm going to have to take you there someday."

"Great."

"It looks like Chester did well this week. Thanks for taking care of him."

"I loved it. Mom even enjoyed having him here."

Nick got back into the SUV and brought out a large bag and handed it to Josh. "What is this?" Josh asked.

"A gift for taking such good care of Chester." Josh opened the bag to see a bow and two arrows.

"Wow, Nick, thanks!"

Nick explained, "It was made by the Cherokee Indians."

"It's so great." He hugged Nick again.

Nick loaded all of Chester's things and asked Josh, "Are you still working tomorrow at the store?"

"Yeah."

"I'll pick you up early and we'll eat at Trudy's."

"Okay. See you tomorrow. Bye, Miss Gabry."

When they pulled out of the driveway Gabry said, "He doesn't seem like the same boy, Nick."

"He's changed a lot."

"You realize it's all because of you, don't you?"

"No. He's just growing up. Vincent has been great for him. Been like a grandfather to him."

Chester was sitting in Gabry's lap. She told Nick, "You're a humble man, Nick."

"God's love humbles us." When she leaned over and kissed Nick on the cheek Chester began licking Nick's face also.

"All kinds of kisses. I'm not sure which one was the best," Nick smiled.

The three of them spent the rest of the day and evening together talking and enjoying the peaceful quiet of the place, loving each other. Nick filled the birdfeeders and they watched the birds return. They watched the sun go down and the moon rise.

~

SATURDAY, JUNE 30TH

Josh and Nick walked into Trudy's Eating Place. Vincent had his table already saved for them. Trudy hurried over and gave Josh a kiss on the cheek and a hug.

Tom yelled, "You didn't do that when I walked in."

"I save my kisses for cute younger men, you old fool." Josh laughed and his smile lit up the restaurant.

"Isn't he a bit young for you?" Tom cried.

"Maybe, but you're definitely way too old for me, you old goat."

"*Na-a-ah,*" Tom mocked. The whole restaurant began doing goat imitations.

"Everyone is so funny this morning. What would you two handsome men like for breakfast this morning?"

Josh spoke up, "I'd like the French toast and sausage links."

"I'll have the same. You seeing Wade this evening?"

"Why do you think I have this large smile across my face?"

"We thought it was for us."

"It partially is," Trudy said as she turned toward the kitchen.

Vincent told Josh about the bear story. How Nick had grabbed the little girl just in time and saved her from running into the bear's arms.

In a few minutes Trudy came back with the orders. Nick got three sausage links and Josh four. Vincent looked at Nick and said, "You've been replaced."

"Apparently so."

Nick and Josh helped Vincent all day at the store. Since the store had been closed all week they were especially busy during the day.

Nick walked into the office where Vincent was sitting. "I'll miss not having our dinner party this evening," Vincent said to Nick.

"It will be different, that's for sure. I think Trudy believes Wade might be the guy she's been waiting for."

"He's a good man." Vincent observed, "It's funny that both of the guys' names started with a 'w.' I keep getting confused."

"I think she's gone through the alphabet. She's at the bottom. All that are left are x, y, and, z and there aren't many of them around."

"You mean Zorro doesn't live in Sleepy Valley. I would like for everyone to find the right person like I found with Maria."

"I've found my Maria," Nick smiled.

"When are you going to pop the question?" Vincent asked. "Pardon me if I'm being too nosy."

"Not at all, Vincent. As soon as I find a good job. I can't ask her to marry me until I have a job."

"I can understand that. I respect that."

"You're welcome to come over this evening, Vincent."

"Thank you, son, but I'm pretty tired. I think I'll rest this evening. You can have an evening alone with Gabriella."

"That would be nice." Nick walked over to the phone and called Gabry.

~

Monday evening Nick was working on his path. He had worked on it Sunday afternoon and all day Monday. It was really coming along and would soon be done. He heard footsteps and voices moving toward him from the cabin. Chester had already romped off toward the sounds. Gabry and Tom soon appeared on the trail.

"Well, hello, Tom. Good to see you." Nick kissed Gabry hello. "What brings you out here?"

Gabry answered first, "Tom called me looking for you."

"I've been by a couple of times but couldn't find you. Didn't know you took up residence in the woods."

"I've been in here for almost two solid days working on the path."

"It's a great idea," Tom complimented him. "I love this place."

Tom looked around at the path and continued, "Principal Sage Nickell at the county high school is looking for a teacher and head basketball coach. The past coach up and retired a week ago. He asked me to have you come in to see him about the position."

"How did he know about me?"

"I happen to be president of the school board. I gave him your name. He checked on your performance in Chicago and wants to see you. The job is pretty much yours if you want it. Not many good coaches banging down the door for a job in these parts."

"Do you have a number for me to call?"

"You have an appointment with him tomorrow afternoon at two in his office. I knew you were taking Josh fishing in the morning."

"I could cancel the fishing if he would rather meet in the morning."

"Nick, nothing is more important than what you're doing for that boy. Enjoy the morning with Josh and see Sage at two. He'll wait."

"I can't thank you enough, Tom. Let's go back to the house and celebrate with a cola."

"I'd love to, but tonight is date night. My wife and I always go out for dinner and sometimes a movie in Pineville on Tuesdays. I can't keep her waiting."

"You're a good man, Tom."

"Don't worry about wearing a suit and tie tomorrow. He likes casual." Tom turned to walk away.

Nick and Gabry hurried to catch up and walk out with him.

The next morning Nick took Josh wading in the creek. The fishing was slow due to the heat, but they had tremendous fun splashing and swimming. Josh went back to the store for the afternoon. Nick went for his interview.

Nick took Tom's advice and wore tan Columbia pants and a blue golf shirt. Mr. Nickell welcomed Nick by shaking his hand and then said, "Walk with me."

They walked down the wide hallway of the school toward the gymnasium. Sage talked about the tradition of the school. "We don't win a lot of games here, Nick. We're a small school, but we do try to do it the right way." Nick looked at each picture they passed. A framed picture of each basketball team since 1950 lined the left wall to the gym doors. The girls' teams were on the right wall. The doors to the gym split two large trophy cases. A few old trophies stood in the case and some basketballs signed by players. Nick stopped and studied the case.

Mr. Nickell opened the doors to an old gym that Nick knew was full of great memories for thousands of people. The old built-in bleaches went high on both sides of the court. The bottom row that almost touched the court sent shivers up Nick's spine. He thought of the screaming crowds cheering on the local team of Friday nights. He imagined his voice going out on him midway through the fourth quarter as he yelled instructions.

Nick walked over to the bench and sat down. "Which is the home side?" Nick asked.

"Your choice, Nick. You're the coach." Sage smiled.

"You're kidding, just like that?"

"Watching you walk down the hallway told me everything I needed to know." Sage had watched Nick look at the pictures and study the trophy case. He saw the look in Nick's face when he walked into the gym and sat on the bench. It was the final thing Sage needed to see. It didn't hurt to hear the wonderful stories about Nick from Tom and Andy. He even called Pastor Hill and Trudy. Nick was a man he could trust to do the best for the kids. The type of man he wanted for the position.

Nick silently thanked God as he walked out of the school building. He was thrilled to have a job and to be head coach of the Pine County High School Fighting Bears. He stopped in Pineville for an hour or so and then drove straight to Gabriella's. He found her in the shop with her hands in clay throwing a new bowl on the wheel. Gabry smiled as Nick made his way behind her and began to slip his hand inside her top.

"I have great news," he whispered in her ear.

"And what would that be?" Trudy had told Gabry that Sage had called her for a reference, so she knew Nick would probably get the job.

"You're looking at the next coach of the Fighting Bears."

"That is great news, Nick."

"How does it feel to be felt up by the head coach?"

"It's actually pretty exciting."

Nick kissed the back of her neck and asked, "Will you go to dinner with me to celebrate?"

"Of course. Let me finish this bowl."

"I'm going to run home to take Chester out for a walk. I'll pick you in an hour."

"Okay, darling." Nick started for the door and Gabry said, "Nick, congratulations."

"Thanks."

Gabriella could tell how excited Nick was in getting the job. She had been hopeful he would teach again and knew this job was a perfect fit.

When Nick walked into his house he noticed the flashing light on his phone's recorder. He hit play and listened to his mom ramble on. She asked for him to call her. It would have to wait till later.

That evening Nick and Gabriella spent the evening at the Oak Club eating dinner and listening to light rock oldies by a local band. They danced to the slow romantic songs, an excuse to hold each tight.

25

JULY 4ᵀᴴ

Nick picked up Josh and took him to Trudy's for breakfast. Nick wanted to spend part of the holiday with him. He told Josh about his teaching job at the school.

"At my school?"

"Yes. Is that a problem?"

"No. That's fantastic. What are you going to teach?"

Nick laughed, "In my excitement, I forgot to ask. I'm the new basketball coach though."

"Cool."

When Nick and Josh walked into the diner everyone stood and applauded. Men gathered around Nick to congratulate him. They offered him luck and of course, suggestions. Nick was very much surprised by all the attention. After everyone returned to their seats, Nick told Vincent, "I guess I don't have to tell you the news. I was going to surprise you this morning."

"No surprises in this town except yours I'd guess, by the look on your face," Vincent said.

Nick got up and walked over to the counter and thanked Tom personally for his help. "I owe you one," Nick told him.

Trudy was refilling Tom and Andy's coffee cups. Tom told Nick, "You could ask Trudy to unbutton another button on that blouse if you would."

Trudy put her hand on her hip and said, "Your heart isn't strong enough to handle that much of a good thing you old fool." Trudy had decided to open the restaurant even though it was the fourth.

She figured people liked to go out on holidays for breakfast and her restaurant was the only place in the village to eat. Trudy was closing the restaurant at eleven but paying Stella and the cooks for the whole day.

Nick followed Trudy into the kitchen and whispered to her.

"Okay," she agreed. She opened the fridge and handed something to Nick. Nick walked back out and got everyone's attention.

"I would like to present a special gift to Tom for helping me get the job at the school. Tom's affection for Trudy's breasts is no secret to anyone here."

"Yeah," Tom whooped.

"It's time we ended his longing. I'd like to present Tom with his own pair of Trudy's boobs."

Nick held the chocolate boobs up for all to see. The crowd erupted in laughter and gathered around to have a closer look.

Tom stood up after everyone returned to their tables. He pulled his handkerchief from his back pocket and wiped his eyes as though he had tears. He removed his hat and placed it on the back of his chair and began, "This is the best day of my life." Laughter filled the place. "I would like to thank all of you involved in getting me to this place in my life. I will cherish this moment for the rest of my days."

Trudy stood on the other side of the counter acting as though she was choked up. She pulled her apron up to wipe her fake tears.

"I can't eat these. I'll keep them under wraps and bring them out when I need them." Everyone was cracking up.

"Lastly, I would like to say, I'll fondle them with care, and I might take a lick every once in a while." Trudy shook her head.

"One other thing, please don't tell my wife I have these." Everyone applauded amid the laughter.

After the laughing died down Trudy said, "You old fool!"

All the businesses in Pine County donated money each year to buy fireworks for the Fourth of July celebration. The county park was where everyone gathered to watch the sky light up. As customers left, they told each other they would see everyone that evening at the park. The small village of Sleepy Valley became festive by attaching flags to the lampposts on Main Street. Windows were decorated with red, white, and blue bunting.

In the park that evening, a few vendors had snack booths placed near a small covered stage where live music played from six p.m. until the fireworks were about ready to begin. Nick and Gabry arrived a little after seven and Nick spread a blanket away from the stage under a tree but within distance to hear the music. A bluegrass band played song after song and closed with "Rocky Top."

They had eaten in Pineville before coming to the park. Gabriella decided she would like some cotton candy, so they walked around searching each booth. Vincent wasn't sure if he would attend, but Wade and Trudy were going to meet them at the park in time for the fireworks.

A familiar voice yelled and then came running up behind Nick and Gabriella. They saw Josh approaching when they turned. He told them he was there with his mom. Finally they saw Wade and Trudy strolling along in front of the booths. Trudy wore a sundress. The top was a swirling red, white, and blue. The skirt showed exploding fireworks in all different colors. This was one of her best. It was right up there with the sunrays drenching the wildflowers she had worn for the party at Vincent's.

"She looks so happy," Gabriella told Nick as they walked toward them and waved. They had to talk loud over the mandolin and banjo.

"He doesn't look very sad either."

After greeting each other Nick said, "Gabry thinks you two look happy."

"And what would Gabry know about being happy?" They all laughed.

"Our blanket is under that tree," Nick pointed. The evening

was perfect for a Tennessee Fourth of July. Nick bought two cotton candies.

Nick asked, "Have you guys seen Vincent?"

"No. Was he coming?" Trudy asked over the music.

"He said he might, wasn't sure. We ran into Josh and his mom. There they are—over there." Josh looked over and saw Trudy and ran back over for a hug.

Trudy introduced Wade to Josh. Josh joked, "You had better be good to Miss Trudy or you'll have to answer to me... and Nick."

"Hey, don't get me involved in your threats."

Josh left to go back to his mom. A new band took the stage and opened with "Rocky Top." Everyone around the stage was singing and clapping with the song, and a few were clogging on the plywood dance floor. Trudy told Wade, "That's the boy that Nick is spending time with that I told you about."

"Seems like a good kid," Wade said.

"He is," Nick confirmed.

They stopped and bought drinks to take back with them to the blanket. As soon as darkness fell on the park, the first explosion went off and the fireworks began. As the sky lit up, Nick remembered Gabriella's story about her favorite holiday. The Fourth she had spent with her mom a month before she died. Nick wondered if Gabry was thinking about it.

Trudy thought about the same thing. Did the fireworks sadden Gabry? Nick had his arm wrapped around Gabry as they lay on the blanket looking almost straight up to see the rockets explode above them. Gabry did briefly think of the evening with her mom long ago. But the thought quickly left her mind when Nick kissed her cheek and said, "I've never been happier."

When the sky exploded with what looked like a waterfall from heaven, the whole park erupted in unison with *oohs* and *aahs*. The show went on for over forty-five minutes. With the last explosions lighting the evening sky the band quickly took the stage and sung

"Rocky Top" again as the crowd of folks made their way to the parking lot and fields full of vehicles. The two couples stayed where they were, letting the park empty and watching the stars put on their own performance in the heavens.

"What are your plans Saturday, sweetheart?" Nick asked Gabry.

"A client is coming from Boston Saturday morning. He should be gone by noon, or one at the latest. I'm all yours after that."

~

Early the next morning Nick's phone rang. "Hello."

"Hi, Nick. I wasn't sure if you would be home."

"Hi, Melissa." His voice was not all that welcoming. Nick wanted to hang up the phone. He didn't want any turmoil in his life. He was happy and his life was back on track.

"I'm sorry I called. I thought about you when I woke this morning and for some reason I remembered how kind you were to me while I was in rehab. You saved my life. I know I would have died without your help." She hesitated to see if Nick was going to say anything. He didn't, so she continued, "I just wanted to let you know I'm doing great. I love my apartment that you and Gabry found for me, and I'm back in church. I've met a guy at church and we're dating. He's a good guy, Nick."

Melissa waited again for a response. "Well, I wanted to thank you again. I hope you're happy. Bye, Nick." Nick was surprised that that was it. He had been waiting for the *but,* or *I need you to,* or anything other than a *thank you.*

"Melissa."

"Yes."

"I'm very happy to hear that you're doing so well. I wish you nothing but happiness. I'm doing well also."

"How is Gabry, if you don't mind me asking?"

"She's doing great."

"She was so nice, and she's beautiful."

"I would tell her you said so, but I don't want it going to her head." They laughed together. "I landed a job at the local high school, teaching and coaching."

"That is so great. It sounds as though we both are doing well."

"Blessed, I would say."

"Yes," Melissa said before she hung up.

Melissa was not as well as she let on over the phone. She had met a man at church and was dating him, but she wasn't that crazy about him. She enjoyed his company and he helped ease the loneliness she felt since leaving rehab, but he couldn't replace Nick. She remembered how much she had loved Nick when they were first married. She wasn't sure when she had stopped being content with her marriage or why she thought she needed more than Nick had provided. She didn't know why she had insisted on more. Now she saw how immature and foolish she had been. Melissa longed to find someone to love her, someone she could love back as Nick had found. She asked herself why she had to lose Nick to realize how much she needed him.

Melissa also struggled with the urges to slip back to the life that sent her to the rehab center. In the lonely evenings when the TV offered nothing she wanted, she could almost taste the powdered relief waiting on the street. It was during that time she found strength in the Bible, in the love that Nick had offered while helping her, and also in her counselor. She spent hours on the phone talking until the urge left her, but it was constantly luring her back. She knew it would always be a struggle.

Nick spent all day Thursday and Friday working on his path. He had cleared the trail almost all the way to the second bridge. Late Friday afternoon, Chester came running up to Nick as he was cutting a bottom limb from a tree. He sat patiently waiting for Nick to notice him. The limb fell and Chester barked with a muffled sound. Nick looked around to see Chester sitting there with something in his mouth.

"What have you got there, Chester?" Nick placed his hand below the dog's mouth and Chester carefully opened it and a baby rabbit fell into Nick's gloved hands. Besides almost drowning in slobber from Chester's oversized lips, the little fellow seemed fine.

"Thank you for the gift, Chester. Where did you find it? His mother is probably worried about this little guy." Chester turned and ran off. Nick decided he had better follow. Chester stopped and looked back to see if Nick was coming. Chester had found the bunny nest and picked the one up when the baby wandered from its home and took it to Nick.

Nick thought the mother might accept the baby back since he had gloves on and hadn't touched the rabbit. Chester led Nick straight to the nest and he placed the baby with the others and covered it with the protective covering the mother had made. Chester just wanted to chase the mother. He had chased her time and time again. It always ended in the same futile result.

Nick decided it was time to quit for the day so they continued to the house. When he walked into his home another message flashed on the phone recorder. He pushed the button and heard Vincent's voice saying he was hosting a dinner party on Saturday evening—same time.

Nick knew it would be pushing his plans with Gabry for the afternoon but still thought they could return in time. Nick showered and he and Chester headed to Gabry's house. Nick knocked on the front door and got no answer. The front window was open so he yelled through the screen, "Gabry! Gabriella! Sweetheart!"

"Nick!"

"Yes!"

"Let yourself in. I'm jumping in the shower." Nick found the key under a rock and unlocked the door. He and Chester walked in. Chester went straight to the bed Gabry had bought him and laid down, making himself at home. Nick walked to the bathroom door and said, "Hello, in there."

"You can come in and talk to me while I shower if you want." Nick opened the door and leaned back against the sink counter. Gabry was standing inside the frosted glass shower stall. Nick could make out the silhouette of her body as the water ran over her head. He could see her hands move slowly along her body as she washed.

"It's too bad I just showered before I came over."

"Yes. That is too bad."

"For some reason though I'm feeling awfully dirty again."

"It could be because you're staring at me through the glass."

"Did you expect me not to watch?"

"I would be worried if you didn't," she laughed.

"Did you get a call from Vincent about dinner tomorrow night?"

"Yes. I told him it sounded great." She suddenly thought of the planned afternoon with Nick. "Was that okay?"

"Yes. We should be back by then. Could you call me as soon as your client leaves? Give us as much time as possible."

"Sure. Where are we going?"

"Surprise."

"Okay. I love surprises. Hey, you want to go out to dinner, or we could have leftover macaroni and cheese."

Nick laughed and teased, "And it's even leftover, huh?"

"Doesn't it sound great?"

"Yes. Going out for dinner does sound great."

Gabry asked Nick to hand her the towel and said, "I knew I could get you to take me out for dinner."

"You probably don't even have leftover macaroni and cheese."

"I do. But it's been in the fridge at least five days." Gabry grinned at Nick and kissed him as she came out of the shower with the towel wrapped around her body and tucked inside above her breasts. "Now go away so I can make myself beautiful for you."

Nick kissed her again and told her, "You're already beautiful."

On the way to the new Japanese restaurant in Pineville, Nick told Gabriella about the baby bunny and the call from Melissa. "What did you make from the call?"

"I think she's struggling. But we knew she would. It will probably be a struggle for a long time," Nick explained.

"Did she want anything?"

"No. She told me how nice and beautiful you were."

"That was sweet of her."

Nick and Gabry sat at the hibachi table with a family of six. They were celebrating the birthday of their oldest child. The Japanese cook came out and began cooking the food in front of them. It was tremendous fun as the cook told jokes and did tricks with the food. He made the onion into a steaming volcano and made happy faces with the rice. The meal was enormous fun, and Nick and Gabriella knew they would have to bring the gang back one evening.

26

Gabry woke up and hurried to get ready for her customer that was to arrive around nine. This was one of her biggest clients and usually bought a large number of paintings and pieces of pottery for her art gallery in Boston and New York.

Nick woke early and began preparing a picnic lunch for the trip. Josh and Vincent were keeping Chester at the store for the day. Chester enjoyed greeting the customers as they entered the store and in return they would bend down and pet him. Nick left the house to take Josh for breakfast at Trudy's. They tied Chester to a bench in front of the eating place. Stella came by to take the orders. "How are you handsome men doing today?"

"Okay."

"Good," Josh said.

Nick looked at Stella and said, "What's the special today—you?"

Stella looked at Nick and bent down and kissed him on the cheek. "That one I actually liked. Best one I've heard for a while. Nick, you might make something of yourself after all."

"Thank you, my sweet Stella."

They didn't have to wait long before their breakfasts arrived. Trudy took Chester some sausages and water.

"You treat that dog better than you do me," Tom complained.

Trudy shot back, "Maybe that dog is better than you."

"I can slobber and beg just as well as him."

"I know. I've watched you do it for years." Everyone laughed. "You slobber on your shirt every time I serve your food and coffee."

Tom replied, "Yeah, and I'd wag my tail and do tricks for you if I ever got that bigger peek."

"Okay, Tom. Here it is, your big chance to see these beauties. There's one trick Chester does—if you can do it, I'll show you my boobs."

Andy patted Tom on the back and said, "You'll be the top dog, Tom. You can do it."

Tom said, "Anything, just tell me what to do. I can fetch, roll-over, or play dead."

The café came to a deathly hush, waiting for the trick that Tom would have to do. It was his chance to finally see the mighty mounds of Trudy, the mountainous peaks of Flynn, the beauts of Sleepy Valley.

Trudy looked around the room studying the Saturday morning crowd and then told Tom, "Chester can still look adorable and cute after licking his privates."

Trudy's Eating Place actually shook from the laughter. The pictures on the walls were left crooked from the shaking. An antique coffee pot fell from a shelf, narrowly missing Avery Cook. The look on Tom's deflated face was priceless. He knew it wasn't a trick, but he also knew he couldn't argue. The crowd had spoken. Finally he laughed and conceded that he had been outsmarted again.

After the laughter died down Andy said, "You'll have to keep staring at the chocolate ones."

"I can't even do that."

"Why?" Stella asked from across the room.

"My wife ate them." Laughter filled the room again. "She didn't realize they were anything special. She just saw chocolate in the fridge."

Trudy walked by Tom, knocked off his hat and said, "You can't teach old dogs new tricks, you old fool."

Later, as Nick, Vincent, and Josh left the restaurant, Chester rose to meet them. Chester watched Nick walk away after a pat on the head and obediently followed Vincent and Josh to the store. Nick went back home to finish preparing the special lunch. He spent time waiting for the phone call, and cleaning the house well for the first time in a long time. Around noon the phone rang, and Nick answered.

"I'm ready," Gabriella announced.

"I'll be right there." Within minutes they were driving away from Sleepy Valley.

"Are you going to tell me where we're going?" Gabry asked.

"No. How did your meeting go?" Nick asked, to change the subject.

"Very well. You're changing the subject."

"Yes. Relax and enjoy the ride."

"Okay." The meeting had gone well. The client loved the new happier paintings, and ended up buying $35,000 worth of Gabry's work and ordered more.

"She didn't," Gabry screamed when Nick told her what Trudy told Tom he would have to do that morning. "In front of the whole Saturday crowd?"

"Yes. I've never heard such laughter."

"That girl will say anything. She has the biggest heart and sometimes the biggest mouth."

Nick laughed. "She's a one of a kind."

Nick placed a Sugarland CD in the player and turned it up. They listened and Gabry tapped her feet on the floorboard to the beat of the songs as Nick drove the familiar roads. As the CD ended Nick was driving through Townsend.

"I take it we're going to Cades Cove." Gabriella had suspicions that this might be the day Nick asked her to marry him. Why else would they be going back to Cades Cove so soon? She tried not to get her hopes up, but she had long ago given her heart to Nick. He was the person she wanted to spend the rest of her life with. She wanted to wear his ring and sleep next to him. Gabry wanted children with him.

"We could be. But maybe not," he said, trying not to give anything away.

Nick turned toward the cove and stopped at the campground for an ice-cream. He then drove around the cove, which was crowded with cars from the weekend crowd. He drove all the way around without stopping until he arrived at the spot where he and Gabry had napped two and a half months earlier. They got out and Nick raised the back door and removed the picnic basket and a large blanket. He led Gabriella across the same field to a spot under a large tree in the middle of the same field.

They walked across the field holding hands. Nick carried the basket and Gabry carried the blanket. It was a warm sunny day, but the shade of the tree gave relief and a nice breeze blew across the meadow. A few clouds floated lazily across the deep blue sky. Nick spread the blanket on the tall sweet grass. He opened the lid of the basket and brought out chilled cheese and strawberries, crackers for the cheese and had cold water and soft drinks. He had small plates and glasses for the drinks. They spent an hour or so eating and drinking and watching small animals and birds come near.

After eating, Nick put the leftovers away and then reached into the cooler and brought out clumps of grapes.

"Are you going to feed those to me?" Gabriella teased.

"I can do that." She laid her head in his lap, and Nick carefully placed the grapes one at a time into her waiting lips. They were large juicy red grapes and tasted better than anything she had eaten in a long time. A squirrel became curious and kept coming closer looking for handouts. Nick threw him a grape, which he quickly stuffed into his mouth.

"This was a great idea. I've come to love this place as much as you do."

"That's why I brought you here. I couldn't think of a better place to tell you something." He looked at her sitting across from him as they held hands.

"What did you want to tell me, sweetheart?" Gabry thought that she must have been wrong. She wanted Nick to pop the question and had hoped this would the day. But she knew she needed to be patient. It hadn't been that long for Nick since his marriage ended. She kept forgetting that fact.

"Please don't say anything till I finish."

"Okay." She was now worried.

He hesitated, wanting to get the words just right, "For the rest of my life I want to watch lightning bugs with you in the summer evenings. Every month I want us to look up into each full moon that shines above our home. I want to walk the path that God leads us on, arm in arm with you. I want to tell you that I love you like I've never loved before."

Tears of happiness were already running down Gabriella's cheeks. She let them fall into her lap. She didn't want to let go of Nick's hands.

"I want to make you happy and comfort you when you're sad. I want to sit for hours and watch you paint. I need you, Gabriella. More than anything I've ever wanted—I want you to be my wife." He reached into his pocket and pulled out a small velvet bag. He opened it carefully and pulled out a solid gold band cut with a beautiful design.

Nick hadn't been looking for love when he'd moved to Sleepy Valley. He thought he wanted just the opposite. Nick knew right away that God had Gabriella wait for him—his angel on earth. He loved her so much. Loving her was so easy. He wanted to spend the rest of his life with her.

He positioned himself on one knee while still holding Gabry's hands and asked, "Gabriella, I love you. Will you marry me?"

Gabriella wanted to say something poetic. She wanted to tell

Nick all the things she wanted for their life together. She felt very blessed to have God bring Nick into her life and wanted to tell him so. Loving Nick was so easy. But all she could do was cry and say, "Of course, I will."

She wrapped her arms around him and kissed him passionately.

After a few minutes Gabriella said, "You had me worried."

"Why?"

"You started out so serious."

"I was serious."

"I have to admit, I thought you were going to propose today."

"You already know me that well, huh?" Gabry was lying on the blanket and Nick leaned over her, kissing her face as they talked.

"I guess I've thought it every time we were together lately."

"I wanted to ask you every time we've been together."

"You have?"

"Of course I have. And sweetheart, you can pick out a diamond ring whenever you want. I thought we should go together to choose it."

"No. No. I love this one. I don't want a diamond. I never want to take this one off. I would have to take off a diamond ring every time I worked with clay. This is beautiful."

"When do you want to get married?" Nick asked.

"Now," Gabriella exclaimed.

"We have to get married in a church, that's my only request. You can have anything else you want."

They talked about the wedding before deciding it was time to head back to Sleepy Valley. They would have quite an announcement at Vincent's party tonight. As Nick drove back Gabry asked, "Where are we going to live, your place or mine?"

"We'll have to think about it. I love my land and the trail."

"I love it too, but my studio is at my place."

"Let's not worry about that now. We can live in a teepee for all I care, as long as I live with you."

Nick dropped Gabry off at her place, and he hurried home to shower and walk Chester before the party. The phone was ringing when he entered the house.

"Hello."

"I knew you would do it."

"Who is this?"

"Your sister. I knew you had to ask Gabriella to marry you soon," Laura said.

Nick was stunned. "How in the world did you know? Do you have someone spying on me?"

Laura laughed and said, "Gabry just called me and told me."

"I just left her a minute ago."

"It doesn't take long to say 'Nick asked me to marry him, and I said yes.' Do you want me to call Mom and Dad or are you going to?"

"Knock yourself out. Tell Mom I'll call her tomorrow. I'm leaving in a few minutes."

"Congratulations, Nick. You done good."

"Thanks, sis. I love you."

Nick walked into Gabry's house and yelled for her. She walked into the room and said, "You looking for me?" Gabriella was radiant. She had put on a skirt that hit just above the knee and a sleeveless blouse.

"You are gorgeous." Nick wrapped his arms around her and kissed her. "I get to marry you."

"You do?"

"Yes. My sister told me so."

"I had to tell her. I love Laura, and I've always wanted a sister. Did you mind?"

"Not at all. She was so excited."

They purposely walked in late so they could tell everyone at the same time. They assumed it would just be Vincent and Trudy. Apparently Wade and his mother Pearl had been invited.

Vincent greeted them and said, "This is the first time I remember you ever being late, Nicholas."

"There's a reason for that. We wanted everyone to be here when we announce…"

Gabry finished the announcement, "…we're engaged."

Trudy was already on her way to Gabriella. They hugged in the middle on the room and spun around like schoolgirls. Vincent and Wade congratulated Nick. Pearl told them how cute they were together.

Trudy had to hear everything. Where, how, when, what did he say, what did you do? "When is the big day? We have to have a big wedding at the church. The whole town will attend. I'll cater it. This is going to be so much fun. Of course, I'll be the maid of honor also. I am so happy for you." Trudy went on and on as she hugged Gabry again.

Vincent opened a bottle of his favorite wine and toasted the couple, "May you love each other forever as you love each other tonight."

Wade said, "You couldn't have picked a luckier day."

Gabriella asked, "What do you mean?"

He explained, "Today is 7–7–7, July 7th, 2007."

Nick or Gabry hadn't thought about it. Nick reply was, "It was definitely my lucky day, she said yes." Gabriella kissed him.

"Okay, that's enough of that. Let's eat, before we lose our appetite," Vincent said while chuckling.

They ate the delicious Italian dinner that Vincent had prepared and then played Pictionary. Later, Vincent played the violin for everyone. Pearl enjoyed it so much. Nick wondered if Vincent had invited Wade and Pearl or if Trudy had brought them. They were tremendous fun. Nick and Gabry both had a good feeling about Wade. Nick could see himself and Wade becoming good friends.

After the party was over Gabriella went back to Nick's house and discussed their wedding. They both decided they wanted to get married soon. No long engagement. They were sure of their love for one another and saw no reason to wait long. They were both so excited about becoming the Stewarts.

~

The next morning at church Josh was waiting for Nick and Gabry at the door they always entered. He smiled, and Nick knew that Trudy had already told him the news.

"So you've already heard, huh?"

"Miss Trudy told the whole class. Congratulations."

"Thank you, Josh," Gabriella smiled.

"Is Nick stilled allowed to go fishing with me?" He laughed as he was saying it.

"So, you've become a little smart aleck, have you?" Nick teased him.

"I just didn't know if you'd still be allowed to come out and play now that you'll have a wife and all," Josh continued. Gabry laughed.

Nick grabbed him in a headlock and said, "Come sit with us during church service."

"Okay, okay. I hope he doesn't abuse you like this, Miss Gabriella. I think you should wait until I'm old enough to get married."

"Hey," Nick objected.

"I'll think about it. That might be a better offer, a younger, better-looking man."

They all laughed as they walked to their seats.

After church they told Pastor Hill their plans and asked if he was available to marry them. "I'm very happy for both of you. I knew it wouldn't be long before you two were tying the knot. I'd be honored to perform the ceremony. I'll mark it on my calendar."

27

Nick woke early, excited for the big day ahead of him. He quickly thought there was a fire outside. The bright red and orange colors came through the bedroom window reminding him of the beauty that surrounded his house. It was the most wonderful autumn he had ever known. The trees were every color imaginable. His property had turned into the Master's landscape. Nick had finished the trail by August, and he and Gabry walked it almost every day with Chester.

Nick was the happiest he had ever been. Life was good. He loved the school and the kids loved him. The school had both junior high and high school in the same building. Nick had been given his choice of several classes to teach and he chose junior high history and a couple of math classes. He liked the idea of getting to know the younger kids when they first arrived at the school and having a relationship with them until they graduated.

Basketball practice would begin soon. He was looking forward to getting back into the routine of practice and the excitement of game nights.

Gabriella's paintings were more beautiful than ever. She had a gift of focusing on something other artists missed. She would turn the painting into a study. A person looking at one of her paintings would stare at it and try to figure out why it held their attention so. In one, a simple bluebird sitting on a small limb in a meadow somehow drew the attention of the eye. A viewer marveled at how that bird became the central point of God's creation in the painting. Gabriella was truly talented and blessed.

Gabry woke knowing she had a full day ahead of her. The day she had been looking forward to for a long time. The weather was perfect for a wedding. She couldn't wait.

Trudy couldn't sleep at all. She had poured everything into the wedding and wanted it to be perfect. In a few hours she would be standing at her best friend's side. She knew she would cry so she had bought some makeup that wasn't supposed to run with tears and hoped it worked. The church would be decorated with every kind of flower they could come up with. She wanted them all. If God created it, she wanted them there. With her own special touch to make it a festive and happy ceremony she ordered hundreds of balloons, every color in the rainbow. They were to be filled with helium and tied to the end of each pew.

Other balloons were to be released when they announced the bride and groom as husband and wife and would fall from the ceiling onto the guests.

A large reception in the recreation hall in the basement would follow the ceremony. A large multicolored cake would sit in the middle of the room with different-colored, paper tablecloths covering the rounds tables seating eight to a table. The church praise band was going to provide the music at the reception.

Trudy wanted it to be the most talked-about wedding ever in the state of Tennessee.

Nick was supposed to be at the church by one thirty. Gabry was already at the church making sure last-minute things were done. She had her hair appointment at ten. He probably wouldn't see her until she walked down the aisle. He knew she would be beautiful as always. Nick's parents were still asleep in the guest room. He decided to take Chester for a long walk. They exited the back door to a world of color. The morning breeze was cool but had a warming hint to it, telling all that the day was going to be perfect. The colored leaves of the maples and oaks and ashes and elms contrasted against the deep green of the pines.

Nick prayed while they walked along the trail. He thanked God for Gabriella, the school, his home, his church, and his friends. He prayed for God's blessings on the marriage. He prayed for guidance, patience, and love. He prayed with humility and for more of it. He prayed again for Melissa.

Nick and Chester crossed the first bridge, and when they got near the clearing, Nick heard noises. He put Chester on the leash and slowly moved to a point where they looked out on the meadow. Two large bucks were snorting at each other in the middle of the clearing. Steam was shooting from their noses. Nick knelt behind a large fallen log and placed Chester beside him. Chester watched the bucks with great interest. Nick noticed a doe standing to the right of him at the edge of the field. She had her head held high and her white tail raised waiting for the victor.

The bucks then lowered their heads and slammed hard into each other's antlers. They locked in tremendous battle. Their muscles rippled in the morning sun. They shoved and pushed with all their might, each knowing what the winner had in store. Nick had been told about the rutting ritual but had never seen it with his own eyes. He had heard it was very dangerous to get close to rutting bucks. They would attack anything that moved. He felt so blessed to see this battle of supremacy and to see it on his property. He wished Gabriella were with him or that he had brought his camera.

Nick noticed something strange. There were always small animals making noise and birds following and flying around him in the woods. But with the rutting going on, it was as though all of creation had stopped their routines to watch this ritual. There was total silence in the woods except for the sounds of the proud bucks fighting over the right to mate with the doe. The battle went on for nearly a half hour before one was forced to his knees. He quickly ran off in defeat while the winner followed the doe into the woods.

Nick stayed there for a while wanting to make sure the bucks were gone. He also wanted to let the image of what he had just seen be absorbed into his thoughts. He wanted to be able to retell the battle just as it was.

Nick and Chester rose from behind the log and Nick disconnected the leash. Chester ran out to where the battle had taken place and smelled the musk aroma left by the bucks. The squirrels began chattering and birds flew throughout the meadow. The trees filled with singing again. Nick was always awed by nature, but never as much as he was on that beautiful October day. Nick and Chester spent most of the morning in the woods.

As they finished their walk Nick thought about the time he had spent in Sleepy Valley. It had become a salvation to Nick in the six months he had lived there. A new life and a new beginning with all the happiness he could possibly imagine. The love that Christ showed him he was able to show others. It wasn't solitude and loneliness he wanted. It was the chance to share his love that he wanted, and to have love shown to him. Sleepy Valley had awakened that realization and opportunity to him.

When Nick returned to the house he saw that his parents had left a message saying they were going to Pineville and would see him at the church. He fixed himself two sandwiches, knowing he would feed one to Chester, and grabbed a diet Pepsi and sat on the front porch swing and remembered the day Andy had delivered the swing. He thought about the joy in Trudy's restaurant and her verbal battles with Tom, the friends he had made and the love he had found in Sleepy Valley.

He thought of the sad times, his disappointment over a failed marriage, Trudy's surgery and how the village had held its breath waiting for the outcome and the month he had spent helping Melissa in Chicago.

He thought of all the dinner parties they'd had on Saturday evenings, sharing their life's secrets together. The fun he'd had fishing with Vincent and Josh. The day he'd walked into the general store and heard Vincent playing his violin. Watching Vincent and Trudy line dance at the Oak Club. All the memories he cherished, but none of them as much as the first time he had laid eyes on Gabriella, his love. Nick thought of their first kiss on her front porch. She had fumbled for her keys and he had somehow found the nerve to kiss her. How he'd wished then he could kiss her again and again. His wish had come true.

Nick looked at his watch and went inside to shower and shave. He had just enough time to ready himself and be at the church at the given time. He put on the tux and shoes and looked in the mirror. He saw a happy man.

He was met at the church by Wade and Pastor Hill. "The big day," Nick said to them. They agreed. They walked to the waiting room where they were to enter after the music was over. Nick peeked out to see Vincent rise to the center of the stage and raise the violin to his chin. He played as if he were playing again in front of thousands. The notes flowed off the instrument as if angels were playing before God. Tears came to Nick's eyes with the joy he felt for having the honor to know Vincent.

The church was filled to capacity. Chairs were placed along the sides for the overflow. Men stood along the back, giving their seats to women who entered. As Vincent finished, Pastor Hill, Wade, and Nick entered from the right rear door and walked across the stage, taking their place. Nick's niece, Molly, walked slowly down the center aisle, dropping multicolored flower petals on the floor as she walked. The matron of honor was next to stroll down the center of the church as a piano played softly. She was a vision of beauty. Her haired glowed as it hung over her shoulders and onto her strapless, soft, yellow dress that stopped before it got to her ankles.

The audience rose as the stunning bride began her entrance with her arm inside Vincent's. The music became louder as though a grand dignitary were arriving to thunderous applause. Nick looked over at Wade and saw a broad smile across his face. Vincent escorted the bride onto the stage and moved off to the side where he picked up the violin and played again.

After the short piece ended, Pastor Hill welcomed the overwhelming crowd to the wedding of Wade Morgan and Trudy Ann Flynn. The crowd erupted in loud applause. Trudy's yellow and white wedding dress was cut low in the back and had straps going around her neck holding the front up. The dress landed at mid-calf and she had on soft yellow heels. Tom and his wife sat in the second row with Andy and his wife. They'd had to arrive an hour early to get the seats up front. Josh and his mother were three rows back on the right.

Stella and Pearl were seated with Faith and Grace. They all were crying already. Trudy's Sunday school class had made a large sign and hung it on the side wall that read, "We Love You and Wish You Much Happiness. Happy Wedding Day!"

As Wade and Trudy exchanged their written vows to each other Nick gazed at his wife standing across from him. She was the most beautiful woman he had ever seen. The soft yellow of her dress brought out even more the beauty of her dark hair cascading down her shoulders. The dark tan of her skin sparkled in the candlelight when the lights dimmed for the ceremony. She smiled at him and winked. She looked at the gentle good-looking man that had become her husband on August the third in Gatlinburg.

Pastor Hill asked for the ring from the best man, and Nick handed it to him. Wade made his promises as he slipped the diamond onto Trudy's finger. Gabriella handed the other ring to Pastor Hill and Trudy placed the ring on Wade's finger as she pledged her love and commitment to him. Wade was instructed to kiss his bride, which he gladly did, and Pastor Hill introduced Mr. and Mrs. Morgan. Balloons began falling from the rafters, surprising the crowd. Laughter and applause filled the church as it always filled her restaurant. Balloons were bounced back up into the air and some men took out their knives and popped the balloons as they fell. The church had become a giant celebration.

Cameras flashed as everyone took pictures of the colorful scene. Pastor Hill had never had a ceremony anything like it, but nothing less was to be expected. With Trudy involved he knew it would be anything but dull. The party continued downstairs. The band played all of Trudy and Wade's favorite songs, country, rock, and Christian. The "Chicken Dance" was a must.

There were finger sandwiches and potato salad and chips, drinks and cake. After the first dance by the bride and groom, Nick got his turn. Trudy threw her arms around Nick's neck and they slow danced.

"How did you know I wasn't the one for you, Nick?" Nick shrugged his shoulders. "Somehow you knew, though. You couldn't have resisted me unless you knew."

Nick did know. Somehow he knew. He couldn't explain it. He knew God had a plan for his life. He knew Gabriella was the one God had for him the moment he saw her. But he knew Trudy would be a great friend to him and Gabriella the rest of his life.

"Who says I could resist you? I still can't resist you."

"Thanks, Nick."

Nick looked over to see Vincent dancing with Pearl. Vincent and Pearl had been keeping company, in Vincent's words, since the party in July. Nick knew that was all they would ever do. Vincent would never give his total heart to another woman other than his Maria.

After finishing the dance with Trudy, Nick looked for his wife. Trudy was quickly grabbed up by Tom. He asked for a dance. Thirty seconds later he heard Trudy yell out, "Tom, you're just trying to look down my dress, you old fool." Everyone laughed as they continued dancing.

Nick found Gabriella talking to Teresa Hill. "May I steal my wife for a dance?"

"Of course," Teresa smiled. "I need to find my husband for a dance."

Nick and Gabriella found a quiet corner to embrace and dance. Nick kissed her softly. "What a great wedding," Gabriella said.

"It is. Do you regret not having the wedding here now?"

"Not at all. This is fun, but I loved our simple wedding."

"I agree." Nick and Gabriella had decided they wanted to get married soon. They became husband and wife in a lovely wedding chapel in the deep woods surrounded by the people they had come to love. They'd set the date for August the third. Gabriella's father had returned from California to be there. Pastor Hill had brought his family, and he'd conducted the marriage of Nick and Gabriella. Trudy had been the maid of honor, escorted by Wade. Nick had asked Vincent to be his best man. Vincent had been so thrilled to be Nick's best man. Even Chester had been allowed inside for the wedding under the watchful eye of Josh. Nick's parents, Mike and Sue had been there, as was Nick's sister Laura and her family, John, Samuel, and Molly. Pearl had also attended the ceremony.

Everyone had worn casual clothes, Nick in his Columbia pants and short-sleeved, white shirt, and Gabriella in a white and pink sundress. After taking everyone to dinner, Nick and Gabry had spent their first night as husband and wife at the Hippensteal Inn nestled deep in the mountains. They had woken up to the beauty of the Smoky Mountains as they walked out on the balcony of their room. That morning they left for a two-week honeymoon in New Zealand.

As a wedding gift to Nick when they got back, Gabriella presented him with the painting she had done. Gabry thought it was her best work, and Nick was astounded. Never had he seen a painting so beautiful. It was a painting of the field in Cades Cove where they had first lain on the blanket and slept and fallen in love, the same field that he had asked her to marry him. She had somehow captured love on the canvas and the vast beauty of God's creation all in one painting.

Nick and Gabry had decided to convert Nick's house into her gallery. It was perfect with the overlooking loft. Their new home would to be nestled into the woods behind the gallery.

They were going to sell Gabry's home to Wade and Trudy, and he was going to use Gabry's studio for his office. Pearl was going to live in the existing house. They had talked the owners of the property next to Nick's into selling them fifteen acres, and were building their home next to Nick and Gabry's land. Wade was then going to build Timberframe homes for both couples.

Nick held Gabriella in his arms and kissed her as they danced. She smiled up at him. She was so happy, her sadness gone. "Nick, we ought to build plenty of bedrooms in our new house." Nick looked at her wondering why she would say that.

She whispered in his ear, "I'm pregnant." Nick shouted with glee.

EPILOGUE

An hour earlier the Timberframe home had been abuzz with excitement. Kids had been running around the house playing games and dropping crumbs of their cake all over the hardwood floors. It was what Nick had always wanted, a family with laughter and love. Friends and relatives had all gathered for Maria's fifteenth birthday celebration.

Nick walked out onto the high porch and sat in one of the three porch swings as the evening sun began to set behind the house. Two of the swings were suspended from rafters and one sat on the porch floor. All were built by Andy. Wicker chairs completed the seating on the porch overlooking the gallery and bird feeders. Wade was already lounging there. He was waiting for Trudy so he could get home. He still had house plans to look over that evening.

Wade said, "It's a great evening."

Nick agreed, "I never get tired of them. Did you drive or walk?"

"We drove. I didn't want to get caught walking back in the dark. You never know how long Trudy will stay and talk." Nick and Wade had built a path from Wade's home to theirs. It joined Nick's path near the beginning. Maria had built a sign and placed it on the trail that read, "This way to Aunt Trudy's and Uncle Wade's house," when she was seven. It was still standing there.

Nick thanked everyone for coming to the party and wished them well as they left for home. Sam Henry Watkins walked out onto the porch with Maria. Maria walked to his car with him.

"See you soon," Sam said to Maria.

"Bye, Sam. Thanks for coming."

Sam was going to be a junior at the high school and played basketball on the junior varsity team his sophomore year. Nick felt he had a good chance of making varsity this year. Nick had coached for fifteen years now. In his third season, the team had brought home the state championship and Nick was named the Tennessee high school coach of the year. He had had only had one losing season and he had been approached by colleges looking for a coach, but Nick would never leave Sleepy Valley. The money they offered trying to lure him away meant nothing to Nick.

Trudy opened the screen door and walked out with her pie plates in hand. "Ready to go, honey?"

"Whenever you are."

Trudy turned and yelled into the house. "Charlie, Gabi, come on. We're going home."

Fourteen-year-old Charlie ran through the door and jumped off the high porch. Gabi followed, still talking a blue streak as she hugged Nick and waved good-bye. They'd adopted thirteen-year-old Gabi in China when she was born. After Gabriella gave birth to Maria, Trudy knew she had to be a mother also. Wade was thrilled with the idea. Wade and Trudy had adopted Charlie when he was four. A church couple had been keeping him as foster parents, and Wade and Trudy loved the sweet little guy, so they adopted him so Gabi would have a brother. "See you guys Saturday evening."

The two families still got together most Saturday evenings for dinner. It had become a tradition, besides they were like family.

Gabriella walked through the door and sat with Nick. Nick placed his arm around her. Maria soon followed her out the door with a photo album in her arms.

"Daddy, will you tell us stories again with the pictures?"

"Tonight?"

"Please, it's my birthday." She knew her dad would do anything for her with a *please* added to it.

"Okay, for a while."

"C'mon girls! Daddy said yes!" She yelled into the house. Thirteen-year-old Ann came through the door followed by their youngest daughter, ten-year-old Lauren.

They all squeezed onto the large swing with Nick and Gabry. Lauren, named after Nick's sister, sat in her mother's lap. Maria handed the special album to Nick and he carefully opened it. It had all their special memories stored for remembering the years gone by. The first picture was of Cades Cove. Nick had taken the family there many times over the years. The girls knew it well, and they loved staying at the campgrounds and hiking the cove or horseback riding.

Nick began, "This is where your mom trapped me into loving her."

Lauren cried, "Daddy, you always say that."

Ann, named after Trudy Ann, corrected Nick, "That's where you both knew you loved each other. It's the same field as the painting over the piano."

Gabriella smiled and nodded in agreement.

"Who's telling the story anyway?"

"But Daddy, we want the real story," Lauren begged.

"Okay, that's where your mom and I knew we loved each other, and it's also where I asked her to marry me."

"Right there, under that tree," Lauren said as she pointed to the tree, although everyone knew which tree it was.

Nick turned the page and there were two pictures of Vincent. One showed him playing the violin at Trudy's wedding and the other of him with the wedding party at the small chapel as best man. The opposite page held the picture Gabriella had taken in front of the Smoky Mountain sign when she and Nick had first went to the park with Trudy and Vincent.

"I miss Grandpa Vincent," Maria said as tears began to form in the corners of her eyes. Everyone nodded in agreement. There had been a special bond between Vincent and Maria. Vincent was very touched that Nick and Gabriella named their first child after his late wife. He had visited Maria every day since she was born.

"You three should thank God every day for Vincent. He taught you all to play so beautifully. He also taught you patience and kindness." Vincent had lived until he was ninety-five. He'd taught each of the girls to play the violin and the piano. His piano stood in the great room inside the house. He had left it to them in his will. Vincent had lived on his own except for the last two years.

Nick and Gabry had finally convinced him to move in with them. He was there every day anyway. The three girls had loved having him in the house. He'd told them magnificent stories, and they'd played music together every day. Music and laughter filled the house. One afternoon Vincent went upstairs to take his daily nap. When Gabry went to his room that evening to tell him dinner was ready, she found him lying still on his bed and realized what had happened. His beloved wife's framed picture was clutched in his hands lying on his chest close to his heart. The same cherished picture still sat upon their mantle above the stone fireplace that had graced Vincent's fireplace mantle for all the years. Gabriella placed a picture she had taken of Vincent with the three girls beside it.

Maria said, "I still can't believe you didn't tell us until after dinner. You let us eat dinner with Grandpa Vincent dead in his bedroom."

Gabriella defended herself by saying for the hundredth time, "He would have wanted it that way. He never wanted a fuss to be made over him."

They all three said as if on cue, "But Mom, he was dead!"

"You still needed to eat."

On the next page was a picture of Nick on the cropped rock

edge at Alum Cave Bluff with his hands stretched to the sky. Ann said, "That was so scary, Dad."

"Don't remind me," Gabriella said. Vincent's will had left most everything he had to the high school for the music program. He had left a few personal items to Nick and Gabry, Trudy and Wade, and Josh. Vincent requested that he be cremated and his ashes placed in the urn with Maria's. He asked Nick to hike up to Alum Cave Bluff and scatter the ashes in the wind. Nick's family hiked up the trail along with Wade and Trudy's family. Nick had placed the urn inside a backpack and made his way up to the top of the cropping and waited for the breeze to pick up and scattered the ashes unto the Great Smoky Mountains. Nick had stood there and cried with his arms outstretched. Gabry had taken the picture.

"That was quite a sight," Maria said.

Ann said, "I'm surprised Mom didn't fix us a little snack so we could all eat while Dad was spreading Grandpa Vincent's ashes." Everyone on the swing began laughing.

When the laughing died down Nick turned the page and there was a picture of Josh smiling with a stringer full of fish. "This was taken at Andy's farm pond. That day was one of the best we ever had. Your Uncle Josh loves to fish. Have I told you about the river otters?"

Maria said, "About a thousand times." Nick told them about the otters for the thousandth and first time. Vincent and Josh had grown closer than a grandfather to a grandson. Josh had worked at the store all through high school, and Josh actually ran the store. Vincent had run the cash register when Josh wasn't there. Josh graduated from high school and had very little money for college but he planned on getting school loans. Vincent sold the store when Josh left for college and actually paid for Josh's entire college education at the University of Tennessee.

Josh was now teaching at the same school as Nick. He was married and had a small child of his own. He'd named his son Nicholas Vincent.

"I like Uncle Josh," Lauren told everyone.

"We all do, silly," Ann said.

Gabriella said, "Little Nicky Vinny is so cute." The three girls had nicknamed him Nicky Vinny. It seemed to stick. Everyone now called him by the nickname.

Nick turned the page, and there was a picture of Trudy, Stella, Tom, and Andy at the counter of the restaurant. "They are so funny," Maria laughed. Trudy still ran the eating place and went in every day to argue with Tom. One day she'd gotten so aggravated with him that she'd shoved an entire fresh-baked, coconut-cream pie in his face. Andy had picked up his fork and began eating the pie from Tom's face. Trudy had tried to charge Andy for it.

"You ate it, didn't you?"

Stella had retired three years ago, and she still lived in the area with her daughter.

Nick turned the page again. A picture of the Victory Road Community Church was on the page. On the opposite page were pictures of Trudy's wedding with all the balloons bouncing among the wedding guests.

Ann said, "I want a wedding just like that."

"When you're thirty-seven," Nick said.

"Dad…" Ann cried.

"That's how old Trudy was. That's how old you girls have to be to get married." He went on to explain how Trudy made a mistake in her first marriage just to get away from home.

"I'm never leaving home. I like it here," Lauren said.

"Wait a minute, I didn't say that," Nick teased.

Maria said, "Yeah, we all three will stay here with you and Mom forever." Deep down, Nick and Gabry would love that. But they knew their girls would live their lives with the heartaches and joy and love that everyone does. They prayed that they were preparing them well for it.

"I loved the old church," Gabry said. Pastor Hill and Teresa were still at the church. It had continued to grow until they eventually had to build a larger building. The church bought the land next door and built there. They kept the old church for the young people to have their own service and for weddings and other functions.

The next page held a picture of Chester sitting tall with his tongue hanging out. The picture next to it was of Nick and Gabriella in Cades Cove holding Chester when he was a pup. It was their first trip there together.

The girls yelled out, "Chester!"

"Look how cute he was when he was a puppy," Maria said.

Nick told them the story about the time Chester brought him the baby bunny rabbit. Chester had lived to be thirteen. He'd died two months after Vincent died. In their old age they would sit together. Chester had loved the girls and protected them, but he was still Nick's dog. He'd followed Nick everywhere, and there was never any doubt that Nick was his favorite, which infuriated the girls. Vincent had talked to Chester like he could understand everything he said. Nick thought he did. Nick had buried Chester in the clearing where they saw the bucks fight over the doe. They placed a memorial stone for Vincent there also.

Over the years, Nick had seen many wonderful things in the home he and Gabry had made and in the Smokies he loved. None of them compared to watching his family grow or watching his daughters laugh and mature. It still thrilled him when Gabriella walked into a room. She was still the most beautiful woman he had ever seen. Maria looked just like her, a beauty with dark hair, creamy skin and lovely expressive eyes. Ann was stunning also with dark brown wavy hair and a gift of kindness. She had the loveliest voice of the three. She sang with the teen praise band at church. Lauren could melt your heart with her smile and light brown hair.

It almost turned a shade of blonde in the summertime. They weren't sure where that came from. She had a giant heart for everyone and everything. Each girl had her own personality and charm. They all loved to paint with their mother. But Lauren was going to follow in her mother's footsteps as an artist.

Over the years Nick had lost touch with Melissa. She had married again and was doing fine the last he had heard anything about her.

Nick continued to touch people's lives. The students that he helped at school were too numerous to mention. Folks at the church were touched by Nick's love and caring. Nick and Gabry's generosity had been used to help many in need. Gabry was known throughout the world for her painting and collectors begged for her artwork. Her painting of the Elkmont fireflies was famous. Nick had talked her into producing prints of it so thousands of buyers could enjoy it.

Gabry had taken a picture of the village of Sleepy Valley. It was the next one they looked at. "It still looks like that," Maria said. The town did still look the same as it did fifteen years before. Some fresh paint, and the trees along Main Street were taller. That was about the only difference.

Nick thanked God every day for directing him to Sleepy Valley fifteen-plus years ago. His life with Gabriella was full of love and devotion. He could not imagine a better life.

The next page showed a picture of the bear and two cubs that Gabriella had taken from the back porch of the old farmhouse in Cades Cove. "Daddy, this is my favorite story," Ann said.

"Mine too, Daddy. Tell us how you saved the little girl's life," Maria begged.

Lauren cheered with excitement, "I love this story."

Nick told the story again.

THE END

The only thing that counts is faith
expressing itself through love.

Galatians 5:6 NIV

Readers,

It's a great honor to have you read my writing. Thank you. Please visit my website: www.timcallahan.net" for information You can email me at: timca121@yahoo.com" with questions and comments. Your comments may end up on my 'Comments' page I love hearing from readers.

May God Bless, and happy reading.
Tim Callahan